To Karina

Acacia Hotel
Hastings
East Sussex
14th September, 2058

My dear Isabella,
This is a book about how I saved the planet. Incidentally, it explains how I helped the Celts to vanquish the Romans in ancient Britain; how, inadvertently, I discovered the identity of Jack the Ripper; how, without meaning to, I prevented a war from happening and how I enjoyed celebrity in a world-famous rock band. Above all, it describes how I was reconciled to you, my sweet, and to your dear mother, the Celtic Tiger.

I hope that the book will explain, if not justify, my long absence from your life, that you will enjoy my stories – they are mostly true by the way – and that you will not be shocked by racier sections. As you grow older and learn my nature – which is passionate but somewhat sedentary – you will come to understand that I did not seek out the role of a Time Traveller (please excuse the capital letters, they seem appropriate, somehow). Fate tapped me on the shoulder; it was my destiny to glimpse the secret workings of the universe, and to intervene in them, like a Deist vouchsafed the mechanism of the divine clock.

Many miracles have occurred in the two hundred years since I arrived in this world – the introduction of wireless telegraphy and powered flight, x-rays, the computer, biotechnology. A destructive capacity was feared in every case; but, in practice, each invention, like Janus, faced towards salvation, as well as damnation. And, ultimately, as I have intimated, the human species was spared from extinction.

However, that is the end of this narrative and not the beginning. Hindsight is a great teacher. I do not seek in writing these words to explain away my failings or moral derelictions but rather to place them in an emotional context, perhaps for my own benefit as much as yours. That is all for now. For it is time to begin.
With much love,
Daddy

The Chosen

The Chosen

William Hatchett

COSMIC EGG BOOKS

Winchester, UK
Washington, USA

First published by Cosmic Egg Books, 2014
Cosmic Egg Books is an imprint of John Hunt Publishing Ltd., Laurel House, Station Approach,
Alresford, Hants, SO24 9JH, UK
office1@jhpbooks.net
www.johnhuntpublishing.com

For distributor details and how to order please visit the 'Ordering' section on our website.

ISBN: 978 1 78279 643 5

A CIP catalogue record for this book is available from the British Library.

Design: Stuart Davies

Printed and bound by CPI Group (UK) Ltd, Croydon, CR0 4YY

All that is solid melts into air, all that is holy is profaned, and man is at last compelled to face with sober senses, his real conditions of life, and his relations with his kind.

Karl Marx, The Communist Manifesto

Chapter One

The Crown of the Wild Olive

I was born, my love, in an upstairs room in a small, fetid house in south London, during a heat wave. We lived in a dark, narrow street, in Camberwell, in the shadow of a workhouse. I can remember little about the house, apart from its gloomy hallway, which was illuminated by a small bright strip of stained glass in the front door. Amazingly, the street is still there. Over the years it changed, almost imperceptibly, from a modest row of artisan's dwellings to a desirable Regency terrace; the workhouse was transformed from a grim bastille into expensive, well-appointed flats. But to me, it is a place full of uncomfortable memories. And I avoid it.

The street was full of cholera, so father moved us to Dulwich, about a mile away, when I was six. Your grandfather was a wine merchant who prospered, while many others were ruined, in the great crash of 1857. Our new house, which was connected to the City by horse-driven bus, could have been a paradise, especially for an only child, like myself, who lived primarily in the world of his imagination. A substantial villa, clothed in wisteria, it had a large walled garden, backing onto an orchard. A short walk away, across pleasant green fields, lived the Ruskin family, in Denmark Hill. Ruskin senior, also a wine importer, was a close friend of my father's. But I can barely remember him, or his house. For my father sent me to boarding school only a year later. I do not think that I ever forgave him.

In moving he may well have saved our lives. For London was a living breathing Thing; a monster endlessly assimilating human beings and other raw materials; ingesting their life forces and spewing out their residues into its sulphurous air and its festering water courses. Families were crammed into endlessly sub-divided houses and cellars, lacking piped water or sanitation. This was bad enough; in the East End they also lived cheek by jowl with knackers' yards, blacking factories, sugar bakeries and coal gas plants, belching out smoke and poisonous wastes.

The city was a heat island, an unholy chemistry set, from whose unplanned experiments local government, council housing and planning laws were ultimately born. And the food! The white flour that is favoured by our unhealthy race was generally adulterated with alum or arrowroot. Milk was thickened with chalk. In the summer, it was rare to find butter and meat that were not rancid. London's limits were prescribed, in my boyhood, by Highbury to the north and Camberwell to the south. Here, in contrast to the misery and filth of the inner city, were market gardens and glass houses serving the metropolis. Dulwich, our new home, was a quiet village in those days, not merely the adjunct of an ever-spreading suburb.

Ironically, some of this rural ambience would return to the great metropolis, London, in the twenty-first century. Once the tyranny of the motor car had been reduced, canals re-utilised and land returned to green uses, the city took on an entirely different character. Many streets were grassed over and the former rigid divisions that were observed between houses and defined public and private spaces became blurred. Thousands of trees were planted. This was a calmer, more verdant place than the city of the preceding century and the one before, an example of *rus in urbe*. However, I am departing from my narrative.

I do not wish to dwell upon the horrors of the educational establishment in the county of Surrey to which I was sent by my father. It was devoted to the task of preparing little boys for grander schools, that would turn them into "gentlemen" (in other words, idle philistines), cannon fodder or other servants of the Empire. I loathed the place from the first day, with its humiliating rituals, orchestrated by endless bells, and its nauseating odours of dubbin, sweat and wax polish. The school engendered in me a dislike of all sports, of heights (we were forced to climb things) and of humbug generally, which has persisted for my entire life.

One hot June afternoon when I was 14, I remember the sports master telling me to be a brave little man, for he had some bad news for me. A breeze blew in from the cricket field, bringing a smell of new-mown grass, which I have always associated with fear and mortification rather than pleasure. I detest cricket. Like Freemasonry, its bizarre customs and practices are never made explicit and I have never wished to learn them. When Mr Hutchinson told me that my father had died, it was easy for me not to show any emotion. For I did not know him, other than as a vague but frightening paterfamilias. Hutchinson seemed relieved by my lack of tears, which he wrongly interpreted as a display of manly fortitude. "That's the ticket," he said, patting me on the thigh.

A feeling of elation began to swell inside me as I walked back to the dormitories. Foremost in my mind was the thought that I would now be spared the tedium of Kennedy's Latin primer. This emotion did not diminish as I packed my few belongings into my trunk and experienced a solemn interview with the headmaster. My departure from the school was to be immediate, for my father's business had collapsed, as a consequence of the Franco Prussian War, and he had been unable to pay the school's fees for several months. I would be met at the gates by Mamma.

If the truth is known, I have few happy memories of my early childhood. In my memory, it takes on the character of a featureless wilderness – a landscape of frustration and passivity, in which I was a helpless agent, subject to the whims of larger forces. Now, as I passed through the iron gates of the school, I tasted a strange sense of exhilaration, and of freedom. Mamma explained, mysteriously, in a cab to the railway station, that my father had died from brain fever. This was also the description on his death certificate; to this day, I do not know the true circumstances of his death. She told me I would now be going to live with my Uncle Edward in Kent, at least while my father's affairs were sorted out. As it turned out, I was never again to live in my father's house, which was soon sold to meet the demands of his creditors. My life now took an entirely unexpected turn.

If Dulwich, in those days, seemed, and was, rural, Spenhurst, in Kent, was the epitome of rusticity. Perched above the Weald, thirty miles from London, it lay in a landscape dominated by deliciously-scented hop fields and oast houses, orchards and flower-strewn meadows. I have said that London was a heat island; in the days before gas and electric light reached the shires, it is hard to imagine the complete darkness that cloaked one at night, and the silence. The stars were bigger then. The world was girdled by the thick creamy band of the Milky Way and the night sky was embroidered with the tails of shooting stars. To me, there has always been a ripeness and fecundity in Kent, with its yeasty smell of hops and wood smoke, that is almost supernatural. Its fields and hedgerows were alive with colour and bird song. My uncle used to say that if you were to plant a walking stick in the rich, loamy soil of our back garden it would sprout.

Edward was the proprietor and manager of a bookshop in Spenhurst high street. The printing business that was attached to the shop never really amounted to anything; most of my uncle's small income derived from selling novels, which he described as "trash" and prayer books. The dismal science of economics was of far greater interest to him. Our shelves brimmed with the works of Hume, Mill, Ricardo and Smith. He also dabbled in evolutionary theory – Butler, Darwin and Spencer – and, of course, aesthetics – Arnold, Newman, Pater and Ruskin. These volumes were of limited interest to our customers but I devoured them, like a hungry man at a banquet. They were to provide the next phase of my education.

My uncle had attended Exeter College in Oxford, where he had studied the divinities, a contemporary of the celebrated artist, poet and designer, William Morris. But, unlike Mr Morris, he had not found wealth and contentment. Poor Edward, never Ted or Ned, carried with him an air of bitterness. In an earlier age he would undoubtedly have toiled harmlessly as a parson in some obscure country rectory but the acuity of his intelligence had made this impossible. With the help of a generous inheritance he had moved to rural Kent in order to sell and write books. But he had not enjoyed success.

Edward was deeply envious of the shrewdness of my father, his younger brother, whom he described, contemptuously, as a "tradesman". He never married. Some people believed that my uncle inclined towards the pederastic inclinations of Pater and the Oxford movement; actually, I believe that he was simply too much of a curmudgeon to marry. It was a shame. A feminine influence may well have moderated his bad temper, and his alcoholism.

We lived in relatively modest apartments behind, and above, the shop. The bookshop was next to a bakery, which lent some delicious smells to my work, and a few doors from the village forge. Our back garden contained a vegetable patch, which I tended diligently for several years. At the foot of the garden, across a strip of nettles and wild garlic, was the River Medway; forming the horizon, on the other side of the river, was the green dome of Saint's Hill.

Edward had claimed to be too poor to send me back to school (this was disingenuous, but let that pass). His idea was that my working in the shop would give him more time to write. In fact, it granted more time to dwell in his interior world. Edward's mood darkened. He brooded in his study, consuming increasing quantities of brandy. Mamma passed away only six months after my father. She never recovered from his death. His personal effects were duly delivered, in solicitor's deed boxes, to Kent. Edward pursed his lips, made a bonfire of my father's papers, letters and diaries and simply burned them.

This was one of the most significant and bitter victories of his life. I watched, clenching my fists, and even said something, but I could not stop him. After that day, I disliked my uncle even more than I had previously.

One Saturday evening in the winter of 1879, I sat in my bedroom with a volume of William Hazlitt before me. Hazlitt is a delightful author, but I was distracted and not in any mood for the task in hand. I had been living uneventfully in Spenhurst for seven years with my querulous guardian, and I was bored. Edward had suggested some careers. The army was one. The idea of my firing off bullets against Zulus or Afghans, before heroically succumbing to dysentery in some distant and desiccated outpost of the Empire, was absurd. In any case, my uncle was far too mean to desire a change in the status quo – my working, he slowly pickling himself to death.

It was dark. The rooks had returned in a great black cloud to their roosts at the top of Saint's Hill; the beech trees at its brow formed a faint pattern of tracery against a quicksilver sky. I was trying to read at the small desk in front of the window, but Hazlitt's disputatious essay on the anarchist William Godwin seemed trivial compared to what was in the foreground of my mind.

From the kitchen below I could hear the rise and fall of my uncle's voice. He was talking to his friend, Doctor Wood. They would be sitting on either side of the kitchen range, my uncle grasping a tumbler in one sclerotic fist, as he gesticulated with the other. They would be discussing the Irish question, the Eastern question, or possibly both. It was an age of questions, my love. But they were rarely amenable to straightforward answers. My uncle and I had stopped talking about politics. Once he had taken Mr Disraeli's side, backing the Turks against Russia in the Balkans, our arguments had become increasingly bitter.

It had been a typical day in the shop. In the middle of the

afternoon, the bell jangled as the local curate, Rupert Winspear, came in. He was a slight, furtive man, with wispy, straw-coloured hair. He headed straight for the shelves containing the work of Richard Burton, the celebrated explorer, but I knew that his interest was prurient rather than anthropological.

Next to the Satyricon of Petronius, in French, and the poetry of Catullus, Burton's *Perfumed Garden*, which, on our shelves, lay next to his 17-volume *Arabian Nights*, was my favourite work in the erotic pantheon and had been borrowed on innumerable occasions for my own nocturnal purposes. Winspear shot me a strange glance as he removed the volume. He was far too embarrassed to buy the book, feigning a sudden interest in medieval architecture to cover his tracks. In fact, he was my only customer that day.

Had I but known it, this night was the prelude to a series of events that would change my life. In retrospect, Edward and Doctor Wood, were at the final stage of their falling out (the urgent tone of my uncle's voice should have told me as much). Edward would now disintegrate, his social persona eaten away by alcohol, leaving me even more responsible for our little world. Their voices rose and fell like the swell of an angry sea. I left my room and stood on the landing, so that I could hear them more clearly.

"Murdering Fenian swine!" Edward declaimed. Charles Wood was a patient man, which is why he had endured my uncle's despotic friendship for so long. His voice was gentle but insistent.

"Edward, please calm down … calm down."

My uncle seemed to compose himself, entering a more measured period. Probably, he was pouring himself another generous helping of brandy.

"Should've let 'em starve, bloody bog trotters. D'you know what those Irish bastards are going to do. They've got Gladstone in their clutches and in no time at all they're going to get their

Home Rule Bill off him. The man is a coward and an opportunist."

"My dear, Edward," said Doctor Wood, such immoderate language is not worthy of you."

"Oh no?" said Uncle Edward. "Well I'll tell you who agrees with me. Your friend, Joseph Chamberlain, that's who?" There was a mocking tone in his voice, I thought.

Doctor Wood paused. They had had this conversation many times before – repetition is the main weapon in the drunkard's tedious armoury – but he was prepared to go over old ground.

"Mr Chamberlain has much to commend him," said the doctor, as if he were delivering a lecture. "As mayor of Birmingham, he ensured that the streets were well-lit and well-paved. The man wears a monocle, which is a sign of ostentation, but I am prepared to allow him that. But on Home Rule, I fear that he is pandering to the ignorant anti-Catholicism of his electorate. He is trawling through the gutter, stirring up base and vile prejudices."

Doctor Wood, who was sober, must have wondered if he had expressed himself a little too strongly. Perhaps he was sensing that the end of his association with my uncle was near.

"You would see the Empire destroyed then!" Edward exclaimed. "Just give it away, to every race of half-baked savages which wants a crack at managing its own affairs."

"If you hold these people in such low regard," said Doctor Wood, "then why do you think that the Empire is worth having?"

My uncle's reply sounded muffled. He must have turned his back on Doctor Wood in favour of the drinks cabinet. Uncle Edward liked to think that he lived in the "real world" and that Doctor Wood did not. In fact, it was the other way round. In the course of his work the doctor visited the poorest and meanest cottages of the village and the surrounding district. He was appalled by the squalor in which people lived, and tried to help them; Uncle Edward's world, on the other hand, was his study, in which he cocooned himself in a lurid patchwork quilt of prejudices.

"Good God, what utter tripe," said Doctor Wood, suddenly. It was unprecedented for him to blaspheme. "I am prepared to allow that you are drunk, sir, but that really is nonsense. It is pathetic."

"I'm pathetic, am I!" Uncle Edward seemed to explode. It had been coming for a long time, perhaps years. I could visualise his face, blotched into crimson patches by the brandy; Doctor Wood's face would be hard and white on the other side of the lamp-lit room.

"I was referring to your words, not your person," Charles Wood said, coldly.

"You said that I was pathetic!" slurred Uncle Edward, rising to his feet.

"I did not Sir!" shouted Doctor Wood.

"You did!"

"I did not! But, by God, Sir, I am revising my opinion. You are pathetic! You are a ..."

It is perhaps fortunate that the doctor was not allowed to complete his sentence.

"Get out of my house!"

My uncle's voice was as clear and sharp as a rifle shot. It was followed by a splintering crash. He must have summoned what was left of his strength to hurl his glass against the wall. I knew that he would later regret this futile gesture and the waste of the precious liquid. I heard the back door open and slam shut. Doctor Wood had left. There was silence, save for heavy breathing from my uncle, which would soon became snoring as he subsided into his armchair. It seemed unlikely that the two men would ever speak again.

Chapter Two

An Apparition

The following day dawned crisp and bright. No reference was made by my uncle to the turbulent events of the previous night. At breakfast, prepared by our domestic, Mrs Brown, he was pale and subdued; he barely grunted as he gulped down his egg and bacon, resisting attempts to elicit conversation. His head must have been pounding and I noticed a distinct tremor in his hands. As I cleared away the breakfast things he melted away, probably back to his bed. Perhaps if Uncle Edward had made more of an attempt to communicate with the people around him he would have been a better writer.

It was exceptionally quiet in the shop that day. At eleven o'clock, the butcher's boy delivered a package wrapped neatly in brown paper. Inside was my uncle's chess set, returned by Doctor Wood. There was no note or explanation. I knew that the return of the set would make my uncle sad, but that, stoically, he would say nothing.

By twelve-thirty, I was suffering from hunger pangs that were made worse by the appetising smells coming from the bakery. I was cutting a book that I wished to read with a paper knife. It may be hard for you to believe but, in those days, books came from the printer only half-finished – one had to separate the pages with a sharp blade. It was a tedious task. I think that the volume was something by Ruskin (an author who my uncle hated).

I read nearly all of his work that winter, which was extremely wet, basking in the warmth of a wood stove as the rain lashed against the window. Patiently, I absorbed *The Stones of Venice, The Seven Lamps of Architecture, The Eagle's Nest, Fors Clavigera* and the rest – Ruskin was a great man for a title and he numbered his paragraphs, which is the affectation of someone who thinks that they have something Very Important to Say.

Why did I, or anyone else, take him seriously? Ruskin's exhortations to the poor to eat from pretty dishes, laid out on well-ironed table cloths, would come to appear patronising; his celebrations of the soaring fan vaults of Gothic architecture would speak, to post-Freudians, of unfulfilled sexual longings and – an embarrassing failing for a man who writes about art – he simply could not draw.

At any rate, the idleness imposed upon me by the shop undoubtedly favoured my intellectual development. I read widely and voraciously and the means of my education were immediately to hand. In retrospect, my time in the shop merges into a blur and it is characterised by a single, pleasurable, sensual impression. In my memory, there is always the wood stove, the rain, and Ruskin. And I cannot think of Ruskin without recalling Lara, for I was immersed in his work when I first met her.

From upstairs, I could hear Uncle Edward's chair creaking. He had got up again and would be trying vainly to write, while thinking about having his first brandy and soda when the sun had "passed over the yard arm" (this phenomenon had assumed an elastic definition in his mind). Soon, it would be time to close up the shop for lunch, although, on days like these, our being open was merely academic. The bell jangled. Looking up, I observed that in had walked an extraordinary apparition.

The girl was tall and slender. I guessed that she was about sixteen. She wore an extraordinary dress of green serge, with crimson edging, draped around her long limbs in loose folds. Her face was pale and slightly freckled with a small, neat nose; her hair, which was abundant, had an auburn tint and was tied back with a narrow black ribbon. Around her neck was a string of amber beads, whose orange luminescence complemented her flawless skin. Later, I would associate her unearthly beauty with the idealised heroines of Rossetti and Burne-Jones. At this time, I had merely read of their school, the Pre-Raphaelite Brotherhood, in Ruskin's flattering essays.

From as far away as the door, I could see that she had grey eyes and that her gaze was clear and steady.

"Could you help me, please?"

Could I help her? I was in love.

"What are you looking for?"

I was now engulfed in her heady perfume. It was a floral scent with a musky note, so sensuous that it made my heart quicken.

"I am interested in poetry," she said. Flames of joy leapt from my heart.

"And in science and art."

"I see." It was a fairly wide area of study.

She stepped forward, allowing me to see that she had a serious expression. It was set in an open and trusting face, which, I judged, had been only marred slightly by trauma. There was a single worry line across her forehead. When Lara was flustered or anxious, two veins would stand out, forming a vee shape on her brow.

"My father has also asked me to purchase some books," she said. "He has made a list for me, which I have here."

As she searched in her small black reticule, I drank from the beauty of her face, like a man dying of thirst. I noticed that she was confident, but also tentative; graceful in a feminine way, but almost ungainly. Sometimes, she would appear to stoop, because she was so tall. Her hands were exquisite – the fingers delicate and slender.

At length, the piece of paper was produced. I have learnt, over time, that women can rarely easily find the objects that they keep in their handbags. It is extremely annoying. The letterhead said, J.Sidgwick, Inventor, Spenhurst Hall, Kent. "Inventor" was printed in a cursive type. On the paper were scrawled some book titles in a scratchy, hurried script.

I perused the list. *De Dis Germanis,* I read, by Elias Schedius, 1648, and *Britannia Antiqua Illustrata,* by Aylet Sammes, 1676. Next was *Stonehenge, a Temple restor'd to the British Druids* by William Stukely, 1740. The list also specified translations (preferably in English) of Strabo and Posodinius, as well as Tacitus' *Annals* and Julius Caeser's account of his Gallic and British campaigns.

"Well, we have the Tacitus," I said, remembering with a shudder my old Latin master. "We may have one or two of the other Latin texts. I know an excellent bookseller who can probably assist us with the rarer works, for example, the Stukely, but it will take time, I'm afraid, and there will be a small handling charge."

"I see." She looked me full in the face. My knees weakened. I knew that it could take several weeks for the rarer books to arrive from London. I could not possibly wait that long until I saw her again.

"You say that there will be a small charge?"

She regarded me brightly, like an inquisitive bird.

"It will be very little," I reassured her, "less than sixpence, I should think. You wanted some other books, miss …"

"Sidgwick, Lara Sidgwick," she said, impaling my soul with her grey eyes. "Yes, but I am not sure which."

"May I help you?"

Very few customers received this level of service, certainly not poor old Winspear. I was unsettled for I had never been in love before, well, only a little, with our maid in Dulwich, but that had been before my sexual impulses had fully awakened.

Walking with her to the poetry section, I noticed that we were the same height and that our limbs had the same proportions; much later I would learn, as I gradually discovered the scents of Lara and the contours of her body; her patches of sweet moisture and her fuzzy secret hair, that our limbs fitted perfectly together, like the two halves of a puzzle. Plato believed that men and women once occupied the same body, but were separated, and that, in all their relations, they are merely trying to merge themselves back into one. It is a theory that has always appealed to me.

Lara told me that she liked Romantic poetry. I drew her attention to Swinburne's new Poems and Ballads, which had just come into the shop. I also commended to her Ruskin's *Sesame and Lilies,* a book I had been reading the previous week. I cannot read it now; I find it insipid. Lara noticed that one of Ruskin's epigrams had been marked by a pencilled under-lining. "You bring up your girls as if they were meant for sideboard ornaments," it said, "and then complain of their frivolity." She seemed to approve of this sentiment. Lara told me that she had recently moved to Spenhurst from Putney, in London. As well as pursuing her own studies, she was helping her father with some important work, about which she was not allowed to tell me.

She left the shop with Swinburne, that decadent corrupter of youthful innocence, and Ruskin, that pious repository of sweetness and light, tucked under her arm. As she went through the door, she turned and smiled, projecting a beam of such intense radiance that it flooded my entire being with joy (I was walking on air for the following fortnight). I knew that I would see her again, and that she wished it so. I could not predict that this chance meeting would affect the whole course of my life.

The rumours and gossip that circulated around Spenhurst high street over the following days fleshed out her story. Her father, it seemed, was an entrepreneur who had made a small fortune from his eponymous invention, Sidgwick's Restorative and Invigorating Liver Pills. The patent remedy was claimed by its manufacturer to have the remarkable property of eliminating virtually every ailment known to medical science. The pills thickened blood that had been thinned by our inclement winter weather and were an infallible cure for night starvation, biliousness and the most jaundiced internal organ. The imposing character of Doctor Sidgwick's brick-built factory, shown in the pills' advertisements, gave credibility to these claims.

Lara, her father and their servants had moved into Spenhurst Hall, a manor house just outside the village. Sidgwick was said to be highly eccentric; his daughter, it was generally held, was beautiful, but aloof. The family was thought to be Jewish. Lara now dominated my life. When I was not with her, I would configure her from the shadows and breathe in her scent, in the long solitary hours in the shop, in my bedroom and in the garden. Never in my life had I been so obsessed with another human being.

It was a filthy night about a month later and I had just spent an evening at the local Mechanics' Institute attending a meeting organised by the Eastern Question Association. I came in through the back door, clutching my wet overcoat. The phrases of the speakers as they denounced the Prime Minister, Mr Disraeli, were still rolling around in my head, like the riffs of a rock guitar.

Uncle Edward was sitting in the kitchen. He would have consumed the meal that Mrs Brown had prepared for him, before she left for the night, in the parlour. Now, he was sitting in front of the range. He was awake. Perhaps he had been waiting for me.

"Hello," I said, entering the room. For me, this was an eloquent speech, for I now barely addressed my uncle.

He made a noise, whose meaning I could not discern. I was hungry. I edged towards the range, wondering if any food had been left for me.

"So, you have been at one of your meetings, putting the world to rights, have you?" he said.

I interpreted this as a mild provocation and ignored it.

"What are your radical colleagues up to these days?" he continued, sarcastically. "Art classes for the indigent; extracting sunlight from cucumbers?"

I said nothing, imagining that my uncle had carefully prepared these choice phrases as he sat alone, brooding over a brandy.

"Did you go see your new friend?" he sneered. His views of Lara and her father were wholly negative. She was exotic and undoubtedly held dangerous ideas (any ideas were dangerous in a woman); her father possessed similar characteristics and compounded these crimes by being rich and successful.

"Oh, and if she comes into the shop again, please tell her to wash first. She smells like a harlot."

I held myself back and was now thinking of abandoning the field. It seemed that there was no food to be had. Probably, Edward had scraped my meal into the dustbin.

"I think I shall go to bed. Thank you for the lovely supper Uncle," I added, sotto voice, under my breath.

Sensing that he had lost his advantage, Uncle Edward sallied, for he had not finished with me. "You may not have noticed, young man, as you right the wrongs of the world. But it is I who gave you a home; I who have provided you with a living and the means of sustenance. I did not have to do this; I chose to do so when your poor father died, and I do not begrudge it."

"Yes you do!" My anger had magnified, having been saved. "You begrudge every morsel of food which is placed on that table. And you may not have noticed, but it is I who am keeping your pitiful life afloat!"

In fact, my work consisted largely of reading. But such an admission would have added little to my argument.

"I see," said my uncle, changing his line of attack. "So you think that you can change the world, do you, with some fine words and a few waves of your magic wand?"

"What about you!" I screamed. "You think that you know everything! Well you don't! All you ever do is to sit in your study pickling yourself in your own bile. You think that you are superior. But you are not. You are a snob! That is why Doctor

Wood has dropped you."

We had never referred to their argument before. I knew that it had affected my uncle deeply.

"So what friends do you have?" he spat out. "A rag-tag of misfits and wastrels!"

"How dare you say that to me!"

"This is my house, young man, and I shall say whatever I like!"

"Don't I know that it is your house!" My eyes scanned the gloomy cave of the kitchen, with its miserable sticks of furniture. Mrs Brown was unenthusiastic when it came to matters of cleaning. Strips of brown wallpaper were coming away from the walls; there were thick cobwebs around the cornices, one entombing a dead butterfly. It had been there for as long as I could remember. In a corner of the room was an etiolated aspidistra. They are virtually impossible to kill, but my uncle's neglect had almost done for it.

"I hate this place. I have always hated it," I said.

"I do not force you to live here." My uncle looked pathetic. It came home to me then that I was his only close relative and his sole companion. And we had come to this. I paused. I then said, "well, I'm sick of it. And I'm damned well leaving!"

Inconveniently, I had thrown down my coat at an earlier phase of the argument and now had to retrieve it. I realised that my eyes were filling with tears.

Uncle Edward seemed to expand. He drew himself unsteadily to his feet and jabbed at me with his finger.

"Oh no you're not, my lad."

I strongly disliked that form of address. "Don't call me that! How dare you call me that!" Now we were glaring at each other, like two animals.

"You have never wanted me to live here!" I exclaimed. "You wrecked my education and you hated my father. Well I hate you! I wish that I were dead!"

"I wish that I were dead!"

I looked at my uncle. With horror, I saw that he too was crying. Nothing was left of his proud words; not a shred of composure or dignity.

I would like to be able to say that this episode formed a catharsis in our relationship; that, afterwards, things were easier between us. But within days, my resentment and my uncle's arrogance had returned, made mordant because of his display of weakness. I think it is sad that the closest we ever came to revealing our true feelings was when we were arguing.

Uncle Edward continued to whimper, but my own tears had vanished. I touched his arm gingerly, momentarily feeling sorry for him. I filled the kettle and we had a cup of tea, which is the English way. Then we went to bed.

Chapter Three

The Willows

"Freddy, why do you hate your uncle so much?" Lara asked me the following afternoon. She had entered the shop to find me subdued following the previous night's argument. She was sitting in her now accustomed position by my side, at the table that served as a counter. It was a bright day – unpredictability is the genius of the British weather. Sunlight was stealing into the darkest recesses of the shop, dappling it with light, like the brush strokes of Canaletto.

She watched me intently with her piercing grey eyes, her chin resting upon her hand.

"I do not hate him," I said, unconvincingly.

"And yet, you speak of him in such negative terms," Lara offered.

"He is slothful, is he not," I said. "He drinks far too much, which makes him morose. He once espoused liberal views, but he is now the most unpleasant and recalcitrant kind of Conservative."

"He is lonely," said Lara. "And, surely, many people are Conservatives."

"Is it any wonder that he is lonely," I said, "given his miserable character and his dreadful misanthropy?"

"Freddy," said Lara, "you are his nephew; his closest family member. Do you not understand that the man is old and ill, which is why he is so bitter, and that he would love to be able to talk to you?"

"By pouring scorn on everything I believe in," I said.

"He likes arguing," said Lara, "as you do. You are very similar, you know."

"What?"

This was not a proposition I was prepared to accept. I had not told Lara about my uncle's anti-Semitism. I could not see the silver lining she perceived in his baleful black cloud. Still, I reflected upon her comments. Over the next few days, I endeavoured to be less critical; to be reticent where previously I would have been scornful or sarcastic. I even tried to make conversation with him on two or three occasions. But my uncle rebuffed these attempts. Remarks that I thought were conciliatory or innocent he turned back on me as evidence of my naiveté. I concluded, with the impatience of youth, that he was unworthy of my efforts and that nothing short of his or my imminent death would change the nature of our relationship. Probably not even that.

I was about to tell Lara that I would try harder to be kind to him, when our conversation was curtailed. For Miss Bain, who was a teacher at the National School, was passing by and glanced in through the window. At that period in history, to see a young woman and man engaged in conversation, lacking an acceptable social context, verged on scandal.

A look passed between us. Lara averted her eyes.

"Freddy?" she asked, suddenly, "what was a Druid?"

The books on the subject that had been requested by her father formed a heap under the table. She knew that I had been reading them and that I had absorbed some of their contents. I had already assumed the role of an oracle in our relationship, passing on scraps of half-understood information in a plausible manner (this was a facility that would later serve me extremely well as a journalist).

"Well, from what I can make out," I began, "they were the wise men and women of our ancestors, the Celts, in ancient Britain. In modern terms, they were a mixture of priests, scholars and magicians. They seem to have officiated at religious ceremonies that took place in sacred groves known as nemetons. There were also female Druids, according to Caesar. He describes a group of them, in black robes, shrieking, on the island of

Anglesey, as they were about to be slaughtered. Why do you need to know this?"

She ignored my question. Despite repeated attempts, I could glean nothing of the purpose of Lara's quest for knowledge. Perhaps her father was organising a fancy dress party. If so, he was going to an awful lot of trouble.

"What does Druid mean?"

I explained that the word's origin might be the Celtic word for an oak tree, duir, although the word had not been found in any pre-Christian text. I said that the Celts had possessed no written language and that Druidism was a secret, oral tradition, often associated with mystery and fear.

"What do you mean?"

"Stukely says that Avebury and Stonehenge were Druid temples, used for rituals. He hints at their apparent practice of human sacrifice."

I realised that I was losing Lara's attention.

"It is awfully stuffy in here," she said, suddenly. "Would you like to go for a walk?"

"Where to?"

"I would like to show you something."

"What?"

"A place where I go sometimes." She smiled, shyly.

"When?"

"Now?"

It was four o'clock. Strictly speaking, I should not close up for another hour. But my uncle would still be snoring off his brandy. He would not wake up until the early evening.

I pondered for a moment. Then I made a small but significant decision. "Very well," I said. "Let us go."

We took the path through the meadow, by the river. In the spring, the fields here became a multi-coloured carpet of indescribable beauty. On that November afternoon, darkness was already falling. The air carried an exciting tinge of wood smoke and wet grass. The pale sun glinted on silver rivulets, churned from the mud by cows' feet. I pointed out my little vegetable patch to Lara as we walked past. I showed her where I had seen my first kingfisher.

"Where did you grow up, Lara?" I said.

Our boots squelched along the path. The hem of her dress and her petticoats were becoming muddy.

"I was born in Soho," she said. "Papa was poor then. He came to England from Paris, with Mamma."

Her expression had become downcast when she had mentioned her mother.

"Is your mother dead?"

"She passed away from tuberculosis, when I was a year old."

"That is very sad."

I did not know what to say. At least when my mother had died I had been fourteen. There was a pause.

"Where did you live next, after Soho?"

"After Mamma died, father abandoned his journalism. He became a doctor. We moved from Wardour Street into a house off Highgate Hill."

"Was it a nice house?"

"I do not remember it clearly," she said. "I was only five when we moved there and we were only there for two years. When I was seven, we moved to an even larger house in Putney. For my father had begun the factory that makes his pills. The house was enormous but the garden was only a yard. Do you know Putney?"

I shook my head.

"It is a very congested place. There are no woods or fields there. Of course, there is Bishop's park and the river."

"How many servants did you have?"

"We had four. There was a cook, a housekeeper, a chambermaid and a groom, Snipe. My father did not have a butler, or a footman. He does not believe in them; he thinks that they are pretentious."

"In what sense?"

"My father says that the people in Putney are narrow-minded and bourgeois – they are only interested in parading the latest kind of carriage and the livery of their servants, like dolls."

"Is he a Radical?"

"I suppose so. He is a follower of Karl Marx."

"Who is Karl Marx?" I had never heard the name before. I was intrigued. Lara told me what she knew of the man.

"Did you go to school in Putney?" I asked.

"I did not go to school. Papa educated me, helped by a governess, Miss Jefford. She taught me French and embroidery. Father taught me Latin and Greek. Or at least he tried to!" She laughed.

"I have a blind spot for languages," she explained. "Papa is so brilliant – he speaks eleven languages, you know, and he could not understand my lack of ability. It is the same with mathematics; it means nothing to me. It is just a soup. Papa was very patient. But he would almost weep with frustration." She turned to look at me. "Did you love your father Frederick?"

"I cannot say," I replied. "I did not know him. Do you love yours?"

"Of course."

"What is he like?"

"He is a kind man, but he is very scatter-brained. Perhaps it is because he is so clever. They say that genius is close to madness."

"Mad people do."

She laughed.

"Why is he reading these books?" I asked. I was carrying Sidgwick's curious collection of volumes in a canvas bag.

"He is interested in history."

"His preoccupations are very specific. Is he an aspiring Druid, perhaps?"

She looked serious.

"Frederick, you must not ask me this. The books are to do with a project that my father is working on. But it is secret. That is all that I can tell you."

"I see."

A silence fell as we walked, our feet sinking into the boggy path. It may seem strange, but this was probably the longest and most intimate conversation that I had ever had with a woman. I had spent most of my time in purely masculine company and was very shy. The women in my life had hitherto been either distant objects of infatuation or servants; in neither case did one talk to them. Lara, however, I found easy to talk to.

We came to a stile, where the path was crossed by a ditch. It posed a dilemma. Lara could only negotiate the stile with difficulty in her long dress. Without a word being said, I crossed it first and extended my arms to help her. She took my hands. As I lifted her, she fell suddenly against my body. The impact of the warmth and quickness of her body; the smell of her skin and the feel of her breath on my face were almost overwhelming. We teetered at the top of the stile and almost fell. It is strange how the really important moments in life often conflate comedy and drama. We managed to save ourselves in time, narrowly avoiding becoming two prone figures, sprawling in the wet grass.

I helped Lara down. I could see that she was shocked but on the verge of laughing. She did not discourage me from looking directly into her eyes.

Without further comment, she offered me her arm. I took it and it seemed perfectly natural. When one is in love one's actions became simple, governed by instinct rather than choice. It was as if a lamp had been lit, illuminating my entire being. My previous existence seemed a dark and complicated thing.

"We are close to the willows, now Frederick, do you see? I adore willows, don't you? They are so beautiful."

The bare limbs of the trees cascaded gracefully over the river, like dryads. They marked the boundary of the deer park that extended to the rear of Spenhurst Hall. I knew that the Latin for willow is salix, which is close to the Celtic name, saille. The Greek term for willow is helice. This gives its name to helicon, the abode of muses, the priestesses of the moon. I knew these things, but I did not say them. I was also aware that the willow is associated with death Goddesses – Hecate, Hera and Persephone – and that the Druids were said to make human sacrifices at the full moon, in baskets made from willow withies.

"They are of the trees of the moon," I said.

"Didn't you tell me that the Druids worshipped trees?" said Lara.

"They did, but not as we kneel before plaster saints or pieces of wood in church; they regarded them as living, breathing, things, with magical properties. Take the willow, example."

She nodded.

"What do you think would happen if you were to break off a willow twig and place it in a cup of water?"

"I do not know."

"Within a few days, it would magically regenerate, producing fresh green shoots."

"Really?"

I explained that the Druids had divided the year into thirteen months, based on the cycles of a lunar year. There was a tree for each month. And its first letter had given them the consonants of their alphabet.

"But you said that the Celts had no written language"

"They did not. The tree language, the Ogham, was known only to the Druids. They used it for the purpose of divination, using sticks. It is very useful, for a magician, to have a secret language. The first tree in their alphabet was the birch, because it is the earliest to come into leaf in the spring. The second was the mountain ash, or rowan. The third was the ash. The ash was associated with lightning. It was used to make wands and spears."

There was a pause. I said that in ancient times our country had been covered with trees and that, essentially, we were a people of the woodland – that was why our houses were about as high as oak trees. I pointed across the river, towards the horizon.

"Doctor Wood believes that there was an ancient encampment there, at the top of Saint's Hill."

Lara paused before speaking.

"I would like to go up there with you, Freddy."

"Would you?"

"Oh yes. I love ancient sites."

"Do you? What about churches?"

She wrinkled her nose.

"I do not like them at all. Cold, clammy places. Please, tell me more about the tree alphabet."

"Well, let me see. The alder represented the fourth month. It was used to make boats and milk pails. When the alder is felled, it seems to bleed, as if it were a man. But that is an unlucky thing to do. I would not recommend chopping one down, unless …"

She smiled.

"I shall try not to Frederick. Did you know that I am a witch?" She spread out her fingers, like talons.

"Look Lara!"

I had seen something – a bundle of blue and orange feathers, moving, like an arrow, down the river. It was a kingfisher, the bird of the winter solstice. It was a startling site for a winter's day in Kent – like a tropical visitation. I touched Lara's waist, feeling my heart beating. The bird vanished into a patch of darkness.

We were now close to our destination. Lara's special place, the boathouse, was a construction of brick and timber, half-veiled by trees. Inside, bobbing against the riverbank, a skiff and a derelict canoe were tethered. In the upper storey of the boathouse, reached by an inside ladder, was a habitable room.

"Would you like to go in, Freddy?" she said. She looked at me.

Was she a beauty? Was the sky blue? "Of course," I said.

The room's three windows, which faced the river, were screened by branches so that its natural light was limited. Lara lit an oil lamp. The floorboards had been painted white. They were partially covered by Persian rugs. There was a narrow brass bedstead, with a dark green coverlet. Pieces of flotsam and jetsam were scattered around – stones and sea-smoothed driftwood – giving the room the feel of a ship's cabin.

Next to the bed was a large trunk, whose lid was open. Spilling from it were pieces of cloth resembling white robes. Were they the costumes for a masque or play? Lara would not tell me. She closed the lid of the trunk abruptly. A battered sideboard served her as a dressing table. Upon it were pictures, as well as pieces of jewellery, shells, trinket boxes and crystals. Women are very particular about such things; their arrangement had the quality of an altar.

Lara sat on a white-painted cane chair, by the windows. A mottled light fell on her face through the curtain of willows. We could hear the river as it gurgled and lapped. It was easy for me to identify the portrait of her mother on the sideboard. A handsome woman with dark, curly hair, she had Lara's features but her face was rounder.

"What was she called," I asked.

"Her name was Chloe. It is my only picture of her. She met my father in Paris, before they moved to London."

"She was very beautiful."

Lara looked away.

"I wish that I could talk to her. Sometimes, when I am speaking French, I imagine that she is correcting my mistakes."

"Who is this?"

Beside the image of her mother was a photograph of a small solemn child, dressed in a sailor's suit. His face was slightly blurred.

"That is my brother. He died the year before I was born. He was four. He had the same name as you … Frederick. There was a pause. "Do you have any brothers or sisters?"

"I do not. This would be your father?"

The photograph had been taken in a studio. Its subject looked confident and impassive. His jaw was squarer than Lara's but one could see a resemblance in the eyes. He was wearing a pith helmet. His feet were resting upon a tiger skin.

Lara came over to me. She picked up the gilt frame.

"That was taken just after Papa had returned from the Congo. We still have that skin."

"Did your father shoot the tiger?"

"Of course not. He would not harm a fly."

"What was he doing in Africa?"

"You are very inquisitive, Freddy. Well, if you would like to know, he was collecting native plants. It was in the Congo that he discovered one of the main ingredient of his liver pills."

"Is that the secret of his fortune?"

She looked away. I felt that I had been impertinent. Standing so close to her, breathing in her scent, was making me feel faint. I noticed the slenderness of her fingers, curled around the picture frame. She asked me whether I liked working in the shop. I said that, yes, I did. But that I was growing more and more impatient.

"What do you want to achieve in life?"

"I have no idea. What about you?"

She looked down at the floor.

"I would like to work with the poor, but I do not know if I am brave enough. Sometimes, I go to the East End, to visit Papa at his factory in Stepney. It is so dark there, and smoky. Papa does not like me walking around."

I had only been to the East End once in my life. But I knew one thing. It exhibited every variety of human degradation and depravity.

She replaced the photograph on the sideboard.

"Freddy, can I draw you?"

It was the first time. Later, we would often sit for hours with pencils or charcoals, scrutinising each other's faces. Lara's work was fluid and subtle. It was true to the essence of her subject as well as its form. My first attempts were woeful. But I did improve under her tutelage. How intensely I analysed her cheek-bones, her brow, her eyes. Each time, I seemed to perceive a different person. In some of my drawings she was Peresphone or Hecate; in others, she was Diana or Venus.

"Do I have to stay still?"

"As still as you can."

She had placed herself on the bed, with her legs aligned in front of her. I sat on the chair. She looked at me and frowned, then glanced down. Her pencil skipped over the paper.

"Do you like Swinburne?" I said.

"Yes, but not as much as Shelley."

"Shelley is your favourite poet?"

"Oh yes."

"Mine too. Will I be able to see what you have done?"

"Perhaps. You must be patient."

My view of the room was limited to a few salient features – Lara's white face in a pool of yellow lamplight and shadows from her objet d'art, flickering across the white floorboards. The prospect of leaving her was a torment. At the back of my mind was a nagging thought that my uncle would soon wake from his stupor, to find that I had deserted him. He would be furious.

I remember telling Lara that I was not looking forward to spending Christmas with Uncle Edward. I explained to her, somewhat pompously, that the occasion was of no interest to me. It was merely a celebration of the winter solstice. Jesus was the Christian equivalent of a Pagan god – Horus, Dionysius or Mithras. All had been born to virgins at Christmas. They were different versions of the same solar myth.

Lara told me that this was no reason not to enjoy oneself. She suggested that I could spend Christmas with her and her father. At first, it seemed a marvellous idea. Upon reflection, there were two problems, both involving my uncle. If he came to Spenhurst Hall, he would sneer at Sidgwick and goad him into an argument; if he did not come, he would convert his envy to spite and make my life a misery.

"You must decide to do whatever is best," said Lara. "But you know that you would be most welcome. Do you still have the books, Freddy?"

"Yes, here by my chair."

"When we have finished, why don't you take them to the hall and give them to my father?"

"Would that be all right?"

"Of course."

I do not know how long it took Lara to finish her drawing, perhaps half an hour. The advantage of being drawn was that it gave me an opportunity to study her face and her body at leisure. Her legs, I speculated, would be lithe and well-formed beneath the green dress. Her upper body was well-proportioned, but she did not have what one would call a bosom. It was fortunate, I speculated, that she could not read my thoughts. Or could she?

It must have been at least half past six by the time she had finished. I had crossed the Rubicon, as far as my uncle was concerned. I anticipated a dreadful assault from him for having left the shop unattended.

"Can I see?" I said.

She frowned. "I am not very happy with it. But yes."

She looked quizzically at her drawing, then back at my face. She laughed.

"What have you done to me?"

"Nothing, Freddy."

I crossed to the bed and stood next to her. I was shocked. Lara had made me look like a satyr. But it was an accomplished drawing, sensitive and sure in its touch; far better than anything that poor old Ruskin could have done. There was an awkward silence.

"Is it all right for me to be here?" I said.

"What do you mean?"

"Well, we are alone and ..."

"This is not my bedroom," she said. "I sometimes sleep here. But that is because I like hearing the sound of the river." She looked down.

"Some people would think it improper."

"Do you?"

"Of course not."

With trepidation, I touched her hand. Her expression was ambiguous. "Lara?"

"Yes?"

"We have spent a lot of time together recently and ..." My heart was thumping.

She regarded my face, as if she were still drawing me.

"I really have grown very fond of you ... very fond." I felt foolish.

She held my gaze. The beauty of her face could have melted my heart. "I know you have."

"I have grown fond of you and, as I say ..."

She looked away. "Come, Freddy," she said. "It is time for us to go."

Chapter Four

A Modern Prometheus

My mind was whirling all over the place as I walked up through the deer park holding Lara's hand. The moon was hidden behind clouds. The lamps of Spenhurst Hall were lit, making it look like a ghostly ship. It was a beautiful stone-built house of the Tudor period, with small-paned medieval windows and a curved oriel above the main entrance. The hall's weathered walls were clad with ivy, honeysuckle and sweetbrier. The building seemed, over the centuries, to have merged with the land, so that it formed a natural, organic extension of it, familiar and well-proportioned.

The house had two storeys, with a third tier of small windows peeping from its pointed gables, and twisted, barleycorn chimneys sprouting from its roof. It was perfectly symmetrical, like a child's drawing of a house. The building was shadowed on one side by a substantial elm tree; on the other was an even more venerable yew. The front drive was bordered by a box hedge and lavender beds.

"That is my room," said Lara, pointing towards the hall.

"I cannot imagine what it would be like to live in such a place," I said. "It is a palace."

"It is only a house. Come."

She walked on, pulling me behind her.

"Those are the stables, where my father has his workshops."

Ahead of us was a group of buildings ranged around a courtyard. We passed through a gateway, into a walled cottage garden. Sufficient light came from the hall to indicate roses clambering along its walls and the tall spikes of hollyhocks. We stopped by the door of the scullery. Lara suggested that I go to the front entrance, where the maid would let me in.

"Aren't tradesmen supposed to call at the back door?" I said.

"Normally, yes," said Lara, "but in your case, we shall make an exception."

There was a look of playfulness in her eyes. The thought that I would have to part from her was painful. We stood awkwardly, not knowing what to do next. I think that the moon put in a brief appearance then. I looked into Lara's eyes for longer than ever before. In fact, I never wished to look away. I seemed to fall into her. I wanted to drown in her soul. It was my first kiss and, I think, Lara's too. It only lasted for a few seconds, because neither of us fully understood the mechanics of breathing. I remember a giddy sensation; I thought that I was going to expire from ecstasy. When it was over, Lara squeezed my hand. She gave me a lingering look. Then she went into the house.

At the front door, I was in the world of the sun, rather than that of the moon – cold, sober and rational. I grasped the bell pull wondering what lay in store for me. After a minute or so, a maid presented herself. She was young and pretty, not quite out of her teens. She wore a neat black dress, with a lace apron and cuffs. I noticed that she had blue eyes, that her accent was Irish and that there was a charming vivacity in her manner, although I spent only a few moments with Mary on this first meeting.

She took me through an impressive, oak-panelled hallway. Music was flooding through it – a lively, complex melody, with a mournful quality. Mary explained that her master, Sidgwick, was playing the fiddle. She told me to wait in the morning room with Sidgwick's books. Then she departed. The music was muffled here but one could clearly discern the verve and confidence of the player – later, I was to become familiar with the piece. It was one of Sidgwick's favourite.

I am an inquisitive person, when it comes to other people's houses. I cannot help it and one day it will get me into trouble. The decorations of this room were unremarkable – its main features were bottle green wallpaper, a piano, a marble fireplace and a small bureau, scattered untidily with papers. However, on the writing table was something interesting – a single sheet of paper that was begging to be examined. It was the headed notepaper I had seen in the shop, covered with the same angular handwriting.

After a moment's hesitation, I read it. The address of the letter's recipient was, 41 Maitland Park Road, Belsize Park, London. It bore that morning's date, the 13th of November, 1879. I read:

My Dear Karl,
I hope that you will not be offended by my desire to communicate with you, on the basis of so casual a friendship, so long ago. It is, indeed, many years since we enjoyed the simple pleasures of the old Red Lion in Great Windmill Street. I believe that the last time we met was shortly after Willich challenged you to a duel, just before the dissolution of the Communist League. Do you remember? Often I think back to those happy times.

You will be aware of my reputation, as I am of yours, and you may feel that it is presumptuous for a quack to solicit the attention of a father of revolutions; but, rest assured, I seek nothing from you, only to convey a piece of information.

In your life's work, you have sought to aid the efforts of those who would influence the course of history. Well, to come straight to the point, I believe that I have discovered, after many years of experimentation, a practical means of achieving this objective. In short …

I should have realised that a quality in the environment had changed, but I had been far too absorbed in my task to notice that the violin had stopped playing. I was about to turn the paper over, when I was startled by a sound behind me. I almost jumped out my skin. Then, when I turned around, I felt mortified by shame and embarrassment. Curiously, the man who had entered the room appeared unconcerned that I had been examining his correspondence. Later, I came to the view that he had wanted me to read the letter.

He wore a black silk waistcoat, decorated by an ostentatiously large watch chain, combined with a long, antique-looking frock coat. His nose, which stood out like a beak from a pale, pock-marked face, was as large and aquiline as rumours had suggested; his eyes were hooded, like those of Mr Disraeli. Sidgwick's grey hair curled vigorously onto his collar. It clung to the sides of his face in the form of abundant side-whiskers.

His manner seemed dreamy and his pupils dilated. I later learned that Sidgwick would take a little opium, in the form of laudanum, most evenings. Only in this way could he sedate his super-abundant brain, as it fidgeted with theorems and equations.

"I have kept you waiting? I am so sorry." There was a faint trace of a European language in his accent. He extended a long, bony hand for me to shake. It was characteristic of Sidgwick to treat a mere tradesperson, for that is what I was, as a social equal.

"I hope that my playing did not offend your ears." He smiled.

"No, on the contrary. It was delightful." I paused. "What were you playing?"

"Vivaldi. His violin concerto in A minor."

"It was beautiful."

He looked at me. "In more skillful hands, perhaps. To me, the violin is a source of relaxation, to, others, I fear, a torment."

"That is not the case, Sir."

"You have some books for me, I believe."

"That's right."

I handed him the volumes and he paid for them. An idea occurred to him.

"Would you like to see the house, Mr …?"

"Frater, Frederick Frater. Very much."

"Than I shall give you the grand tour. Shall we start with the drawing room?"

Sidgwick led me through the hallway. The former banqueting

chamber with its minstrels' gallery and commanding stone fireplace had been converted into a comfortable Victorian interior, which was tasteful without being pretentious. This was my first experience of the aesthetic school of interior design, for I had lived, hitherto, in a world of flock wallpaper and ugly mahogany sideboards. The Oriental carpets with their lush patterns of vermilion and gold, the lacquered furniture, the Doulton vases and the Japanese prints were a wonder to me; all the more because such a grand space had been so completely domesticated. Sidgwick told me that his daughter had been a prime mover in this creation, inspired by frequent trips to that excellent shop, Liberty's in London and to the show rooms of William Morris and Company, in Oxford Street.

"I understand that you have you spoken with my daughter?" he said. I imagine that I went red. I blush easily. "She is very artistic. I think that you would get on." He studied my face for a moment. "Tell me, would you like a glass of something, Mr Frater?"

I murmured my assent, with a sense of excitement tinged with doom. Sidgwick was the kind of man who could speak for hours. It was already at least seven o'clock and my uncle would be purple with rage by now. However, there was no going back. My fate was sealed.

Sidgwick and I sat in comfortable, chintz-covered chairs, in front of a cheerful fire. We drank Madeira and ate fruitcake, served by Mary. I must have spent five hours listening to him, for by the time he had finished, it was long after midnight.

When he had first arrived in London from Paris in 1849, he explained, he had stayed in the German Hotel near Leicester Square, with a motley collection of Poles, Germans, Hungarians, Italians and Russians. He had been born in Poland, to a Jewish orthodox and well-to-do father, but the family had been propelled by religious intolerance to Germany. Here, the precocious young Sidgwick had studied mathematics and physics at Dresden University. His father, he said, had been a manufacturer of optical instruments and an inventor.

After a month, Sidgwick, who had now anglicised his name, moved into rented rooms in Soho, with his wife. Their son, Friedrich, was born here soon afterwards. Sidgwick was writing articles for various German newspapers and making a small living from his pen. He came from a far more affluent background than the other members of the German Workers' Educational Association, with whom he congregated in their club in Great Windmill Street – most were carpenters, compositors, shoemakers, watchmakers and the like. A prominent member of the group, he explained, was the impoverished German exile, Karl Marx.

In Europe, this was a time of revolutions, my love. Sidgwick's band of friends formed a close-knit group, devoted to self-improvement and political education. Within their society was another, more secret group, the Bund der Grechten, or League of the Just. This was later to become known as the Communist League. The group would often be found quarrelling and carousing in public houses off Tottenham Court Road, disputing the rival merits of English and German beer.

After Friedrich was born, the family moved frequently, always selecting tiny lodgings of two or three rooms, one step ahead of the bailiffs. It was while the family was living in Wardour Street that Friedrich's brief life was terminated by scarlet fever, in 1862. Sidgwick was inconsolable. He told me that he could not work or sleep for a year.

Lara was born in 1863. The sudden death of her mother a year later precipitated the next phase of Sidgwick's career. By an extraordinary act of will, he managed to qualify as a doctor. And within five years, he, Lara and their housekeeper had moved into a small villa, off Highgate Hill.

The creation of Sidgwick's Liver Pills was the result of a

sojourn in 1868 to the Ivory Coast and the Congo. Here, Sidgwick had discovered, through his researches, a curious native plant. Used in magical ceremonies by the Bwiti people, the plant was said by them to induce dream states, allowing them to visit their ancient ancestors.

An alkaloid in the plant, said Sidgwick, accounted for its psychoactive properties – basically, the relief of pain and hunger, whilst one was suspended, lucidly, halfway between wakefulness and sleep. William Gladstone was always said by Sidgwick to be a secret devotee of the pills. He often maintained that Gladstone made some of his longest speeches when under their influence.

At The International Working Men's Educational Club, in the East End, Sidgwick had made the acquaintance of a Lithuanian Jew, named Jakov Vynodsy. The two men became friends. They used to discuss the Talmud together in Yiddish. Jakov had a son called Nathaniel, a businessman in the sugar trade. Nathaniel, who had adopted the surname Vane, was more money-minded than his father. It was he who provided the working capital for Sidgwick's first factory. But it was not the grand premises shown in the pills' advertisements. In reality the product was made in a dingy warehouse beneath some railway arches in Stepney.

Every month, shipments of the African plant would arrive by cargo boat in Dover and be transported by train to London. The sweet-smelling stems and leaves were boiled in big copper vats – their vital ingredient extracted by the addition of (*here a word has been scored out. Ed.*) and distillation.

Vane became Sidgwick's business partner. He was a tall, suave man with a luxuriant black mustache – charming but single-minded. Sidgwick abandoned medicine for his pharmaceutical enterprise in 1870. Within two years, he and Vane were rich men. The peculiar properties of Sidgwick's Liver Pills made them fantastically popular – they were said to be three times more powerful than laudanum. Sidgwick moved to a larger house in Putney. Vane acquired a valet and a coachman and swaggered like a lord, in a mansion in Finchley.

"The pills," I said. "How do they … I mean, do they?"

Sidgwick looked at me queerly. He reached into his waistcoat pocket and removed a small twist of paper. He offered me the packet.

"See for yourself," he said. "But do not, on any account, take more than three."

We both looked at the fire. It had died down to glowing embers.

"So that is my life," he said, "providing an opiate for the proletariat, while I masquerade as a gentleman." He looked at me curiously. I suspected that there was a lot more to it; something hidden that had not yet been divulged.

"Good grief," he said, looking at his pocket watch. "I have kept you far too long with my stories. I am so sorry."

"Not at all," I replied.

My head was spinning as I walked through the pitch-black lanes, back to the village. I sensed, intuitively, that my circumstances were about to change. I need not have worried about my uncle, for he did not ask me where I had been the following morning. He had little curiosity about anything beyond the purlieu of his own prejudices. His manner was only a little more irascible than usual.

It was not merely to keep up with Sidgwick but also out of curiosity that I now entered a new intellectual universe. First, I nibbled at the French utopian socialists. These were preliminary courses before the main dish, Marx's *Communist Manifesto,* which had been published by the English Chartist, George Julian Harney, in his estimable journal, the *Red Republican*.

I now discovered that revolution was inevitable. The middle class would be devoured by the ravenous beast it had inadvertently created, the proletariat, which, of course, had nothing to lose but its chains. And the collapse of the capitalist system would augur a heaven on earth.

I fear, Isabella, that, emboldened by a new way of thinking, I became the worst kind of zealot. My uncle bore the brunt of my scorn. Ruskin's limpid works now seemed like a heavily-diluted cordial, compared to the deep drafts of revolutionary liquor that I was imbibing. Uncle Edward saw through the whole business. To him it seemed axiomatic that such a dogmatic, purportedly empirical theory, would produce evils when tested against reality, and, I am afraid to say, he was right. But I could hardly have known that at the time. I also began to write poetry. This combination of the political and the lyrical may seem strange to you, but was not Marx intoxicated by the Romantic poetry of Heine? And, also, remember that I was in love.

One morning, a week after my first visit to the hall, I was startled by the shop-bell. I was in a state of dreamy intoxication, induced by a handful of Sidgwick's pills; my head was full of dreams and metaphors. It was Lara.

"Hello, Druid," she said. We were using nicknames, I am afraid. My name for her was the Venus of Putney.

"What are you doing?"

"Nothing," I said. I pushed my book aside, a political work in French.

She made a strange expression. She found such volumes dreary.

I turned the book around and showed her the flyleaf. Upon it, I had inscribed her name, nestling in a superstructure of acacia leaves.

"Your drawing is really coming on," she said.

I smiled. There was, indeed, a vitality in my embellishments. We laughed.

That week Lara had begun to teach embroidery to girls from poor families at a Ragged School in Tonbridge. The following day, she would begin giving them lessons in copying. She placed a book of steel engravings on the table. I remember a particular work that we looked at that day – Burne-Jones' Laus Veneris. A damosel swoons in front of a mediaeval wall hanging. There is a crown upon her knees. At the foot of her divan are four melancholy ladies-in-waiting; glimpsed through a window one sees five knights. The symbolism is heavy handed and the composition stilted. But I love that picture.

"My father speaks highly of you, Freddy," said Lara. She looked up from the book. We are having a dinner party tonight, did I tell you? We would love you to join us."

"Is anyone else coming?"

"Doctor Wood, I think. Do you know him?"

"My uncle knows him more than I do. Or at least he did."

I recalled the awful night of their arguments.

"Is he a friend of your father's?"

"Oh yes." Lara smiled sweetly.

"What time shall I come?"

"We shall be dining at eight o'clock. But you may come earlier, if you wish."

"Thank you."

I looked at her face. There was something curious in her expression; I could not quite divine it.

As I shut up the shop that evening, I could hardly contain my excitement. Uncle Edward was in a particularly bad mood. It deteriorated even further when I told him that I had been invited to the hall for dinner, provoking mingled feelings of resentment and jealousy. Poor Edward, who always managed to get everything wrong, had transferred his political allegiance from Gladstone to Disraeli at the nadir of the latter's success and popularity – I sometimes think that he liked to be on the losing side; it fed his sense of bitterness. The following year, Gladstone was to trounce Disraeli in a famous general election – an event that I would not witness.

Following my walk through the lanes, the lights of the hall beckoned me at the end of a long drive. The lamps behind its leaded casements cast a soft orange glow. I was wearing my best clothes. The stiff, unfamiliar collar strangled my throat. As soon as I crossed the threshold most of my anxiety left me. Mary took my overcoat, moistened with drizzle. I was keenly aware of Lara, in a white dress, with a blue sash around her waist, her hair restrained by a copper clasp. But this was not a moment to be intimate with her.

The table had already been laid in the dining room. Lara had placed a large vase of white lilies on the starched tablecloth, complementing the simple forms of the blue soup bowls. The silver cutlery and napkin rings had been polished to a mirror finish that sparkled in the lamplight. I had not realised, as I took in the room's decor, that Doctor Wood was already in situ. He was masked from view, seated in a high-backed leather dining chair, in front of the fire.

"Frederick." He rose to greet me. "It is good to see you again. You are looking very well. How is your uncle?"

Their angry exchange flashed through my mind. Again, I heard the tumbler crashing against the wall and the back door slamming shut.

"My uncle is in fine fettle," I lied. "He sends you his best regards."

Doctor Wood seemed satisfied with this disingenuous reply. It is curious that the English people, who say that they value sincerity, can dissemble with such facility; but then hypocrisy is their primary vice.

"Frederick!" Sidgwick was as warm to me as Doctor Wood had been, perhaps excessively so. I suspected that he was beginning to regard me as a replacement for his lost son, Friedrich, who had been born in the same year as me, 1858. Sidgwick's eyes were bright. I guessed that he had prescribed one or more of his pills for himself.

He bore down on me with a bottle of claret and filled my glass. Then Lara came in. Her demeanour that evening was shy and reserved. She spoke very little, but I was keenly aware of her, especially during the highly charged moments when my knee brushed against her dress beneath the table.

Although Sidgwick shared with Doctor Wood a medical training, neither man was a bore and they carefully avoided talking shop. There was a sense of gaiety and lightness in the air, rather than the gloom of the dissection room. To my relief, art, culture and politics were on the agenda.

Over soup, we discussed the merits of Whistler's abstract paintings, compared to the realism of Watts and Millais. At the time, I did not understand Sidgwick's predilection for Whistler; I was sympathetic to Ruskin's view, exercised in a celebrated libel trial two years before, that the American artist was a charlatan – a coxcomb who had, "flung a pot of paint" in the face of the public. But in later years, I changed my mind. I came to find much of the Pre-Raphaelite painting, championed by Ruskin, cloying and false in its notes. And I detected an insincerity in its sentimentality. If you study photographs of Ruskin's friend Rossetti, you will certainly notice that there is something unpleasant in his expression – he has the eyes of a sexual predator.

Our conversation flowed through the stages of the meal. I had become, somewhat unwillingly, Ruskin's champion in the Whistler controversy. This role continued as Mary served us our main course of braised lamb and the theme widened into politics. "How can you read him?" said Sidgwick, provocatively. "I cannot abide the man. He is a simpering bourgeois who merely wishes the working classes to adapt to their slavery. Ruskin wants to make them beautiful prisons." He paused for effect. "But Marx and Engels wish to set them free. Besides, he is such a stuffed vest."

"Shirt, Papa," Lara corrected.

"Thank you."

"That is unfair," I began. "And, besides, to my knowledge, Marx and Engels are from similar social backgrounds to Mr

Ruskin."

"If I may intercede." Doctor Wood, who was one of nature's diplomats, entered the fray. He said that he, personally, was sympathetic to the practical and philanthropic side of Ruskin; but that he could also see Sidgwick's point. Ruskin's political views were naive and tended, perhaps unintentionally, to serve the interests of the ruling classes.

"However, I do feel," said Doctor Wood, studying his glass, "that the views of your friend Marx, are far too, mechanistic – that he applies empiricism where it is not warranted. I know that you believe that his predictions will be fulfilled – that the proletariat will empower itself and seize control."

Sidgwick considered the doctor's proposition. For him Marx was a real person, not a mere name on the spine of a book – the two men had got drunk and played billiards together.

"No, not inevitably," he protested. "Marx has a saying on this subject in his *Theses on Ludwig Feuerbach*. It is this – 'The philosophers have only interpreted the world in various ways. The point, however, is to change it'. At certain points in human history, it may be necessary for external agents to intervene in human affairs. And in this case ..." He stopped. "But we have grown far too solemn. I fear that Lara will die of boredom if we persist." He laughed. "Perhaps she would entertain us with a song at the piano?" Lara blushed. I felt for her.

Less portentous topics were broached as we ate desert. Doctor Wood, who was a vegetarian and who barely drank, allowed himself a small glass of moselle, but declined brandy. He took his leave at about eleven-thirty, explaining that he was visiting some cottages in Poundsbridge early in the morning. We were all cheerful – the evening reverberated with a sense of success. What a contrast to the miserable and fractious meals that I had taken with my uncle. Afterwards, it was as if Lara, Sidgwick and myself formed a family. We agreed that the evening had been a pleasant one, that the flowers were lovely and that Doctor Wood's conversation had been interesting.

Traditionally, women retired before men after dinner, leaving the latter to their cigars and ratiocinations. I was disappointed, for I would have loved to have gone into the drawing room with Lara in order to enjoy a more relaxed conversation. I would have loved even more to explore the treasures of her sweet body, hidden beneath complicated layers of cotton and muslin. Actually, I think that her departure had been pre-arranged, leaving the field clear for her father.

He looked at me seriously. "Come, Friedrich," he said, "I have something to show you."

Outside, it was pitch black. The feeble glow of a hand-held lantern had little effect, pitted against the illimitable darkness. Our feet crunched upon gravel. Soon, we reached the outbuildings to the rear of the house. We stood before a door secured by a large padlock. Sidgwick silently unlocked it.

He used a match to light a paraffin lamp. It is here, Isabella, that my story leaves the realm of the prosaic – the world of omnibuses, headache pills and brass fenders. I do not expect you to believe everything at once, but I do ask you to come with me. As the interior of the room came into focus, I gradually perceived two round objects against the far wall. They were extremely large. Each was perhaps fifteen or twenty feet high. Later, I formed the analogy that they resembled over-sized diving-bells.

"Go on." Sidgwick motioned me forwards.

In front of each device was a set of metal steps, giving access to an oval entrance. Each sphere had a metallic, silver surface that seemed to glow faintly and was girdled at half-height by a broad black band. I detected at once the ponderous but practical workmanship of the village blacksmith, George Watkins.

"What on earth?"

"These are the chronospheres," said Sidgwick, proudly. "This one is the Daedalus, and that is the Icarus. Don't be shy, Friedrich, let me show you."

Chapter Five

Letting Go

The interior was bright and surprisingly spacious – I cannot remember if we had climbed into the Daedalus or the Icarus, for the machines were virtually identical. Ample illumination came from a luminous white hemisphere that was set into the ceiling. I was never able to discover the source of this light, and Spenhurst Hall was not yet supplied with electricity but this was one of the chronosphere's minor mysteries.

"Good grief," I said. "What …"

"It is a travelling device," said Sidgwick, "which functions, if you like, in the temporal rather than the spatial dimension. I understand that you will find the concept a little strange, at first."

I did, especially, as the scene before us was as comfortable and homely as a housemaid's parlour. I recognised the pastoral wallpaper with its floral motif as a product of William Morris and Company, as were the two armchairs, upholstered in velvet. My eyes took in walnut-veneered cabinets and, behind a carved wooden screen, a narrow day bed. A raised wooden dais to our left Sidgwick described as the bridge, for this was where the machine's controls were located – an arrangement of gleaming brass, owing more, one felt, to plumbing than to navigation.

"Come, don't be bashful."

"But, Sir," I protested, lingering in the doorway.

"You are behaving as if you have never seen a time machine before, my lad." I did not resent the appellation coming from Sidgwick. We had already formed a close connection and, after all, we both loved Lara. I could detect her hand in the chronosphere's richly-textured rugs, the lace antimacassars and the scattered turquoise and red cushions.

"You will be curious as to how it works," he said. "I understand that. I shall try and explain."

He had stepped onto the dais, to which he beckoned me. There was a self-satisfied look in his eyes of complete mastery. I do not think that he had demonstrated the potentialities of the machine to anyone else, although many hands must have been involved in its manufacture.

"The first is this ..."

Here, my attention began to wander. I must confess, I have never had the slightest interest in the stern disciplines of science and mathematics – others may find them as fascinating and colourful as the Russian ballet but, to me, they have always been far too difficult, and, to be honest, excruciatingly boring. Many years later, I picked up by chance, a little quantum mechanics from a casual acquaintance who, between puffs of Indian hemp, tried to explain to me what is known as string theory. I believe now that Sidgwick must have stumbled upon the secret of dark matter or anti-matter. The chronosphere's mechanical heart, its gravatron, enabled it to move through space and time as easily as a knife through butter; although, as Sidgwick explained, a better analogy for the multi-dimensional universe would be to imagine it as a giant brain, and the chronosphere as a thought.

"Calibration of the diatronic configurator." Sidgwick concluded a long and complicated sentence, to which I had not been listening. I have always had a useful ability to feign an interest in subjects I do not understand.

"I see." Briefly, I made eye contact, to give the illusion that I had been paying attention. "But how does one actually activate the device? And why are there two of them?"

Sidgwick pondered my questions. He had the same clear grey irises as Lara and the unblinking stare of a bird of prey.

"Well, Friedrich, one simply chooses the time one wishes to visit and the place." He manipulated three large calibrated dials. "Then one pushes this lever. Forwards to go there; backwards to come back."

His long fingers briefly alighted on the mechanism – a polished brass rod with an ebony handle. Historical tableaux now paraded through my mind, like the pages from an ancient, ink-stained text book – Diogenes in his barrel, brave Horatius guarding the bridge, the charge of the Light Brigade, Lady Godiva riding, naked, through the streets of Coventry.

"But we are not going to put the machine through its paces tonight, for it is far too late and I have kept you from your bed for far too long. You have been most attentive and I am gratified by the interest which you have shown."

This short speech concluded the demonstration. We now returned to the drawing room, where we enjoyed a night-cap of cognac, as the fire made by Mary died down. There was little conversation. Sidgwick was subdued; his eyes like dark coals.

As I walked back to the shop, a full moon loomed huge over the hedgerows, guiding my steps, its shadowed face had not yet been defiled by man's footprints. I thought of the civilisations that had risen and fallen in the blink of an eye and of the numberless generations that were yet to be born. I thought of Lara in her bed, of the rise and fall of her sweet breasts and of the moon shining through her casement, onto her sleeping form.

A strange odour greeted me as I entered the kitchen of the shop by the back door – a smell of burning. It would not be correct to say that Uncle Edward's feet were on fire, but they were certainly smouldering. I realised at once what had happened. He had fallen asleep, dead drunk, with the soles of his boots resting upon the kitchen range. Over several hours, the leather had reached a sufficient temperature to convert to charcoal, filling the room with an acrid smoke.

I shook Uncle Edward roughly by the shoulders. As he regained consciousness and became aware of his pain, he let out a blood-curdling scream. My uncle's feet were badly injured. He must have been hobbling around for days afterwards.

"Get off me!" he growled. Now, pain combined with mortification as he realised what had happened. Like most slaves to alcohol, Edward refused to acknowledge his addiction, and attempted to involve others in this self-deception. His story was that he had simply fallen asleep, unassisted by a quart of brandy, never mind that his face was as red as a sugar-beet and that his breath was short and stertorous.

There was some terse conversation between us – he did not ask me whether I had enjoyed my evening – then he painfully climbed the stairs, like a walrus on an ice floe, refusing my offer of help.

I was supposed to be stocktaking the following day, a Saturday. But this was a misnomer. The shop's sales, which were theoretically recorded in a thick black ledger, had dwindled to almost nothing; meanwhile, its stock had expanded in proportion to my new interests. The political economy section was now swelled by the writings of radicals, anarchists and revolutionaries, in several languages. Their books would never catch on in Spenhurst, unless its rustics were seized by an improbable desire to storm the citadels of power.

I knew that my uncle would be furious when he found out and was dreading this happening. Christmas was fast approaching and the thought of spending it with him filled me with apprehension. My uncle begrudged the joy and prosperity of others and in that season, which legitimised his drunken torpor, he became particularly misanthropic.

As I sat at the table in the shop, bleak and wholly negative thoughts engulfed me. In general, if you had asked me whether I was happy, I would have said yes, for Lara and her father had come into my life. But, at this moment, I was shrouded in a blanket of gloom.

Seeds of resentment were germinating in this dark medium. I knew that my mother had set up in her will a small trust fund, with what remained of my father's estate after the sale of his assets, and that the money was held in the custody of two trustees, Uncle Edward and my great aunt, Agnes. Agnes, unfortunately, was mad. Uncle Edward paid me no salary, arguing that in feeding and watering me, as he put it, he was discharging his familial duty.

Now that I was twenty-one years old, I suspected that the money from the trust fund should be mine; or, at least, that I should know when I would come into my inheritance. Agnes, who lived alone in a huge, gloomy house in Sevenoaks, was in la-la land. It seemed highly probable that Uncle Edward would cheat me of my inheritance, or, if he could not, would attach onerous conditions to my acquiring it.

I sat with the ledger before me, its sparse columns of figures adding up to months of futility, and several ideas popped into my mind in quick succession. First, what was the purpose of my working here when I did not want to? Second, I loved Lara, what should I do about it? And third, where was my money?

Suddenly, I stood up. It was one of those moments that change one's life. I abandoned the table, the ledger and the shelves, never to return to them. I flung open the door that connected the shop to the kitchen.

Uncle Edward was seated at the table, his head cradled in his arms, next to a half-empty bottle of brandy. It was not even eleven o'clock, by the grandfather clock, but he was in a complete stupor, dead to the world.

My words must have cut through his fogged brain, like a shard of ice.

"Where is my money? I want my money!"

"What are you talking about?"

"The trust fund. I am talking about the trust fund!"

My uncle twisted around to face me. His feet were swathed in bandages, which could almost have been a comic sight.

"What trust fund?"

"You know damned well what I am talking about. The money my father left me, of which you have charge."

"You would be well advised not to use such language in my house, young man!" Edward shot a look of pure venom at me, with a hint of fear beneath it.

"I shall use whatever language I damned well like," I said. I do not know where my courage had come from; perhaps from the fact that I had burned my boats; whatever happened, my days beneath his roof were numbered.

Uncle Edward considered my statement and moderated his tone. "I do not know to what you are referring. But I suggest that you come back when your mind is less disturbed and you can talk to me in civil manner." His voice was slurred. His eyes were bloodshot and rheumy, like those of an old bulldog.

"How dare you!" I do not think that I had ever been so angry. For a moment, I considered smashing the bottle over his head – "Ghastly slaying of bookseller – nephew to hang".

"You will not fob me off with this nonsense," I exclaimed. "You know that it is mine! And I will no longer stand for this!" I advanced upon him menacingly and somewhat ridiculously. Perhaps a Darwinian instinct for survival intervened. For he now conceded the point.

"A certain sum is indeed entrusted to me, young man, which I may, at my discretion, allow you to have, in the fullness of time. If I feel that you will exercise sound judgment and spend it wisely then I may, in these circumstances …"

"You swine!"

I had reached the edge of language and could not untangle my disordered thoughts. I held back, suspended between word and action, glowering, at a red-faced man with a torn bed-sheet wrapped around his blistered feet. I stood back and took a few deep breaths.

"Listen! I work and save for you in that excuse for a shop and what is my reward? Nothing. I am simply asking for what is mine, so that I can decide what to do with my life. Is that so unreasonable?"

"If you spent more time working and less dreaming after that painted harlot I would be more disposed to listen to you. As it is …"

"That is your last word?"

"It is not my last word. It is the condition that I impose upon your request."

Anger continued to well up inside me. There was no hope with my uncle of appealing to his better side because he did not have one.

"Then you shall be hearing from my solicitors."

I do not know where the phrase came from. I had no solicitor; the only professional man I knew was Charles Wood.

I took my coat off the peg and paced to the back door, giving my uncle a final baleful glare. As I left, I slammed the door, satisfyingly, with just enough force to rattle the plates on the Welsh dresser. I am surprised that the door remained on its hinges, what with all of the rough treatment it endured over the years. At any rate, I walked away and I did not return.

The cool air braced me and helped to clear my head. I knew that I could no longer live with Edward, but where was I to go and how was I to make my living? For a moment, I contemplated joining the Royal West Kent Regiment. The idea passed quickly; its main attraction was the thought of my uncle learning of my death in a brief, matter-of-fact telegram from the War Office and of him being overcome with grief and guilt. On reflection, Edward would have felt no such emotions; he would merely have sliced off the top of his breakfast egg, and got on with his day. No, the army was out of the question.

There was only one place I could go. My steps guided me, almost unconsciously, down the high street to the path by the river. I remembered my walk here with Lara, on the day that we had drawn each other. A heavy darkness was settling over the afternoon. I plodded disconsolately along the sodden path, which had scarcely dried out since the summer. I walked slowly but purposefully, rehearsing how I would broach the topic of marriage to Lara and of my prospects in life, which were non-existent, to her father. I reached the boathouse and made my way through the deer park to the rear of Spenhurst Hall.

It seemed unnaturally quiet around the stables for a Saturday. There was no sign of the handyman, Snipe. I pulled on the front door bell, my heart pounding with anticipation.

Mary, too, was out of breath. "Sir, thank heaven that you are here!" The words tumbled out in a strong Irish brogue.

"What is happening?"

"They are gone Sir. They are gone! The master and Miss Sidgwick. I went into her room, Sir, five minutes ago. But she is nowhere to be found!"

"Doctor Sidgwick is gone too?"

"Yes, Sir."

She was flushed and out of breath.

"Where have they gone?"

"I don't know. They were here this morning, at breakfast. Mrs Murdoch saw Snipe with the master, in the stables."

"Show me."

Mrs Murdoch, the housekeeper, was hovering in the hallway, unsure of what to do. We went upstairs and I saw Lara's bed – curious things happen at times of crisis. The pillow was still indented where her head had lain and the damask coverlet was thrown back. Lara's characteristic scent was there, but indubitably, she was not. I descended the staircase with Mary.

"Did they perhaps leave together in the carriage?"

"No Sir, for it is still here."

I now asked to see Sidgwick's study, suspecting, correctly as it turned out, that it could offer some clues. It could have been deemed improper for a stranger to be allowed such a liberty; but, for some reason, it did not seem unnatural that I had taken charge of the situation.

There was a masculine smell of leather and cigars in the room. The fact that Sidgwick's books and papers were neat and orderly did not surprise me. His genius required, as a precondition, a certain predictability and order. Where would Leonardo have been without a ready supply of charcoals? But I sensed that he had left the room midway through a task. On the desk, was a copy of that excellent volume, Lempriere's classical dictionary. It was left open at the curious chronological table that prefaces the work.

In his famous table Lempriere, with a certainty that now seems touched with pathos, locates the beginning of the world precisely. The date which he authoritatively attaches to this event is 40004 BC, or the 710th year of the Julian period. Next to this year, Sidgwick had placed a question mark. His pen had hovered over other actual and mythological events placed in a historical sequence by Lempriere – the birth of Moses, the voyage of the Argonauts, the building of Alba Longa and of Rome (20th April, 753 BC, says Lempriere. "Rome was not built in a day," Sidgwick had added, dryly).

Caesar's expedition to Britain, in 55 BC, had attracted an underlining, as had his murder 11 years later. Some more notes had been added by Sidgwick in a tiny, crabbed hand. I read in the margin: AD 43 invasion by Claudius; AD 47, Aulus Platius first governer of Britannia, Fosse Way built, Cogibudnus of Sussex becomes Roman citizen; AD 60 Druids of Anglesey slaughtered; AD 80 conquest of England and Wales complete. The word Anglesey was under-scored and embellished with an exclamation mark. I guessed, or some instinct told me, that the fate of this remote island, off the north-west coast of Wales, was of crucial importance as far as Sidgwick was concerned. It had been the Druids' most important stronghold.

The Romans, I knew, had done their best to crush the Celtic

tribes of Britain and to obliterate, or assimilate, their magical, nature-worshipping belief system. But what if events had taken a different course? If the Celts had unified their scattered forces and mounted a serious resistance to the Roman legions, Britain's subsequent history may have been entirely different.

It would seem paradoxical to associate Sidgwick, a master of science and mathematics, with the irrational, moon-drenched society of the Celts. But I knew that he felt that the human race had been diminished by its separation from nature and had gone down a false path. His genius, I believe, in contrast to the stern Jehovan rigidities of Marx, was to acknowledge the magical and to merge it with the empirical. He wished for a softer world in which humanity was in touch with, rather than alienated from, the forces of nature.

It may seem fanciful to believe that the pre-eminence of the Romans in Britain had led, ineluctably, to the iniquities of the nineteenth and twentieth centuries, as well as the steam train, the electric telegraph and the gramophone. But Sidgwick clearly regarded the first century AD as a point in history at which his intervention could profoundly influence subsequent events.

My mind immediately flicked to the chronospheres and to the open stable door.

"I think we had better go outside," I said.

There was no need to light the lamps in the stable. A shaft of winter light sliced through the darkness, gilding swirling clouds of dust. We could see immediately, that where, previously, there had been two chronospheres, there was now only one.

"Holy Jesus," said Mary, softly. We both looked up, to see if there was a large hole in the ceiling. There was none. The chronosphere, we reflected, could not conceivably have been removed through the door.

"Is Snipe around now?" I asked Mary.

"No Sir."

There was a cool look in her eyes. She told me later, the reason for her dislike of the man. He had clumsily tried to seduce her in this very stable – a not uncommon phenomenon with regard to young female servants. She had fought him off. After that, Snipe, who was described by Mary as a, "miserable streak of nothing", had been insolent and offensive.

I did not learn exactly what had happened until much later. I guessed, however, that Sidgwick and Lara had not intended to travel back to the first century without telling anybody and that Snipe had somehow been involved in their precipitous disappearance.

"Mary," I said, "please go back to the house. I shall join you in a few moments."

What happened next was not of my conscious volition; it was as if an invisible hand was guiding my actions. I climbed the steps of the second chronosphere, the Icarus. Fortunately, its door was open.

The machine's homely décor was flooded by a harsh white light. When I opened one of the cabinets, I was not at all surprised by what I found there – a long white robe, apparently designed for someone of my precise dimensions, with flowing sleeves. There was also a bronze-coloured headpiece, a large neck ornament of the same material and a sword, whose hilt was encrusted with gemstones. The Druidic garb was completed by a wig of flowing grey locks and a false beard. Since I have never been able to grow anything more than a sparse stubble on my chin this particularly appealed to me; I tried on the wig and wig and beard.

After a few moments of hesitation, I removed my clothing and put on the rest of the costume. Robes are very comfortable, I must say, compared to the restrictive clothes normally worn by men. I cannot account for what I did next. It was madness. Having closed the door, I crossed to the dais. Two assumptions governed my following action – firstly, that the chronosphere's mechanism had already been set, in preparation for a predestined journey, and, secondly, that the curious costume had been made for me by Lara, appropriate to its destination. I grasped the ebony knob of the Time Lever.

Slowly, I pushed it forwards, to its full extent. The lever settled into its final position, like a ship coming slowly to rest against a harbour wall. My head seemed to expand into an infinite space and to fill with stars, as if a new universe was being born – which, indeed, it was. A darkness engulfed me. I blacked out.

Chapter Six

A Journey to Hell

Consciousness slowly returned, accompanied by a headache pounding at my temples, like a vile hangover, and a feeling of nausea. The light in the chronsophere had dimmed, so that I could barely recognise my environment. I know now that the journey I had made had drained energy from the machine's power source, the gravatron. It would take a little time to charge up again.

I was standing when I came to, clenching the Time Lever in two hands, my legs barely supporting me. Feeling dizzy, I stumbled back to one of the armchairs, which was an oasis of comfort. I closed my eyes, unable or unwilling to accommodate the new reality.

Prometheus had stolen fire from the gods to liberate the human race from darkness; had Sidgwick achieved a second stage of emancipation, in conquering our oldest enemy, Time? As I settled back into the chair, I could not have imagined that, in the twenty-first century, we would be able to take the essential ingredient from a jellyfish and make a potato that glowed in the dark; that many diseases would be eliminated through the science of genetics, and that the human race would stand at the threshold of immortality, one of the primary characteristics of godliness, through the prospect of transplanting consciousness to new bodies. Neither did I know that everyday implements would become intelligent; that virtual reality would knock on the door of the physical world and shake its hand, or that one day we would invent miniscule organic machines that could repair our bodies.

In a later age, such developments would require philosophical speculations as cybernetics and biotechnology raced ahead. What would life mean without birth and death, the cornerstones of existence? Would a brain in a jar, metaphorically speaking, still be a human being? And what if the contents of a human mind could be re-located to another physical vessel?

Few such thoughts were in my pounding head at that moment; in reality, I felt awful. I would dearly have loved to have sunk into a feather mattress and gone to sleep. Suddenly, there was a ping; it seemed to be a ricochet as a projectile hit the chronosphere's strong outer casing and bounced away – later, I realised that it must have been a stray bullet. That was what got me to my feet. There was nothing else for it. I would have to see what lay outside.

The door opened smoothly – as evenly-balanced as any expensive, well-crafted mechanism. It arced outwards on its well-greased hinges, to reveal a tract of open countryside on a bright summer's day. Before me, was a landscape of gently curving hills and valleys – the chronosphere must have carried me a few miles to the South Downs of Sussex, I thought. The sky was azure; the sun blazed almost directly above. Somewhere, a skylark was making a mellifluous ascent to the heavens. At the end of a sunken road, curving to the horizon, was a village with a square-towered Norman church.

The chronosphere, I now observed, was resting just beneath the lip of a huge hole that had been gouged in the landscape – a scar of dazzling white chalk. At first my eyes were blinded by its brightness; then I saw black shapes, twisted like crushed ants, littering the bottom of the crater. I realised, with horror, that they were corpses. I now perceived that, crossing the fields below, what looked like dark hedges were actually thickets of barbed wire. On the wire were more bodies, dangling in grotesque shapes, like moles on a game keeper's gibbet.

The chronosphere had entered this Stygian scene during a lull. For, suddenly, a ridge to my right became smudged by smoke, spitting flashes of light. A second later, came a long, low rumbling, like a colossal surf. The air seemed filled with sulphur and pulverised chalk, as artillery shells detonated in the crater below me, tossing the corpses around like grains of chaff. Presently, I heard a deep-throated roar as hundreds of men spilled from the crest of the ridge, like a dark liquid oozing from the top of a jar. The men were wearing drab uniforms, the colour of mud.

There was a chattering sound, like a magpie. As I watched, the line of men was scythed down as a gunner ranged his lethal enfilade along its length. All the while, shells rained into the crater, cutting the mutilated bodies to ribbons, accompanied by the crack of rifles.

Alerted by a curious noise over my head, I looked up to see a weird, stiff-winged bird – a peculiar hybrid of a heron and a pontoon. There was a man sitting inside it, wearing goggles and a leather helmet. He must have seen me before the whirring contraption vanished into the smoke haze above the ridge. It was a shock. Remember that I had left the nineteenth-century, before the infernal combustion engine had blighted the English shires; I had never even seen a safety bicycle, let alone a single-seater Sopwith Pup, equipped with a Vickers machine gun.

An explosion showered the outer casing of the chronosphere with fragments, like a violent hailstorm. I looked down, straight into the eyes of a soldier, who was standing upright, some thirty feet away. Miraculously spared from the maelstrom of shrapnel and bullets, he must have been secreted among the corpses, waiting for his moment, when fate had strangely introduced to the battle a man in a white robe with a long grey beard, standing in a doorway. He lifted his rifle to his shoulder and took aim.

I shouted, "Don't kill me!" or something similar. Then I said, "For God's sake man, get in!" The soldier examined his possible courses of action as a bullet lifted a cloud of chalk dust inches from his feet. It was an easy decision. In a gap between explosions, he ran towards me and clambered up the ladder. I shut and secured the door. Quickly assessing the situation, I decided to pull the Time Lever back to its original position, hoping that this would remove us from the scene, before we were blown to kingdom come. My hands closed around its ebony knob.

The man was fast asleep on the bed. This time, the journey had not caused me to black out. I had remained conscious as the gravatron came to life, with a whirring vibration that died down once its work of transporting us through Time was completed. I surveyed the prone man and his clothes. His sallow face was filthy and his khaki uniform was streaked with blood, down to his puttees and boots. A steel helmet, a rifle and a haversack lay next to the bed.

I gave him a gentle shake in order to rouse him.

"Jesus Christ," he said, opening his eyes. The man took in his environment with the incredulity that I had experienced on the battlefield. "I'm in bleeding heaven."

"No you're not," I said. "I don't think so anyway."

"So you're not an angel?"

"No."

"Thank Christ for that."There was a pause. "Have you got a smoke?" He had a Cockney accent, but not strong. It was the voice of a clerk or a policeman.

Fortunately, like a club in the West End, the chronosphere was furnished with tobacco and brandy. The soldier's hands were still trembling as I helped him to light up an Abdullah, the expensive cigarettes that Sigdwick had chosen. He sucked in smoke appreciatively and swigged greedily from the flask. Colour was returning to his cheeks.

I found out that his name was Alfred William Thomas and that he came from the East End of London. Strictly speaking, in terms of the military's ineluctable hierarchy, he was Private Thomas of the 16th Battalion of the Middlesex Regiment, part of the 86th Brigade of the 29th Division of the VIIIth Corps of the

Fourth Army.

"Who were you fighting?" I asked.

He looked at me uncomprehendingly. "The Germans."

"In England?"

"Don't be bloody stupid. In France."

"When?"

He regarded me as if I were a simpleton.

"In 1916, of course. July the first, 1916"

The words hit me like a hammer blow. All I could think was, "Good God, it works!"

Was it merely a misfortune that the chronosphere had delivered me into the heart of a savage battle? Had some malign agency, knowing the course of history, deliberately sent the chronosphere to hell? For the moment, the question remained unanswered.

Mortal fear had gone from Private Thomas now and adrenaline was no longer coursing around his body. As he became more reflective and his desire for alcohol less urgent, he began to recall past events. I learned that the scene I had just witnessed was merely one skirmish in a titanic conflict engulfing the whole of Europe. Its routes lay in a dispute between the Austro-Hungarian Empire, which was allied with Germany and Serbia. Britain was on Serbia's side, with France and Russia.

Thomas had been working as a porter at King's Cross Station when the war began. He had recently married his sweetheart, an East End girl called Emily. He had managed to get himself into the Middlesex Regiment in 1916 and had trained in Chatham.

Alf, as he was known, was a Welsh Cockney, a Taffy. One could clearly hear the intonations of the Welsh valleys in his voice, especially at moments of heightened emotion. His father, he explained, had moved to London from Pontypridd. The family lived in the East End.

He was a novice to this, "fighting lark", he explained. In fact, he had only arrived in France a week before the battle I had seen.

"So where were we exactly?" I asked, "when I picked you up."

He stubbed out his Abdullah on a brass ashtray. I offered him another.

"You were in a mine crater. You see, we let off this huge landmine just before we went over the top. Our division, the 29th, was to take this village, see, Beaumont Hamel. Well, our engineers tunnelled under No-Man's Land and put a mine under the German position, the Hawthorn redoubt. There was six lorry loads of dynamite under there. Bloody enormous it was.

"They blew the mine ten minutes before the attack. You should have seen it, this massive column of earth, awesome it was. The trouble was, in them ten minutes the Boche got back into their trench. Their machine guns were going like mad. Well, our lads had to go straight into it."

Later, I established the details of the colossal engagement. Half a million British soldiers had faced the Germans along an 18-mile front, to the north of the River Somme. But the artillery bombardment, which had pounded the Germans continuously for the previous eight days, had failed to destroy the thick rolls of barbed wire protecting their trenches.

The British soldiers had been ordered to walk, not run, across No-Man's land, in the mistaken belief that the German defences had been obliterated. Each man was weighed down by heavy equipment. As well as his rifle, he carried a gas helmet, ammunition, Mills Bombs, sandbags, a spade, wire cutters and flares – up to seventy pounds of kit.

Half of Alf's battalion fixed bayonets and went over the top in the first wave of the attack. The lives of nearly four hundred men were snuffed out in the next fifteen minutes as they floundered on the wire, vainly searching for gaps. The German simply fired belt after belt from their machine guns, picking off their slow-moving targets at will, like geese in a farmyard.

Alf's section had made its way from the transport lines, almost jauntily, the previous afternoon. The men had sung cheerful songs to keep their spirits up. He lounged back in an armchair, recalling the scene through a twist of blue smoke.

"I'll always remember, we marched past our company commander, Captain Doubleday. He says, 'don't worry lads, the German wire's all been cut. It'll be a piece of cake'. Then he says, 'I'll see you in Pozieres, tomorrow afternoon'. But the thing is, there was tears streaming down his face."

They had waited all night in the assembly trenches, crammed together and unable to sleep. As dawn arrived, a light shower of rain fell. The parched and terrified men tried to catch the drops in their helmets and pour it into their canteens. Some speculated, half with relief, half with dread, that this would mean that the attack would be delayed; it had already been postponed for two days because of heavy rainfall. But it was not to be. They were now told that the attack would begin at 7.30, in broad daylight. They knew, from rumours that had drifted back from the front line, that the British artillery bombardment had failed to breach the German defences.

By six o'clock a perfect summer's morning had arrived, bringing a cloudless blue sky and a light mist, clinging to the valley bottoms. The men were served with coffee from petrol cans, laced with thick, treacly rum. They joked nervously. Some polished their bayonets. Some wrote letters, with stubby pencils. Many prayed. At 6.25 the silence was broken, as the British artillery barrage began. The men cheered as the shells went over their heads, smashing into the German lines. Perhaps it would be a piece of cake, after all. The rum was having its effect. For some men, it was their first taste.

At 7.20, the barrage stopped and, seconds later, a British land mine pulverised the Hawthorn redoubt. The explosion flattened the soldiers' ear-drums. It threw a plume of chalk thousands of feet into the air, spreading out into a swirling cloud, like milk in water.

How can one imagine the mortal terror of those moments – the mens' heads spinning from the sickly rum; the deafening impact of explosives; the rattle of machine guns. Some would be shivering and crying, others stoically clenching their jaws. Alf told me that he was less afraid now than in the previous hours, because he was at least certain of his fate and almost resigned to it.

"I said the Lord's Prayer and I crossed myself. A lot of the lads done that. I thought of my missus, Emily. I thought, well that's it like. I'm going to die. Simple as that."

The moment of attack came with the shrill blast of a whistle. As if in a dream, Alf climbed onto the fire-step and heaved himself over the top.

"All I could see in front of me was dead and dying men. It was horrible. I saw Lieutenant Dixon up ahead. He was our platoon commander. He was waving his revolver, encouraging us on, like. Well, I ran like buggery. To be honest, I'd dumped most of my kit by then. I got to Dixon, and he says, 'well done lad'.

"Just then Dixon got hit in the thigh. He was screaming with pain, like, but I managed to drag him forwards. I managed to reach this shell crater and I thought, thank God for that. There was four blokes in there already, all from D Company, and one dead one. They were not happy to see us, I can tell you.

"Dixon's leg was bleeding like a fountain. I took out a field dressing and made a tourniquet but he was in a really bad way. He kept saying, 'leave me, leave me' but where was I going to go? There was this machine gun up ahead and it must have known where we were, because when the corporal from D Company stood up a bullet went clean through his helmet. It didn't kill him though."

Alf paused.

"What happened next?" I asked.

"Dixon died," said Alf, calmly. "He must have bled to death. Before he passed on, he gave me these." He reached into his pocket and pulled out a cream envelope and a gold pocket watch. Alf passed the watch for me to see. It was a beauty – a half hunter.

Engraved on the back were the initials JD.

"I suppose it's mine," he said. "I don't really want it; it seems wrong somehow. I think I'll give it to Dixon's missus, with the letter, if I can find her."

He indicated that I should read the letter. I removed it from the envelope. It was written in pencil, in a neat, copper-plate hand.

Near Beaumont Hamel
July, 1st, 1916

Dearest Claire,
It is the morning of the big push at last and I write this at first light with the Platoon around me. I shall leave this letter in my pocket, trusting that, by one means or another, it will get to you. Perhaps when you read these lines this nightmare will be over and I shall be safely returned to the Battalion dug-out.

If the truth is known, we are all sick to death of this War. Those who lead us have no conception of its dangers and are negligent with our lives, in pursuit of a few pitiful yards of captured ground. The men care not one jot whether Germany has Alsace, Belgium or even France too and, I must say, even their religious faith is tested. How could a beneficent God allow such evils while the Generals dine on succulent banquets and sleep in clean sheets far back from the front line?

I am lucky that my own faith has survived these doubts, as does my love for you. I want you to know, my sweetheart, that I truly love you and the little ones; I pray that you keep safe and that you will not worry about me too much, for I am in God's hands now and my fate can only be decided by His providence. I fear that I must go now. Kiss the children for me. I send you, and them, my most tender thoughts.
All my love,
James XXX

Alf did not know how long he remained in the shell hole with the two dead men. It may have been for two or three hours. There was little chance of going forward and the British attack had been halted. The air was filled with the moans and cries of the wounded. Occasionally a British aeroplane would fly overhead, looking for evidence of life. Every so often came a burst of machine gun fire, as those who were not in sheltered positions were picked off by the Germans. From what Alf could tell, his battalion had been annihilated. It no longer existed.

Just before midday, the 1st Newfoundland Battalion was ordered to attack the same ground. The soldiers did not make their way to the front line through the communication trenches, but went straight over the top from the reserve trench. The German machine gunners opened up on them immediately. Most of the Newfoundlanders were killed on British barbed wire; they did not even make it into No-Man's Land. The battalion was wiped out in forty minutes. Alf and his four comrades were among the few Middlesex men in forward positions who were still alive. They now decided to take their chances, while the Germans were occupied elsewhere. But Alf was the only one who made it into the vast hole that was all that remained of the Hawthorn redoubt.

There he hid in a pile of bodies which were swarming with flies, hot in the midday sun. He had drunk all of the water in his canteen and was almost mad with thirst. He told me that he was now on the point of giving himself up. He was about to make his blood-sodden vest into a white flag and wave it about. But he was almost certain that the Germans would kill him – had not the British soldiers been told by their commanders to take no prisoners, or as good as?

When Alf saw the chronosphere he thought at first that it must be a piece of ordnance, perhaps an unexploded mine. But how could that be? His sighting of me, in a white robe, in the doorway, had fazed him. Perhaps he was dead, he reflected, and this was a celestial being. What would happen if he killed an angel?

We had already become firm friends. The flask was now empty. Alf was drunk but still lucid. The air was thick with cigarette smoke. Wherever the chronosphere had landed, at least we were not in the middle of a battle. It was quiet outside.

"My God," I said, "what a story."

I thought of the two vast armies that were dug into the ground like termites, devising new and ever more gruesome ways of killing each other.

"Mr Frater," said Alf, "I've got to go back to my battalion, like. As it is, I'm in deep trouble. They'll probably court martial me."

"Look Alf," I said, "there's a small problem. The thing is, I don't know exactly where we are, or in what year. Where we may be is in the village of Spenhurst, in Kent, in December 1879. That's when I left."

"But I was born in 1890," said Alf.

"Oh dear". There was a long silence.

"It may be 1879 or it may not be," I said. "We'll just have to find out."

I crossed to the door and placed my hand on its opening mechanism. "Here goes."

It was dark outside and icy cold. My nostrils were greeted by a familiar smell – that of horses. At least we were back in the stable. I made my way down the ladder. "Come on Alf," I said, "follow me."

The stable door was unlocked. We could see lights in the windows of Spenhurst Hall. That was a good sign. Strangely, there was a faint sound of cheerful music floating from the house. We made our way towards the hall, wondering what we would find.

Chapter Seven

The Masquerade

At the front of the hall, light cascaded astonishingly from every window. I stood and gaped – you see, it was my first experience of electric light. Alf and I pondered on what to do. We knew that we looked incongruous. I was still wearing a white robe with a bronze collar and crown and the beard, which I had grown strangely fond of. Alf's filthy uniform would have disgraced him on parade, if not on Spenhurst High Street. But at least I had managed to persuade him to leave his rifle in the chronosphere, saying that we would go back for it.

I should also point out that we were both starving and that Alf, with most of a bottle of brandy inside him, was several sheets to the wind and barely able to stand upright. Through the partially open door, we could hear the sound of a small chamber orchestra, set up in the drawing room. I speculated that Sidgwick was having a party, although it seemed out of character. My heart quickened at the thought of seeing Lara.

"Don't worry, Alf," I said, "we'll soon have you fed and into a hot bath."

As soon as we reached the door, a footman appeared to greet us. He was wearing knee breeches, a jacket embellished by large buttons and gold braid and a top hat, all in a shiny blue material. He was enormous and towered over us. The footman did not seem at all disconcerted by our dress. Without a word being said, he led us into the house.

I wish you could have been there. The hallway was festooned with colourful paper chains and at the foot of the stairs was a large, elaborately decorated Christmas tree. Its silver decorations coruscated with reflections from an electric chandelier. The orchestra was playing a polka – a form of music that was new to me and whose violent syncopations had an immediate and disturbing effect upon Alf's psyche. I was now holding him up and his eyes were rolling.

The hallway was full of people in small animated groups, talking and laughing. I say people. In front of us, a Roman legionnaire wearing a kilt of leather strips, was conversing with a foot soldier from Wellington's army. The latter was dressed in white duck trousers and a gleaming red coat, criss-crossed with white straps. He wore a lace ruffle and a flat-topped peaked hat, or shako. His muzzle-loading, India pattern musket would have been no match for Alf's Lee Enfield, but that is another story.

The two infantrymen instantly recognised each other as confreres, although they did not speak; meanwhile my attention was drawn by two ladies coming down the stairs. They were Medusa, her hair a writhing nest of serpents, and the Goddess, Artemis – a stout lady in a beige tunic, carrying a bow and a quiver of arrows. At the top of the stairs, Nefertiti, the Goddess of the Nile, was talking to a pantalooned clown, possibly Mr Grimaldi. Robin Hood hovered at the edge of their conversation. Alf gripped my arm, his eyes wide with amazement. But my own grasp on the situation was becoming attenuated.

At that moment, another soldier came bounding towards us. He was also red-coated but wore a spiked helmet rather than a shako and dark blue trousers, with a red stripe. His costume was completed by a white leather waist belt. High on his back was a stiff black pack, which was known, in the Victorian army, as a valise.

His luxuriant black mustache was greased into military points and his cheeks glowed red in a waxen face. I would say that he was in his early forties. But he had the sprightly manner of a younger man. He extended a white hand for me to shake.

"Good evening. Vane, Nathaniel Vane," he said, brightly.

There was a hiatus. This, then, was Sidgwick's partner in the pill-making business. He was clearly doing very well. He carried with him an air of sleek, complacent prosperity.

"Frederick Frater," I replied.

Alf said nothing. He was transfixed by the chocolate soldier's helmet badge. For he had recognised it as that of his beloved regiment, the Middlesex, which was nick-named "The Diehards". The uniform was, in fact, as familiar to him as his own; it was that which had been worn by the Middlesex before it adopted the khaki and webbing kit that it took to Flanders.

"Well, I must say, you both make an absolutely splendid show," said the chocolate soldier. "Those blood stains are awfully realistic. May I touch?"

He reached towards Alf's sleeve. Alf shuddered and let out a kind of growl. I managed to disguise this as a joke, but it was a close thing.

"Elspeth!" the chocolate soldier exclaimed, "you must come and see these two, they're absolutely priceless. What are you supposed to be by the way – Old Father Time, is it, or Triton the God of the Sea?"

"A Druid," I muttered.

"A Druid! How terribly original!"

A woman approached us, carrying a long shepherd's crook. She wore a yellow silk dress and a necklace and earrings of real-looking diamonds. The dress was laced tightly at her waist and ballooned voluminously around her posterior, under the influence of that curious late-Victorian invention, a bustle. The effect of her pale, powdered face, with its rouged cheeks and painted beauty spots was grotesque, particularly as she was not beautiful. But her crowning glory was a gigantic blonde wig. It was as tall as a guardsman's busby and garnished with flowers and pieces of fruit.

"May I introduce you to Madame la Pompadour," explained the chocolate soldier. The woman gave a silly giggle, covering her mouth with a white-gloved hand. I have noticed that the characters adopted by the guests at fancy dress balls are an infallible indication of their true natures. I must say that the eighteenth century has never appealed to me. I view it as a time of darkness and ignorance and I find its manners and much of its art stilted – to me, there is nothing more depressing than the sound of a harpsichord. At this moment I was at one with the Jacobins, who had guillotined Marie Antoinette and butchered her silly sheep.

"Elspeth," said the chocolate soldier. "This gentleman is a Druid and his companion is a …"

Alf was now scowling at our host in a most disconcerting manner. He had guessed, correctly, that the chocolate soldier had never been near to a barrack room or a parade ground. He was also forming a view that the man, by his very existence, was insulting his regiment and his fallen comrades.

Elspeth giggled again, this time conveying a sense of anxiety.

"Gentlemen," said the redcoat, covering his embarrassment. "Could I offer you a glass of champagne?"

"We would love some," I said.

The chocolate soldier led us across the hall to the drawing room. On the way, he introduced us to Adam and Eve and to a medieval knight, who seemed rather depressed. He then left us to greet more guests. Up in the minstrel's gallery, the string players were sawing away at a Viennese waltz, but no one was dancing. Medusa was talking to a Samurai warrior, who, I noticed, was carefully avoiding looking into her eyes. This was not the same room that Sidgwick had shown me. Lara's subtle aesthetic furnishings had been stripped away; in their place were elaborately ugly artefacts in that pretentious style often favoured by the nouveau riche, known as Louis Quinze.

I am sure that you can imagine the mother of pearl inlaid cabinets; the gilt-legged, marble-topped sideboards; the silk-covered chaise-longues and the panelled walls, painted in grey, white and gold. There were also some oil paintings, in a style of bastardised Watteau. They were so hideous that I do not wish to describe them. I now understood the beaming pride of Madame La Pompadour and her chocolate soldier, for this was their kingdom.

At least there was food. A table to one side was heaped with delectable fare. It strained beneath the weight of turkeys and geese, game pies, risottos, cheeses, baskets of fruit, cakes, trifles, and much else besides. Alf became suddenly animated. Remember that he had been living on corned beef and biscuits for the previous year. Like a man in a trance, he headed for the table. Well, that will keep him occupied for a while I thought. I must confess that, at this moment, I desperately wanted to relieve my bladder. As I left the dining room, Alf began to cram food into his mouth with both hands, watched by unbelieving guests.

I would not have left him for so long had it not been for an extraordinary coincidence. On the first floor landing I met another Druid! After I had admired his sickle, we talked shop for a while. He told me that he was the Chief Ovate of the Banstead Lodge of the Ancient Order of British Druids. I think that he gave me his address. Unfortunately, I mislaid it somewhere.

Anyway, by the time I returned to the drawing room something terrible had happened. The music had stopped. Inside, deities, demi-gods and historical personages were standing in a tense, silent group, all looking in one direction. Madame La Pompadour was sobbing.

I saw that the chocolate soldier was lying full-length on the floor, with a thin line of blood dripping from the corner of his mouth. He was absolutely still, obviously unconscious. Alf stood over him, exhibiting an expression that was half defiant and half guilty. Food was smeared all over his face. A look exchanged between us. No-one attempted to apprehend us, not even the giant footman. We ran down the drive, as fast as our legs would carry us, Alf leaving a trail of bread rolls and chicken legs from his bulging pockets. We did not stop until we reached the road to the village. There was a frost on the ground and our breaths came out in thick white plumes. Alf recovered more quickly than I did. He told me what had happened.

"I decked him, Mr Frater. The man was an idiot. I was just eating, see, minding my own business, when he comes over and he says, 'would you like a shovel?', all sarcastic like. I says, what battalion are you in mate – and he just looks at me funny. It turns out, he's never heard of the Middlesex Regiment. He doesn't even know what uniform he's wearing. Well, I got really angry, Mr Frater. This mist came over me and I hit him, see. He went down like a skittle. Lovely it was."

Alf rubbed his bruised fist and smiled. I smiled too. Something snapped and we laughed hysterically until our lungs hurt. A startled pheasant clattered across the dark fields. I formulated a plan. We would sneak back down the drive and return to the stable, where the chronosphere was housed. In the morning refreshed by our rest, we would return to my uncle's shop.

When dawn finally came, we were both blue with cold. I had slept, if that is the right word, on the bed in the chronosphere. Alf had enjoyed a warmer night, for he had buried himself in malodorous straw, in a horse's stall. He was the first to get up, for he was used to rising at dawn. I was still trying to open my eyes and to reconcile myself to a raging headache when I heard an animated voice.

"Look at this, Mr Frater!"

At the side of the stable, beneath a dust-sheet, Alf had discovered an interesting object. The cause of his excitement was, essentially, a metal box. It was mounted on an exposed chassis, with leaf springs and wire-spoked wheels, the rear ones larger than the front. The device had a bench seat and various fascinating-looking appurtenances, including a pair of coach lamps, long rear mudguards, a steering tiller and a hand brake.

"Would you like to go for a drive?"

"For a what?"

Since this was the first time that I had ever seen a horseless carriage, I was somewhat at a loss. Alf explained to me that the machine did not require an animal; it was propelled by a hidden engine, which ran on petroleum. Ah, the motor car! If only I had known then, Isabella, what havoc this innocuous-seeming device – this specimen was the first in Kent – would wreak upon the twentieth-century. The car was a liberator, at the heart of the planet's project of social enlightenment, but it was also a means of enslavement. It despoiled the environment and removed the innocence and tranquility from the English lanes, yet those who decried it were viewed as cranks and told that there was no going back.

"Lovely, isn't it Mr Frater?" said Alf. He adored all machines. He was never happier than when he was tinkering with one, preferably underneath it on a cold winter's day, his hands covered in oil, with an unlit Woodbine protruding from the corner of his mouth. He had already clambered up onto the seat.

"My mate Chalky told me about these. It's two horse-power and it's got this special gear for hill climbing, see. It's a Benz Ideal. You see this funny thing here. That's the steering tiller. They didn't have steering wheels in them days. A man with a red flag had to walk in front of you and you wasn't allowed to do more than four miles an hour!"

What an excellent idea, I thought. For a moment, the idea of us travelling to Spenhurst in this metal object crossed my mind. It would have been the first car theft in Britain – a significant milestone. I dismissed the notion, although Alf was keen, arguing that we were in enough trouble already.

We retrieved our belongings from the chronosphere and walked back to the village. I can remember little about the journey except that we were ravenously hungry and thirsty and that, during it, Alf told me, hesitantly, that he no longer believed in God.

Imagine medieval man. He crawls around in the mud and

slime, beaten into submission by his fear of a sadistic deity who has the eternal flames of hell at his beck and call. In the nineteenth-century, life becomes marginally easier and there is a scientific enlightenment. The middle classes largely break free from God, with the help of John Stuart Mill, who formulates the useful philosophy of utilitarianism, but the malleable Protestant religion is retained by the state, with its panoply of mumbo jumbo. Challenged at the edges by Catholicism and Non-Conformity, it cements British society together in the colourful triad of Church, Parliament and Crown.

Alf had now broken free or, at least, was peering over the parapet of his subjugation. He had seen that his so-called betters were no better than he was; that, in fact, many of them were contemptible. His religion may reassert itself. The desire for the divine is, I believe, a natural human impulse. It must never be denied by a cold rationalism. But a niggling doubt from his days in the trenches would always remain, on the basis of "how could a god allow such things". It would be there in the back of his mind, even on Coronation or Armistice days. But on these occasions a lump would also come to his throat and tears to his eyes. The larger the sacrifice, the bigger the myth that is needed to sustain it.

It must have been six or seven o'clock by the time we reached Spenhurst. It was a cold, clear morning, with no wind. No-one was about. The milkman's dray, clopping slowly down the high street, was the only sign of life. I had noticed that things were subtly different – a changed shop front here, a new window there. There were also signs of the Christmas season, in the form of wreaths and sprigs of holly, displayed around the village. But I was not at all prepared, psychologically, for what greeted us when we reached Uncle Edward's shop. I found that I could not open the door, for the locks had been changed. The window was empty. There was not a book in sight; only a dead spider and a small hand-written notice in the bottom right-hand corner. It read: "Owner deceased: please address all inquiries to Dr Charles Wood, Prospect Cottage, Old Sweylands."

My heart sank through my boots. Uncle Edward was dead!

"What are we going to do, Mr Frater?"

Alf's voice brought me back to my senses. I felt numb and emotionally anaesthetised. This was far worse than when my father had died, for Uncle Edward had been a real person. I had actually known him. "What does the sign say, Alf?" I asked, weakly.

He read the sentences slowly and falteringly, like a child.

"It says, 'please address all inquiries to Dr Charles Wood, Prospect Cottage ...'"

"Then that is what we shall do."

I don't think that there is any more agreeable home in England than Doctor Wood's cottage. It is reached at the end of a twisting lane, off the Poundsbridge Road – a narrow green tunnel that you could easily miss, if you were going by too quickly. The lane is bordered by blackthorns and elders. In the summer, there is nothing more pleasant than to stroll down it, listening to the metallic chirrup of chaffinches and the mellifluous songs of chiffchaffs and willow warblers. The cottage, an ancient construction of lath, wattle and thatch, appears, unannounced, after a final sharp bend.

There is usually a twist of smoke rising from the chimney, if the doctor is at home, for the only demerit of the cottage is its cool, sheltered position in the lee of a patch of woodland. That, though, is also a blessing, for the back garden, an island of emerald sward, shades imperceptibly into a delightful sylvan world of bluebells, badgers and woodpeckers.

I knocked on the door, hoping that the concussion would be loud enough to wake the doctor, but soft enough not to alarm him. He did not recognise me at first. I must have looked ragged and dirty. Alf was done in, from all the walking. His face was as pale as chalk. He was at the final stages of exhaustion.

"Frederick!" Recognition dawned. "Can it really be? My dear lad! Come in!"

I saw that we had raised the doctor from his bed, for he was wearing a paisley dressing gown. His face was considerably older than I remembered it. It was lined and drawn and his fair hair was streaked with grey. Immediately inside the door, a single large space had been knocked through from three rooms. This served as the doctor's living room, parlour and study and adjoined a small kitchen. It was dark but cosy in the cottage; I always thought that it smelled of old leather, dampness and cured ham. Electric lighting did not reach the end of Doctor Wood's secluded land until well into the twentieth century. Reliance on lamps became part of the cottage's charm – it made one far more aware of diurnal sounds and rhythms that were obliterated by synthetic means of illumination.

Doctor Wood served us with copious quantities of tea. Alf took a few mouthfuls then immediately fell asleep. He slumbered so deeply that it was almost impossible to rouse him. God only knows what he dreamed about.

"How did he die?" I asked.

"Your uncle?" The doctor poured me another cup. "It was a brain haemorrhage brought about by chronic alcoholism, I would say. It was I who examined his body."

"He drank himself to death?"

"Yes."

"When did he pass away?"

"Didn't you know? Only eleven days ago, I'm afraid."

"In what year?"

The doctor looked surprised.

"Well, it was almost ten years to the day after you left – December the 14th, 1889."

I almost dropped my cup. I had just lost ten years of my life. For I had left Spenhurst in the chronosphere in December 1879.

In theory, Alf had not even been born yet.

"Where on earth have you been for all these years, Frederick?" asked the doctor, earnestly.

I did what most people would have done in this situation. I told the first lie that came into my head. I said that I had run away to sea ten years before, because I had been so unhappy. Doctor Wood seemed content with the story, improbable as it was. I added that I had just met Private Thomas at Tonbridge Station.

"Was he in the Sudan?" asked the doctor, alluding to a Colonial skirmish which I did not know anything about.

"Oh yes. It was terrible … terrible."

"Indeed." The doctor looked grave. "You know, it was a curious business how you, Sidgwick and Lara all vanished at the same time. You know about Sidgwick do you?"

I shook my head.

"Of course not, you have been out on the ocean wave. Hearts of oak and all that."

Alf snored. Every so often, his body convulsed and he cried out, as some ghastly memory came into his mind. We chatted pleasantly over tea. The doctor told me that he had continued with his philanthropic work. Recently, he had been researching housing conditions in the locality, with a view to improving them. At length, the conversation turned to an entirely unrelated matter.

"Has anyone told you about the Ripper?"

I shook my head.

"Really? You had better see this."

The doctor reached to the side of his armchair for a newspaper and handed it to me. It was a copy of the Evening News from the previous week. Newspapers did not have photographs then, only columns and columns of dense type. I do not know how we managed to get through them, particularly as the light was so bad. At the top of the page was the following headline: *Alien preys on English flesh: Beast from Poland named in Ripper case.*

The story said that a Polish Jew, formerly a resident of Kent, Jan Sadowitz, also known as John Sidgwick, the celebrated pill manufacturer, was almost certainly responsible for the sadistic murders of five women in Whitechapel, in the East End of London, carried out between August and October, 1888. The fiend had butchered them and removed their vital organs, using surgeon's tools.

The proofs for this hypothesis seemed irrefutable: a) Sidgwick was Jewish and therefore sinister. b) He was a doctor and possessed the anatomical knowledge required for the women's mutilations. c) His modus operandi was the East End. His factory in Stepney was only a few minutes' walk from Whitechapel. d) He was missing from his former home in Kent and no-one knew of his whereabouts. The newspaper said that his business associate, Nathaniel Vane, had supplied convincing evidence to the police of Sidgwick's evil nature and of his nefarious practices.

Vane's allegations were reproduced almost verbatim, covering most of an inside page. The gist of them was that Sidgwick had been conspiring with other Polish, Russian and German Jews to bring down the British government for several years. He had introduced a toxin into his patent remedy, Sidgwick's Liver Pills, and had attempted, by this means, to weaken the moral fibre of the nation. Sidgwick used the pills himself, in the ritualistic deflowering of virgins, carried out in his Castle of Evil, Spenhurst Hall.

Special Branch, said the story, which had been established to keep an eye on seditious activity among aliens, had been closing the net around Sidgwick since 1887. In order to taunt his pursuers, he had taken to sending them letters, written in blood in spidery handwriting.

Doctor Wood told me that Sidgwick had been represented in more lurid papers, like, The Illustrated Police News, as a hook-nosed vampire, lurking in London's shadows, where he waited to pounce upon English maidens; he had even been implicated in that ill-defined phenomenon, the white slave trade. He had become, in short, a bogeyman, using whose name generations of children would frighten each other in school playgrounds.

"This is preposterous," I said. "Sidgwick would not harm anyone! He is no more capable of murder than he is of flying to the moon." Strictly speaking, this was not true; I am sure that if Sidgwick had set himself the task he could easily have flown to the moon. But I did not say so.

"I know that Sidgwick is a peaceful man," said Doctor Wood. "But I fear that his former associate, Vane, has deceived everyone with this tarradiddle. You see, it serves his purpose for Sidgwick to be portrayed as a wicked monster and a charlatan. Do you know, I never liked that fellow, Vane. He claims that he has reformulated the pills by the way. While denigrating Sidgwick, he is living the life of riley up at the hall, with his dreadful wife."

"Is she called Elspeth?"

"Yes, that is she."

"A vapid woman with a silly giggle?"

Doctor Wood nodded.

"Do they own a horseless carriage, do you know?"

"What is one of those?"

"Never mind. It does not matter."

I reflected for a moment. "Do you know where Sidgwick and Lara are now?"

"I am afraid that no-one does. They have been gone these ten years. They appear to have vanished from the face of the earth."

Alf stirred in his sleep, his body stiffening with some horror.

"He has been through trying times," I said. "It will take him a long time to recover."

With great difficulty, Doctor Wood and I carried Alf upstairs. We laid him out in the spare bedroom. When he was awake, the doctor would examine him.

The doctor lived by that admirable maxim, *de mortuis nil nisi bonum*, or, do not speak ill of the dead.

"I often think of your uncle," he told me, downstairs. "You know, he was not a bad old stick. He was stubborn, certainly, and, latterly, many of his views were obnoxious; but I think that, in many ways, he was a victim of his own intellect."

I said nothing. My own views of my uncle were still wholly negative.

A log fire flickered fitfully in the grate. Doctor Wood had slipped some whisky into my tea.

"I think that the poor man actually died of loneliness," he said. "That is what they should have written on his death certificate."

"Did Gladstone win the election?" I asked, changing the subject.

"Ah Gladstone," the doctor's eyes twinkled. "Yes, he did, Frederick, in March 1880. But he made a complete pig's ear of things, I'm afraid. He has pushed many of his followers straight into the arms of the Radicals."

"Why?"

"Well, he made elementary schooling compulsory, he gave married women rights and he reformed parliamentary elections. Those were the good things. But as to his foreign policy ..." Doctor Wood jabbed at the fire with a poker. "The man exhibited the jingoism and bombast of Disraeli, adding his own incompetence."

I nodded. The doctor continued.

"First, he flexes his muscles in the Transvaal like some tin-pot Colonialist and then he bombs Alexandria, merely to protect the interests of the stock-jobbers and their precious Suez Canal and in order to slight the French. That disgusted many people, although I am sure that it would have delighted your uncle." He smiled. "Then there was the Sudan. Thanks to Gladstone's ineffectual dithering, poor General Gordon had his throat slit by the mad Mahdi."

"And Ireland?"

"I'm afraid that Ireland, just as your uncle predicted, contributed to Gladstone's downfall, even more than the siege of Khartoum."

The doctor explained that a dreadful murder had taken place in Phoenix Park Dublin, in May 1881. Fenian terrorists had butchered the English chief secretary and under-secretary with long surgeon's knives, while the two men were out taking a stroll. This had played into the hands of those who opposed Gladstone's policies. He had failed to introduce a Home Rule Bill after the '85 election.

Joseph Chamberlain, now a loose cannon, had broken away from the Liberals to form a Unionist party in '86. That was it for poor Gladstone, Doctor Wood explained. The game was up and his Government fell."

"So who is Prime Minister now?" I asked.

"My dear boy, you have been away for a long time haven't you." The doctor smiled. "It is that elegant Conservative, Lord Randolph Churchill. You know, the former Chancellor."

There was a pregnant pause. "Now, lad. I want you to tell me of all the ports that you have visited, and the hearts that you have broken. I want a detailed description of your adventures. I always knew that there was a dash of seawater in your veins. Oh and, by the way, Happy Christmas. You do know that it is Christmas day don't you?"

I now blurted out the whole story. It was impossible not to. I told Doctor Wood about the chronospheres, explaining that they certainly worked; about the circumstances of Sidgwick and Lara's disappearance on that grey December morning; about my trip to the Somme and the comic fracas at the fancy dress ball.

The doctor seemed to accept the idea of Time Travel quite readily – he told me that he had long suspected that Sidgwick was up to something of the sort. As a man of science he was used to testing fantastic and delusional ideas by means of physical corroboration. This I could supply. We would be able to go to Spenhurst Hall, I suggested, where I would show him the battle-scarred time machine. Perhaps, if my nerves allowed it, I would attempt a practical demonstration.

We speculated on where Lara and her father had disappeared to. I offered the implausible-sounding theory that they had travelled to the first century AD, to help the tribes of ancient Britain in their resistance to the Romans. But I explained that I did not know how to set the controls of the Icarus so that we could find them.

Doctor Wood said that he missed Sidgwick. He was going to make sure that the architect of his downfall, Nathaniel Vane, got his come-uppance and would do his damnedest to rehabilitate Sidgwick's shattered reputation.

"I will not rest," said the doctor, "until I have drummed that Judas out of Spenhurst Hall."

While we were talking a possible explanation occurred to me of why I had returned to Spenhurst Hall ten years after I had left. When I had pulled the Time Lever back to its original setting, it must have stopped fractionally short of its final position – a tiny gap equating to a decade of sidereal time. I did not appear to have aged in those ten years. While the doctor's jowls had sagged and his face had grown more creased and lived in, I had not changed at all. This was another proof of my fantastic hypothesis.

It was the battle I had just witnessed that seemed to interest Doctor Wood the most. During our walk to Prospect Cottage, Alf had described, from his somewhat limited perspective, its political and diplomatic background.

"So the whole of Europe is involved in this conflict?" said the doctor.

"The whole world really," I replied. "Britain is not just fighting Germany in France and Belgium. From what Alf tells me, we are also up against Serbia and Bulgaria in the Balkans.

We fought with the Turks in the Dardanelles and we are tussling with them for the Suez Canal and southern Mesopotamia."

"Is Russia in this war?"

I nodded.

"And India and the colonies?"

"I am afraid so."

Doctor Wood was matching this geo-political map with the one which he already knew.

"Which side is Russia on?"

"Ours I think."

"Thank heavens for that." There was a pause. "Would you like a piece of cake, Frederick? You must be famished, my dear boy."

While Doctor Wood was in the kitchen, the reality of my situation suddenly struck home. I had no family, no job, no home, and, for all I knew, no possessions. Lara and Sidgwick were gone and nobody knew where they were.

The doctor appeared in the doorway. "Look," he said. "You and Mr Thomas must stay here for a few days, while you sort yourselves out. It won't be the best Christmas you have ever spent, but I can offer you a goose, some plum pudding and some rather fine whisky. How about it?"

The doctor was right. It was not my best Christmas (it is not a celebration that I particularly like) but it was far from the worst. Thanks to his rest, Alf recovered his strength to a certain extent, although he was deathly pale and his face had acquired a nervous tic. While the goose roasted, we played cards. This occupation had helped to get Alf through his time in the trenches; it calmed his nerves.

The goose, served with roast potatoes and parsnips and a succulent gravy, did not disappoint. Alf and I drank rather a lot of whisky with the pudding, which was delicious, while the doctor abstained. Alf's face was glowing. He said that the pudding was the most excellent thing he had ever tasted. He must have felt, at that moment, like a warrior in Valhalla or the

Elysian Fields.

There was a silence – the culmination of the meal.

"A toast," said Doctor Wood, lifting his glass. But it did not happen. Quietly at first, Alf was crying. He was mortified but he could not stop himself. Soon, he began to sob as I have never seen a man sob before, drawing air into his lungs in deep, heaving gasps. I put my arm around his shoulders and told him that it was all right.

The doctor was very good about it. We took Alf back up to the bedroom and left him to sleep. We carried on talking until darkness had entirely engulfed the little cottage.

Chapter Eight

Following the Ripper

Ten months later, in October 1890, I was sitting in the shop reading a newspaper. Quite a bit had happened, which I had better tell you about. My uncle, in a final act of misanthropy, had died intestate. Since I was his sole remaining relative, I became his executor. Eventually, after months of financial and legal complications, I was able to gain access, with the help of Doctor Wood, to the trust fund that my father had left me, or at least what was left of it. We discovered that more than half of the money was missing. I do not know whether my uncle spent the money on brandy or on the collection of erotic prints that I found hidden beneath the floorboards in his bedroom – probably both. My anger subsided after six months or so and I enjoyed the erotica. Had I kept it, it would probably have become quite valuable.

You should also know that the Icarus, which had delivered me to the Somme, as Alf's guardian angel, was gone. I discovered, on a surreptitious visit to Spenhurst Hall, that it had vanished from the stables. I came to the conclusion that Nathaniel Vane knew, or at least suspected, what the chronosphere was and had destroyed it. He was carefully obliterating any trace of Sidgwick as he became the sole beneficiary of their pharmacological empire.

The disappearance of the Icarus could have made me look like a lunatic in Doctor Wood's eyes. But it did not. He continued to believe my story. After all, he conceded, although I was 32 years old by my birth certificate, I was still a fresh-faced young man. Alf and I wondered whether the war in which he had fought would now take place. We monitored events and compared them to those that he remembered or his parents had told him about. We soon began to notice discrepancies. Minor at first, they became larger and more significant. Ultimately, as I shall explain, came a conclusive proof that this was not Alf's nineteenth century, but an entirely different one.

There was just enough money left from the diminished trust fund for me to continue renting the shop, to pay back what I owed to Doctor Wood and to set up a business. But what kind of business? I racked my brains. The books would have to go, for there was no money in them. I decided at length, with the encouragement of Alf, to open a bicycle shop.

Don't laugh. Cycling was all the rage at that period. Motor cars had not yet made the lanes hideous with dust and the safety bicycle, with pneumatic tyres, had replaced the inherently unstable penny farthing. Spenhurst, with its pleasant watering hole, the Green Man, and its pretty village green, was a favourite destination of bicycle tourists from Tunbridge Wells and even London. They would disport themselves on Saturday and Sunday afternoons on the lush grass around the market cross – apprentice lads, old codgers in Norfolk jackets and shy, blushing maidens – laughing and drinking bottles of lemonade.

Alf was ideally suited by his skills and temperament to be a bicycle mechanic. He would far rather have sold and repaired cars but that task fell, progressively, to George Watkins, the blacksmith, Alf's friend, whose forge, inevitably, became the village garage. That summer, Alf divided his time between the bicycle shop, the forge and the public bar of the Green Man. He and George talked about horseless carriages from morning until night. And I became just as familiar with Alf's feet, which were invariably sticking out from beneath a chassis, as I did with his upper body.

The Benz that we had seen at Spenhurst Hall would be merely the advance guard for other, more powerful models – Peugeots, Clement-Talbots and Humbers, to name but a few. The men of Kent adopted the horseless carriage with enthusiasm. Their hero was the mayor of Tunbridge Wells, Sir David Solomons.

Solomons would scandalise the county in 1895, by driving his single cylinder Peugeot along a public road, without a man with a red flag walking in front of it!

Alf never understood why I did not share his enthusiasm for cars – to me they were just metal boxes, imbued with no magical spirit. Nor could I understand his love of cricket. For as well as a fixture in the Green Man, he became the demon spin bowler of the village team – the "Welsh wizard" they called him. Bicycles were far more to my taste than cars, or cricket. They were now a common sight in Spenhurst. One even saw ladies riding them. The bustle had by now almost died out. The disappearance of the bustle and the whalebone corset allowed women a physical freedom they had previously been denied. And this accelerated the bicycle craze.

As I say, it was an October afternoon and I was sitting alone in the shop. I hoped that nobody would come in. The premises were filled with primitive bicycles – bone shakers, we called them. Alf had kitted out the back of the shop with neat wooden cabinets, each packed with spanners, pliers and the like. There was also a work-bench. But this equipment was of little interest to me. Alf was down the road, at the forge. He and George Watkins would be tinkering with a motor car. My feet were resting on the counter as I studied, intently, that week's issue of Commonweal. You see, I had become a member of William Morris's political organisation, the Socialist League and this was its weekly organ. At that time, the paper was serialising Mr Morris's utopian novel, *News from Nowhere*, and in this issue was the final chapter.

I should explain that the League was an early advocate of revolutionary international socialism – "from each according to his capacity, to each according to his need". It held that ownership was iniquitous and that all land and property should be nationalised and redistributed, so that those without would no longer be reduced to economic slavery. Did it not strike me as odd that Morris, who owned a substantial furnishings factory at

Merton Abbey, and who lived in a lavishly-appointed mansion, should have been promulgating such a philosophy? Why not? Now, I realise that the league was impractical and, in reality, somewhat elitist. It held that mundane institutions, such as parliament and trades unions, were mere palliatives; they were irrelevant to the revolutionary cause. Wood carving and folk singing, it believed, were more important than the ballot box. This, of course, was utter rot.

That very Sunday, Morris was to give a lecture entitled "Art for the People" at the Athenaeum Hall, at 73 Tottenham Court Road. I had underlined the announcement in pencil.

Doctor Wood, as I have said, took a keen interest in national and local politics. He was later to become a councillor. He held that local authorities should be able to build subsided housing, paid for by the rates, for the poor. I am embarrassed to say that, echoing the utopian views of William Morris, I disagreed with this proposal. I held that such a measure would be counter-productive; it would delay the appropriation of power by the dispossessed. How misguided.

The shop bell rang. It was three o'clock. Alf came in, smiling. His forearms were covered in oil.

"Did you hear it?

'What?'

"The Panhard. We got it going lovely. We done twelve miles an hour!"

He explained that he and George had been conducting an unofficial speed trial up and down the high street in a two-cylinder Panhard et Levassor. They had been "tuning up" the motor for a local landowner. To later eyes, the vehicle would look like a motorised biscuit barrel but to Alf and George it was the ultimate in mechanical sophistication. Their experiment had been a great success.

Alf looked around the shop. "Any customers?"

I shrugged. He saw the Commonweal upon the counter and

looked at me disapprovingly, although he would never have said anything. Alf, a true son of toil, betrayed a complete indifference to international socialism. Like most working men, he was far more interested in beer.

"Let's have some tea," I said. Alf brightened. We agreed to close the shop for the remainder of the day.

The kitchen was not the gloomy abode that it had been in the days of my uncle. Thanks to Alf's decorating skills and to the subtle vibrations of our friendship, its atmosphere had changed entirely. Picture a light, airy space, with white walls, pine shelves and a few simple decorations. My uncle's tattered wallpaper and the pallid aspidistra were a distant memory. We had extended what, formerly, had been a dingy scullery into a spacious conservatory with a floor of warm yellow flagstones. It was full of plants. I love growing things and was now able to indulge my passion fully.

That evening, as we ate in the kitchen, Alfred told me that he had seen Mary, Sidgwick's former housemaid at Spenhurst Hall. He said that she was now working as a housekeeper for the vicar, Winspear. He added that she had asked after me and that he thought that she was "sweet" on me. He winked. I imagine that I blushed.

"I'm only passing it on, like," he said. His expression suddenly became downcast. He looked down at his plate. I knew what he was thinking. "I miss my Emily something desperate," he said, softly. Alf's former wife had cropped up frequently in our conversation in recent days. "She had lovely black hair. Her skin was as white as milk."

"I know, Alf," I said.

"Do you think that I …"

Should he attempt to find her? I reminded Alf, for the hundredth time, that if the Emily that he had left to go to war still existed, she must remain many years in our future.

"But, Mr Frater," he said, "I still think that I should go back to

Spitalfields. My ma and da moved there in 1889, that's last year. I think that I should go and see them, like, to see how they are."

He interpreted my questioning look. "I know what you're thinking," he said, "It's almost my birthday. My ma will be eight months pregnant, with me. I shan't tell them it's me. I shall just say hello and ask after their health."

He smiled weakly. He could not be discouraged. We agreed that, soon, we would both travel to Fashion Street, where his parents had lived, in the heart of the East End. So as to make him look more presentable, I agreed to lend Alfred one of my old suits. There was a small problem. Alf was far shorter than I was and the trousers flapped around his ankles. The following day, Alf went round to the vicarage to ask Mary if she would be so kind as to adjust them.

She came into the shop on Thursday morning, bearing a paper package, with the trousers neatly wrapped inside. I was aghast. In place of the callow maiden I had met at Spenhurst Hall in 1879, here was a fully-grown woman. She was wearing a pale blue blouse and a cobalt dress. Her hair, which was an unusual shade, midway between auburn and red, was brushed forward from the back of her neck and gathered at the top of her head, in the French style.

Mary exhibited an unusual energy – her movements were quick and direct. One immediately noticed a vivacity in her blue eyes and that her teeth were very white, for she was always smiling. Although she was small – she would reach barely to my shoulder – she seemed to fizzle, like a fire cracker. Later, Mary told me about her exploits on moonlit nights in County Meath. For the want of a son, her father, had schooled her in the masculine arts of poaching. She told me of her heroic childhood labours – hewing pails of water down long lanes and digging mountains of peat. They were tasks, accounting for her compact strength, that would have challenged the endurance of a grown man. We did not exchange many words on this first morning.

Mary handed me the white package.

"I have done the alterations, Sir." She looked at me directly – she was fearless – holding the gaze just a moment too long. Only a trace of her Meath accent now remained.

"Thank you, Mary," I said, taking it. "We have met before, have we not?"

"Oh, yes," she said. "It was more than ten years ago, before Doctor Sidgwick and his daughter disappeared."

"I remember it well," I said. "You were a little thing then."

"Was I?" She smiled.

There was an awkward pause. I do not know what came over me. For I now asked her, of all things, if she was married.

"Oh no, Sir. I am in service, for Mr Winspear up at Holly End."

I pictured the fellow, shuffling through the damp, draughty manse. I thought of his lank yellow hair and his unhealthy reading habits. She, his servant, was worth a million of his sort.

"He's a rum cove," I said.

"He is that, Sir." She laughed.

Our business was done. I placed the package beneath the counter. Mary's eyes scanned the shop. I could detect that she was curious about the bicycles. In the following few minutes, I demonstrated the safety bicycle and its rudimentary brakes. She said that the machines were very clever. I told her that one day, soon, I would show her how to ride one. She was ecstatic. At one point, I put my hand on her shoulder. Close to, she smelled of clean fresh linen. When she left the shop, with a final smile and flash of teeth. I could not get her out of my mind. I was bewitched by her.

From my current vantage point – the balcony of a clean white building overlooking the sea – it is hard for me to summon up an image of London in the closing years of the twentieth century. But I must try. You will probably not have heard of a poem called The City of Dreadful Night by one James Thomson. It is a lurid and melodramatic production. But Thomson does not exaggerate the miasmic vapours rising from London's sluggish river; her filth-strewn streets and the pale faces of her scurrying crowds. One Friday morning, we took the London Bridge train, second-class, from Tonbridge. It cost us sixpence each. Alf was kitted out in a black jacket and the trousers modified by Mary. I was also wearing a dark suit and a felt hat with a wide brim. I love hats.

We arrived at London Bridge in the late afternoon. From here, we took a four-wheeled cab to Spitalfields. The vehicle threaded its way through a tide of carriages and people, trudging slowly across the river to the station. Alf was growing nervous. He was turning his cap around in his hands, like a charm. This was not his city. It was that of a generation before, with subtly different noises and sensations. His eyes were searching for motor vehicles. But they were not there. London was still in the slower, gentler world of the horse.

At one point in the journey, he whispered in my ear that he was afraid.

"Don't be ridiculous, Alf," I murmured. I thought of the Somme – of skylarks singing and bodies twitching on barbed wire. But I did not wish to convey this picture to him. "We shall be fine," I said. "Do not worry."

We were quiet then, until the cab turned into Whitechapel High Street, where, at last, our ears and nostrils could detect the ululations of the East End. Here, beneath the flaming gas lights, costermongers and cab touts plied for trade. Men were lounging in shop doorways, smoking evil-smelling pipes. Women with bare heads and arms beneath their aprons sauntered along in twos and threes. I paid the cab driver, who was wearing a black dress coat and a white cravat. Alf seemed uncomfortable. I think that both of us had been softened up by our life in Kent.

"Up here, Mr Frater, Sir." He gestured with a twist of his head that we should walk up Commercial Street. "It don't seem natural, do it?" said Alf. For, even though it was almost night, the street was alive. It was vibrating with commerce – here, being transacted, were crockery, carpets and oil-cloth, second-hand boots, furniture and artificial flowers. I often think of that time – of its dangers, smells and delights. It may seem curious to feel regret at its passing, for we live in a safer world now. But, sometimes, like a half-remembered dream, I do miss it.

"Don't go down there, Sir." Alf tugged at my arm. We passed, quickly, the end of notorious Wentworth Street. It looked like the mouth of hell.

"Thank God it's there." Alf had spotted a familiar landmark. It was his local public house, the Ten Bells, close to the end of Fashion Street.

"You have a drink, Sir, and I shall find my ma and da's house," Alf said. "I shan't be long." He smiled nervously. I agreed to Alf's plan and watched, anxiously, as he crossed the road to confront his destiny.

With its gilt, polished wood and frosted glass, the Ten Bells was a palace of oblivion. A printed handbill had been pinned to the door. It was offering a £100 reward for the apprehension of the perpetrator of the dreadful Whitechapel murders, the notorious Jack the Ripper. The prostitute, Mary Jane Kelly, his final victim had met her grisly end in lodgings nearby; indeed, this pub had been one of her favourite haunts and she had trawled for business outside.

A blast of noise, warmth and stale smoke almost pushed me back as I entered the public bar. The place was a watering hole for the most degraded specimens of East End life – gaudy street walkers, flush lightermen and sozzled clerks. Children clutched at their mothers' skirts. Eyes regarded and then dismissed me. Pushing my way through the melee, I bumped into a huge fellow. He turned and spat abuse at me in a language which I did not recognise – Polish or Russian.

A woman in a ragged black dress was ahead of me at the bar. A hooked nose protruded from her ruined face with its almost purple cheeks.

"'Ere give me a blue ruin, woncher?" I heard her demand. Blue ruin was a slang name for gin. She looked me up and down, assessing me as a candidate for a back-street copulation.

"Garn!" she cackled. "E's a gentleman 'an no mistake. E'll do!"

Upon this signal the brute who had previously accosted me began to berate me in broken English. I assured him that I had no interest whatsoever in his lady friend. But the man bombarded me with abusive epithets in his native language as the harridan cackled with glee, egging him on. I cursed Alf, as I waited for an age for my pint of beer to be served. I selected a table close to the door. I had no intention of lingering in this hell-hole. In fact, as soon as I had finished, I would meet Alf outside.

Just then I saw him – a pale-faced man, with ringlets of black hair spilling across his collar. His hair glistened with Macassar oil. He had put on weight since our last meeting. As he leaned back in his chair I noted a waistcoat of silver brocade stretched across an ample abdomen. There was no mistaking who it was – Sidgwick's former business partner, Nathaniel Vane! It was no surprise that Vane was sitting alone, for there was an aura of hidden and unspeakable things about the man. His fleshy face had a sinister quality, a composite of the lascivious mouth, the black side-whiskers, curving like scimitars, and the cruel, narrow eyes. Even his laugh was unpleasant.

I pulled down the brim of my hat, so that he would not recognise me. Just then, Alf came in through the door. I realised, at once, from his disappointed expression that he had failed in his quest. He had not found his parents, or anyone who had heard of them. I was not surprised. Alf confirmed my suspicions with a few words, as Vane downed a small glass at one gulp. He then took up a silver-headed cane and a black leather bag. He was leaving.

Quickly, I thrust a half sovereign into Alf's hand. I told him that he should stay the night in a lodging house and return to Spenhurst the following morning, where I would meet him, for I must follow Vane. Alf protested but I insisted. Vane scraped back his chair. Ostentatiously, he attached a black cloak to his shoulders. He punched a collapsible top hat into shape and placed it on his head. Alf looked crestfallen. But he would get over it. I pointed to my unfinished drink and then to Alf's mouth. You have it, I mimed.

Vane must have known these streets intimately, for he did not stick to the principal routes. He turned, almost at once, into one of the narrow thoroughfares that feeds into Commercial Street from the east. Here, around dark courts, were the cheapest lodgings, only one step from the casual ward of the workhouse. They were the abodes of wretchedly overcrowded families, sweated labour and prostitutes. Gas lamps did not pry very far into their dark secrets. I slid in and out of pools of darkness, carefully tracing the steps of my quarry. Not only was the air raspingly cold; coal fires and gas lamps were filling it with a dense, yellow fog that stuck to one's clothes like tar. Vane scuttled across Brick Lane like a spider, into another maze of dark streets. I knew that we would soon reach the Whitechapel Road.

I now think that he was attempting to kill time. For we had entered a milieu of people and light. The road was a long series of brightly-lit gin palaces, public houses and music halls, each establishment spilling its raucous crowds onto the pavement. Vane stopped where a barrel organ was cranking out a crude melody. He reflected before paying a penny to enter the Pavilion Theatre.

It may be hard for you, who will have enjoyed far more sophisticated pleasures, to imagine this establishment. Essentially, it exhibited alleged freaks and deformities of nature alongside recreations of historical scenes, all rendered in wax. One would have seen, for example, hairy men and hairless dogs, gorillas, aztecs and five-legged panthers. One of its attractions that night was the English Giant, lately exhibited at Mile End Gate. But I never saw him. My quarry had probably been drawn to the Chamber of Infamy, whose main attraction was a grisly tableau of one of the recent Whitechapel murders. He indulged his morbid curiosity for about twenty minutes. I did not follow him into the theatre, but lingered outside, shivering in the cold.

At the end of Berner Street, he engaged in conversation with a prostitute beneath a gas lamp. She was a slight, pretty girl, in her late teens, wearing a grey bonnet and a pale blue dress. She looked incongruous here, I thought, like a statuette of Little Bo Peep. My heart was pounding. I was barely twenty yards away. Why had I not suspected until now, the awful truth? Nathaniel Vane was the guilty man – the ripper.

Clutching his black bag and cane, Vane followed the girl through a dark entrance and into a mysterious yard. What on earth could I do? I hesitated. Should I pursue them? Of course. But how could I defend myself?

I am afraid that the denouement to the story is almost farcical. Suddenly, I felt a rough hand grasp my shoulder. I turned to discover a police constable. He had been following Alf, who had been following me, all the way from the Ten Bells, suspecting the worst. The policeman was now holding Alf, who was looking sheepish, by the sleeve of his coat.

"Sir," he said, "did you know that this man …"

"For God's sake," I cried, "a murder is being done!"

I broke free and dashed across Berner Street, towards the yard. Fortunately for me, there was only one way in, and one way out.

"There," I said, pointing to a patch of blue, in the shadows.

The girl screamed as Vane dropped his hands from her neck. He decided to make a run for it, leaving the tools of his trade in his leather bag. Alf rugby tackled Vane as he shot out of the yard like a bolting horse. His top hat sailed across the road and his cane clattered into the gutter. The cane, as readers of The

Illustrated Police News were later to learn, concealed a razor sharp bayonet in its handle – an ideal instrument for slashing a human throat.

I am happy to say that the swine, Vane, bloodied his nose on the muddy cobbles. Alf sat on him with the expression of a defiant mastiff upon his face. The constable blew his whistle, as if he was calling the last trump. Soon, other officers were converging upon Berner Street from all sides, also emitting shrill whistles and illuminating the mystery with their flashing lanterns. It took only a few minutes for news to spread through the gregarious social establishments of the East End, and from thence across the city, that the notorious perpetrator of the Whitechapel murders, Jack the Ripper, had been apprehended.

Chapter Nine

The Other Side

Nathaniel Vane was hanged that December. His trial, in the central court of the Old Bailey, did not disappoint the newspapers, which were clamouring for fresh sensation and lascivious detail on the Whitechapel slayings. Vane pleaded not guilty of the attempted murder of the prostitute Molly Price that October (the crime that I had witnessed) and to the slaying of five women in the autumn of 1888. He claimed that he had merely been conversing innocently with the girl and that there was no actual evidence linking him with the other deaths.

The fact that he was carrying a bag stuffed with surgical instruments and a sword stick flecked with dried blood when he was caught weighed heavily against him. An incriminating piece of white chalk was also discovered in his bag. In September 1888, on a night when two victims had been found, a message had been discovered in Goulston Street. It said, "The Juwes are the men that will not be blamed for nothing". The barrister for the crown suggested that Vane had scrawled these words on the wall in order to foment anti-Semitism and point the finger of blame at Sidgwick.

The barrister also suggested to the jury that Vane had killed Elizabeth Stride, his third victim, close to The International Working Men's Educational Club, a meeting place for Polish and Russian socialists, because it was one of Sidgwick's former haunts. Vane's alibis were far from robust, and his manner, which was alternately sneering and pathetic, did not endear him to the jury, which could easily imagine that he took sadistic pleasure in killing women. It took the twelve men less than two hours to find him guilty. Six weeks later, his feet were dangling through a trap-door in Wandsworth prison.

Briefly, Alf and I became famous. A succession of disreputable characters came out to Spenhurst on the train to "interview" us, although our exact words were rarely used. We became accustomed to seeing our names in print. I was the Whitechapel hero and Alf was my steadfast companion – the man who had refused to be left behind. Much of what was printed was tosh; it gave me a great insight into how events are distorted and exaggerated as they work their way from personal experience to history.

After his death, Vane's effects were sold by auction to settle his debts, including Spenhurst Hall and other assets of the company that he and Sidgwick had founded. Because of Sidgwick's notoriety the general public had stopped buying his pills – the business was, as a result, on the verge of bankruptcy. One fine March morning, I was able to purchase the Benz that Alf and I had discovered in Vane's stable on the night of the masquerade. It was knocked down with dozens of other lots, by a ruddy-faced auctioneer, in the drawing room of Spenhurst Hall.

I had no interest in Vane's pretentious paintings or his nouveau-riche furniture, but the car was a treasure. Alf painted the name of our shop, Frater and Thomas, on the side and used it as a run-around. He was delighted with it.

Changes were coming over me. For one thing, I was becoming less preoccupied by politics. It increasingly seemed to me that the squabbles of the Socialist League and its rival Mr Hyndman's Social Democratic Federation were like squalls on a duck pond.

It was at this time that I wrote my first newspaper article. It was published in the Kent Messenger and told the story of Hiram Maxim's flying machine. It was an extraordinary tale. In a hanger between Bexley and Dartford, Dr Maxim, an American millionaire, had created a steam-powered, propellor-driven aeroplane. The four-wheeled device, which looked like an attenuated bedstead, propelled itself along an iron track. My article was sceptical as to its potential (I did not reveal that I had seen an aeroplane used as a weapon of war); however, in 1894, Maxim's machine would slip the surly bonds of earth and achieve an altitude of a few inches, before crashing to the ground.

The article was re-printed by Mr Stead's Review of Reviews. My uncle's face would have curdled with envy. Other published pieces followed – on bicycles, dress reform, hop picking and allotments. Allotments were on my mind, for on the west side of Spenhurst, a portion of land had been set aside to enable working men to grow vegetables. This had been done at the instigation of Doctor Wood. And I was one of the first people in the village to be given a plot.

That winter, I worked my way through the rimed turf to reach black loam, usually with a robin or a thrush for company. The rhythm of the spade as it sliced through the soil seemed to liberate ideas for poems and articles from deep in my mind. The allotments were laid out so as to overlook the titanic sweep of the Weald. It was the best view in Spenhurst, Doctor Wood used to say. From here, one felt within touching distance of the hop fields and meadows, with the conical roofs of oast houses pointing through, like witches' hats.

On lucent winter evenings, the sky was mottled with red and gold. The vast plain of the Weald darkened beneath the gaudy canvas of sunset. As I dug, my spade would often turn up bits of clay pipe and fragments of ancient pottery. I felt that I could touch history and that I could hear and smell it – Stone Age cave dwellers, Roman legions and woad-painted Celts. All had trodden the lanes of Kent and had felt the same sun on their back.

The Christian rituals of St Thomas and St Stephen pointed back to the old gods; in my mind, the ploughman in his smock, leaning upon a stile, was coeval with the Neolithic farmer. I knew, as I broke through the stiff earth, that little had changed for thousands of years and that the summer would bring laughter and hay-making, jugs of amber beer and over-loaded wagons, swaying tipsily down the lanes.

By a happy coincidence my allotment was located next to the vicarage – the house in which Mary lived. I saw her first one February morning when I was planting broad beans. Mary was leaning over the garden wall. She was wearing a white dress. Her eyes were like chips of sapphire.

She smiled and said that it was no work for a gentleman. I told her that, on the contrary, cultivating vegetables was a delightful occupation. She said that her father and grandfather had grown potatoes, the latter before the great famine.

"Anything would grow here," I replied. "They say it is the most fertile soil in England."

Mary laughed. She offered me refreshment, which I accepted. I climbed awkwardly over the wall and we took tea in the scullery where she was wringing the vicar's washing through a mangle. It was the first of many such occasions. I came to associate Mary with the smell of soapsuds. I would lay out my ideas to her, falteringly, and she would cock her head to one side, listening. Mary was of the soil but she had little time for it – it was associated in her mind with poverty and indignity – while I would rhapsodise about my potatoes and runner beans. I would also tell her of books that I had read, giving voice to ideas that had formed, unconsciously, in the long hours in my uncle's shop.

Mary told me of her first experiences in London, explaining that she had arrived in the East End at the age of fourteen and fallen in with a gang of costermongers in Stepney. Sidgwick had seen her in an alley one day, close to his factory. He had rescued her from an altercation with a street Arab. Soon afterwards he had offered her a job as maid at Spenhurst Hall, on a stupendous salary of £12 a year.

She was fifteen then. She had worked for Sidgwick's housekeeper, Mrs Murdoch, who was a hard task-master, but fair. That summer, our conversations were frequently conducted on bicycles, riding through the lanes. Although Mary was compact she was uncannily strong. I was more interested in the songs of birds and in the flowers in the hedgerows than in arriving at any destination and often struggled to keep up.

One October evening in 1891, I was up at the allotments. I had been digging and was about to go home, but I had one more task to perform. The vicar, Winspear, kept a few chickens and a pig at the end of his garden. Mary liked the birds but detested the pig, so the task of caring for it had largely fallen to me. I must say, I had grown very fond of Hector – he was a sensitive creature, intelligent in his way. I could hear him snuffling around. He was hungry. I heaved some turnip tops over the wall to furnish his dinner – pigs, as you may know, will eat virtually anything.

Although it was nearly dark, I lingered then, looking over my little kingdom. Beyond the newly-turned sods was the Weald, like a dark inland sea. Plumes of wood smoke rose from a thousand hamlets, perfuming the still air. To the east, I could see, almost on the horizon, some patches of grey stonework melting into the dusk. These shapes were Spenhurst Hall. Though you could not tell from here, it was boarded up. Seeing the hall made me think of Lara and her father.

"Mr Frater!"

A sharp voice interrupted me from the other side of the wall. It was Mary. She was swaying.

"Mr Frater, I ..."

She leaned over Hector's sty. The smell must have made her feel nauseous. And I think that she had been drinking. I heard a heaving sound. Mary mumbled something I could not understand as I guided her, tottering, down the path. In the scullery, she bent over the sink as I placed my arm around her shoulder. I bathed her face in cold water, with a towel. She leaned back. Her blue eyes locked into mine. I saw that she was mortified with embarrassment. She started to apologise. I said that there was no need. I noticed, then, the symmetrical perfection of her features and her pale, flawless skin.

Her eyes were wide open. She murmured something. Our

faces moved together. In a trice, we were kissing, passionately. The matter did not end there. To this day, I do not know exactly how, or why, the following astonishing event occurred. For Mary, at length, led me from the scullery up some creaking stairs. Her tiny bedroom was squeezed beneath a sloping ceiling. It was mostly taken up by a black metal bedstead. It had a white coverlet. But I do not think that we actually climbed beneath it. To avoid your blushes, I shall spare the details of what happened next.

A few days later, I was at home, with Alf. Extraordinary ideas were taking shape in my mind. They were only half-formed. Could I be happy? What if Mary and I …

"Mr Frater?" Alf's voice interrupted my thoughts. We were sitting at the kitchen table.

"Do you think that dead people are still alive?"

"I'm sorry?"

It was a Sunday afternoon. We were lounging in our shirt sleeves. Alf cradled a delicate tea-cup in his sausage-like fingers.

"The thing is, I've been reading this."

On the table was a pamphlet. Its title boldly proclaimed: *Scientific Evidence that the Dead Still Live.*

"Tell me more."

"This book, it says that when we die, like, our etheric body goes out through the top of our head and into the spirit world, in a blaze of yellow light."

"I see." For a moment I wondered whether Uncle Edward was hovering balefully in the vicinity. "And where is this spirit world?" I asked.

"It's on the other side."

"On the other side of what?"

Alf's brow furrowed in concentration. Often he did not realise when I was ribbing him.

"I don't know, Mr Frater. I've only got to page seven. I wondered if you could read it to the end and tell me what you think."

I took the small green pamphlet. On its cover was an illustration – a serpent cradling a six-pointed star, with an Egyptian ankh at its centre. There was a motto beneath: "Truth is our goal. Love is our way".

This was the first time that I had encountered the literature of the Theosophical Society. Theosophy, which flourished in the twilight of the nineteenth century, was a peculiar mixture of science, religion and philosophy. It purported, in fact, to represent the universal truth of each. A sub-group of Spiritualism, Theosophy was at once, rational and mystical. People in Theosophy were free agents, not merely the playthings of a monotheistic God. Its key text, which I later read, was a dense tome called *The Secret Doctrine,* by Helena Blavatsky. The Theosophists held that there was a Great White Brotherhood – a group of initiates who understood the secret workings of the universe. Members of the brotherhood walked among us, but we did not always know who they were. The first Theosophists, wrote Madame Blavatsky, the curiously-named Philalethians, lived in third-century Alexandria. They were followers of Pythagoras, Plato and the lost Orphic and Egyptian mysteries. Later, traces of the creed could be detected in the beliefs of the Rosicrucians and the Knights Templar.

This is queer stuff, you will be thinking. But it does not end there. The Theosophists thought that the characteristics of all life forms derive from the properties of seven rays originating in the constellation of Ursa Major, the Great Bear. Human beings, they believed, have astral as well as physical bodies. In the astral realm, they said, dwell fairies, elves, gnomes and the like – the little people of folklore.

They believed in karma and in reincarnation. Our souls, they maintained, migrate between bodies, moving towards higher and higher forms of consciousness. The earth and all of its life forms, they held, are evolving towards the ultimate state, a civilisation of light, in which hatred, crime, pollution and suffering have been eliminated – a heaven on earth. In the late 1960s, the sun, said the Theosophists, would leave Pisces and enter Aquarius. At this point, the seventh ray would become stronger than the sixth. This would signal a shift in energies towards love, understanding and harmony – the beginning of a so-called New Age.

Now all of this, with its overtones of incense and table rapping, may seem totally mad. But is it any more so than believing that you will go to hell if you eat a bacon sandwich on a Friday?

"If we are surrounded by dead people, Alf," I said, "why can't we see them?"

"Ah, I know that one." His face brightened. "It's because we are not tuned in to their vibrations. They are there all around us, like, but they are invisible, like electricity."

"So who can?"

"Psychic mediums, Mr Frater. Clairvoyants."

Alf could sense that he was beginning to lose me. He continued enthusiastically. "You know the scientist, William Crooke? Well, he done these experiments with this eighteen-year-old girl. She stayed in Mr Crooke's residence for a week and they never left her alone, not day or night." Alf was now reading directly from the pamphlet.

"No cabinet was used except the curtained end of the library. On this particular occasion, seven witnesses were present. Five photographic cameras were in position and no device that could assist in testing the genuineness of the phenomena was neglected. So perfect were the arrangements that the temperature of the room was automatically registered as the time passed. Under these conditions, the most satisfactory materializations occurred."

Alf was convinced that this account, written by one L.W. Rogers, was genuine. The specificity of the detail – seven witnesses, five cameras, four and a half inches – and the simple authority of the print on the page had done the trick. I saw at once that such a conflation of science and mysticism would exercise a powerful attraction upon the credulous; especially those who had been made receptive, like Alf, by the loss of a loved one. Death is not the end, claimed Theosophy; it is merely the portal through which one enters an invisible kingdom; the dawn of a brighter day. There is always something ineffable, I reflected, beyond the reach of our understanding, and we seek to read in it different ways.

"Mr Frater ..."

Alf's voice pulled me back from my speculations. He poured more water into the teapot from the big black kettle.

"You know my Emily. Well, I think that she is there, like, on the other side."

"I see, Alf." I did not want to dash his hopes. Why should I? I mean, who would have thought that travelling through Time was possible.

At that moment, there was a tap on the back door. It was Mary. She was carrying a basket of eggs.

"I'm sorry I am so late, Sir. The vicar ..."

"It does not matter. Come in."

I kissed her on the cheek.

Alf looked uneasy. He poured Mary a cup of tea. But he seemed uncomfortable. Alf and Mary never hit it off, I am afraid. Perhaps Alf, my best friend, was jealous of my intimacy with her. Also, they were of two different nations. The Welsh tend to be reticent, unless they are in chapel or singing, usually with tears in their eyes. Their non-conformist religion is as dour as their climate and tends to promote feelings of guilt and misery. The Irish on the other hand, benefit from a gaudy religion, which is pre-occupied with forgiveness. And their relationship with alcohol is open and unabashed, not like the furtive, hole and corner affair of the Welsh. Alf left on some assignation in the workshop. I complimented Mary on her beautiful dress. She had made it herself, she said. Smiling, she walked across to me. I placed my hands on the small of her back. I drew her towards me. Hungrily, we began to kiss.

I have no doubt, dear Isabella, that my relationship with Mary would have deepened but for the subsequent turn of events. There would have been more leisurely bicycle rides through the lanes and long conversations. The following summer, we would undoubtedly have married. I would have prevailed upon Alf, despite his strong reservations, to be my best man. However, these events were not destined to take place.

At the end of October something happened that changed the course of my life. I received an unexpected letter. I picked it up on Saturday morning on my way to the allotment. It was an extraordinary thing. The envelope reeked of a sickly perfume and was covered in an alarmingly large, curvilinear script, composed in violet ink. It was from great aunt Agnes.

In her looping hand-writing, Agnes explained that she had become a Spiritualist and that her new moniker was Anya Petrovska. This, she said, was her Armenian name. It was news to me. Agnes was from London. Her father had been a greengrocer in Bromley. She expressed regret for the death of my uncle, saying that she hoped that his troubled spirit had finally found contentment – although she doubted it.

Finally, she invited me, to my great surprise, to an "emanation" at her house in Sevenoaks. It was to be held, she said, on the night of Samhain, or the Feast of the Ancestors, when the full moon entered Scorpio. She said that I could bring a friend or companion. There would be a small "consideration" in order to pay for refreshments, but we could settle this when I arrived. At the end of the letter she alluded to the beneficence of the God Horus. There was a peculiar squiggle next to her autograph – I recognised it as a Theosophoical symbol, derived from the Hindu religion. I carried the letter in my pocket that day, its smell lingering on my fingers.

Alf was sceptical but also curious, because of his newly-aroused interest in life beyond the veil. Mary said that Agnes was clearly, "as mad as an owl" but that she would like to go, for a laugh. I was fascinated by the whole business. For these reasons, I accepted my aunt's peculiar invitation.

Chapter Ten

Call me Madam

A few days later, the three of us stood on a pavement in Sevenoaks, in front of my aunt's surprisingly ordinary-looking house. We all felt nervous, despite the stiffeners of whisky we had gulped from Alf's hip flask. We had been uncertain of the dress code – what does one wear to a seance? We had opted, finally, for our Sunday best, on the basis that this was a quasi-religious experience. Alf seemed uncomfortable in the suit that he had worn to the East End in search of his parents. He hated formality. But Mary was radiant in her new, pale green dress with a matching hat. She loved dressing up.

The house, which was called Brightlands, was a modest bay-windowed affair, with net curtains and a small front yard. The young woman who opened the door appeared to be a creature of this planet. Her hair was cropped short and she was tall and slender. She had a pale complexion, high cheekbones and clear grey eyes. Mary recognised at once, in her trusting, open features, an Irish physiognomy and felt immediately at ease. But the girl, Nuala, appeared nervous as she led us through a cluttered hallway and into the parlour.

Here, the presence of my aunt was palpable, although she was not yet visible. The aroma of incense, the same smell that had permeated her stationary, was overwhelming here, at its source. It clung to our clothes for a long time. A gentleman was already present in the room and a lady, in an oxblood-red dress. The man was remote and self-contained in his demeanour. He barely acknowledged us, while the lady greeted us shyly.

There was a noise; it lay somewhere between a breakfast gong and a Tibetan temple bell, and Aunt Agnes, or Anya Petrovska, as I should perhaps call her, swept dramatically into the room. What a transformation! My great aunt had always been amply proportioned, but she was now even more so. Her dress was of deep purple velvet, trimmed with lace. There was a string of amethyst beads around her neck; her plump white hands were festooned with silver rings, some with turquoise stones.

My great aunt had a dignified bearing, commanding respect. Her eyes were dark and deep-set, like points of jet. These hypnotic instruments, I came to realise, were the principal tools of her trade. Her hair, although you could scarcely call it hair, was a helmet of close-cropped curls, glistening with a sweet-smelling oil.

"Nuala!" Her commanding voice made us all jump. "In the name of Isis, why did you not tell me that the guests had arrived? Don't just stand there simpering girl. Go! Can't you follow the simplest instruction!"

Nuala squirmed and fled from the room. We felt for the poor girl. My great aunt treated her like a slave. She now turned a sickly smile upon us – the sudden transformation in her manner was disconcerting.

"Now, I must introduce you. Frederick, this is Mr Leonard William Rogers, from Hammersmith. He is a renowned Theosophist and this is his lady wife, Sarah." Rogers nodded vaguely in my direction. What a curious coincidence. Here, in person, was the author of the little pamphlet that had converted Alf to spiritualism. Clearly, he was blessed with extraordinarily high self-esteem. His wife seemed pleasant enough – she was a well-padded matriarchal woman.

After effecting these introductions, my aunt turned to face us. Suddenly, she gasped. Her pendulous chins quivered. "Oh my goodness," she gasped. "Look at him!"

The object of her attentions, Alf, became sheepish. He had removed his hat but did not know what to do with it.

"Look at his monads!" my aunt hissed. "Can you not see, the brightness is shining out of him!"

My aunt ran one of her bejewelled fingers through Alf's brilliantined hair. He looked like the traumatised prey of an Indian cobra.

"I have never seen such a pronounced aura. This man is a chela. Do you not see it, Mr Rogers?"

Rogers stepped forwards. He made a great play of inspecting the Welshman, looking him up and down and murmuring something. But I could see that he was as blind as a badger to Alf's alleged luminosity.

My aunt continued to simper. "I shall be watching you very carefully," she said to Alf. "Few are blessed with such inner light. Now. Sit!"

My aunt's voice brooked no opposition. We perched on dining chairs. They were covered with a scratchy, tapestry-like material and were extremely uncomfortable.

"Before we proceed to the Temple of Horus, I must detain you with a few words of caution," said the clairvoyant. "Please listen very carefully." Her eyes bored into us. "The ancient forces, which we may, or may not, invoke, are extremely powerful. If my Spirit Guide wills it, then an ectoplasmic liquid will enter all of our bodies. Mr Rogers has experienced this phenomenon many times before, as has Mrs Rogers." A smug look crossed the man's features. "But for you others, it will be the first time. I must warn you that an insertion of ectoplasm can be uncomfortable and sometimes even dangerous, especially for those who are morbidly sensitive."

She regarded Alf with a peculiar expression on her face. He squirmed in his seat. Mary was half smiling, a mixture of amusement and scepticism was evident in her expression. I could tell that she was enjoying the experience.

"The spirit world is not like a Sunday picnic," continued Madam Petrovska. "Look at me! All of you! That's better. You will obey my instructions at all times. Is that clear? There is one more thing. It is a sacrilege to enter the Temple of Horus under the influence of alcohol and I will not allow it, under any circumstances. Has anyone been drinking?"

Her beady eyes swivelled from person to person. None of us was brave enough to admit our apostasy. "Good. I have explained what you must do. Are you now ready to partake of the sacred rites?"

"Yes," we muttered.

"Yes, what?" My aunt scowled.

"Yes, Madam," replied Rogers, obediently. He was clearly familiar with this ritual.

"Good God," said Alf, too softly for the psychic to hear. "Mr Frater, if you don't mind I ..." But it was too late. The mystical gong sounded again. It was struck by Nuala, who must have been waiting nervously for her cue.

"Initiates of the Ancient Wisdom," hissed Madam Petrovska, "you may now proceed to the Sacred Temple. Follow me!"

The Sacred Temple was little more spacious than a box room. It was dark and confined in there. The smell of my aunt, whose exotic perfume masked her other more natural odours, made our eyes water. We squeezed ourselves around a circular table. A few small candles flickered on a sideboard, where incense was burning. My heart was thumping. I don't know what I was expecting – a little automatic writing, some levitation, a few mildly diverting bumps. Certainly not what happened. Alf was gagging for breath; he would have welcomed, no doubt, a means of escape, but none was available. We now heard the sound of a heavy velvet curtain being drawn across the outside of the door. Madame Petrovska lifted her small white hands. She had arranged the six of us around the table so that the sexes were alternated. Mary was to my right, Mrs Rogers, the padded matriarch, to my left. We joined hands. I could hear Alf wince as my aunt squeezed his knuckles like a vice.

"Silence!" she commanded.

In the quiet that followed, we could hear my aunt's hoarse

breath, and we could smell it. It was rank with garlic, or onions. Nothing happened for a long time. Significant silences are as important to the mystic as their staring eyes. Our arms, which were held above the table, soon began to ache.

I could sense, from Mary's posture and her expression, that she had suspended her disbelief. She was going along for the ride, as they say. Poor Alf! The more intense the experience became, the tighter my aunt gripped him. His hand was in agony, he told me later. For all of us, the feeling of tension combined with bathos was becoming unbearable. I think that Alf would have cut his losses and broken away if nothing had happened for much longer.

Just then, to my great surprise, the table began to rise. Slowly, but steadily, it actually lifted from the floor. The table began to undulate fractionally, like a yacht bobbing on a swell. Mary's breathing quickened. I could sense that she was becoming excited. Rogers was as calm and placid as a bank manager. What happened next was equally surprising. A thin, rasping noise began to issue from my aunt's throat. It was not her own voice, but that of Oblovsky, her Armenian Spirit Guide. We gathered this information because he told us so. He sounded, I thought, like a parrot with bronchitis. But he shared Madam Petrovska's irate disposition.

"Are they here?" he rasped. "For five long centuries you keep me waiting! Arkhhhh!" At this point, he fell silent, as if a piece of cuttlebone had caught in his throat.

Nothing happened for perhaps ninety seconds. It seemed that Oblovsky had decided to call it a day and had gone back to the Other Side. I was disappointed but also somewhat relieved. Alf would be thinking, "Thank Christ for that; we can all go home". I looked around the table. To my astonishment, I saw that a shimmering corona of white light was glowing around my aunt's head. Faintly pulsing, it was growing brighter. The air became icy and my fingers began to tingle. A tight band seemed to wrap around my chest. Mary felt this too. Her grip on my hand tightened. I was becoming light-headed. I shut my eyes but this did little to restore clarity. When I opened them, a peculiar sight was revealed. Mr Rogers had grown horns!

The man's face was gradually transmuting, in a swirling pattern of molecules, into a snarling mask of evil. And his body was contracting, as it adapted to the curvature of an animal's spine – an animal with cloven hooves. The transformation of Rogers into a devil was a relatively short step, for the greed, cunning and wickedness that manifested in his features were not too far from the surface. In a later age he would no doubt have prospered as an estate agent or as a "personal financial advisor". I seemed to see into his soul; I could taste his vinegary thoughts and feel his rancid breath, hot upon my skin.

It was of little surprise that my aunt's features had now transmuted into those of the most hideous crone on the face of the earth. Her eyes had become reptilian, set in a face of ancient wrinkled parchment. Her purple dress had turned to black. A horrible croaking sound now issued from her gnarled throat; it made Oblovsky sound like a choirboy. As to Mrs Rogers, on my immediate left, her breasts had swelled like melons and burst out of her dress, which was now a vivid shade of scarlet. Her face was serene, almost beatific. She seemed a benign, universal matriarch; one wanted to bury one's head in her bosoms.

Suddenly, the air was rent by an almighty crash, as what appeared to be a bolt of lightning jolted through our bodies. The table shot away – that is the only way I can describe what happened. One moment it was there; the next it was gone. The heavy mahogany object passed cleanly through the ceiling, leaving a neat circular hole. It traversed the upstairs room and exited through the roof.

The explosion had also removed most of an internal wall. Nuala was now revealed, sprawled in the rubble, in a space beneath the stairs. There was a splintered wooden cabinet in front of her, trailing some wires. She must have used an electric current, I realised, to levitate the table. But how could she have made my aunt's head glow and turned Rogers into a devil? These phenomena were hardly the charlatanism of a suburban occultist.

There was a shocked and guilty expression on Nuala's features. She had also, and this was perhaps more significant, become the most beautiful woman on the planet. Imagine Isis merged with Cleopatra, the PreRaphaelite damosels and all music hall sirens and cinematic goddesses you have ever seen and that would not come even close to her heart-stopping gorgeousness. Admittedly, most of Nuala's clothes had blown away, leaving only a few wisps of white silk clinging perilously to her shapely form. But her attractiveness was not merely of a carnal nature; it was a magnetism permeating every particle of her being. One would have died for her; one felt privileged merely to be allowed to gaze upon her loveliness for a few seconds.

Time had been slowing down since I had seen my aunt's halo. Now it had almost stopped. I looked at Mary and Alfred. They were still holding hands. Their mouths were opening. But if they were speaking, it was infinitely slowly. Suddenly, I felt someone tapping on my shoulder. I looked behind me.

It was Sidgwick.

"Friedrich," he said, "I need to talk to you."

"You could have come in through the front door," I replied. "Where on earth have you been?"

Sidgwick appraised me closely. His eyes were red-rimmed, with dark shadows. I could see that he had been through a terrible ordeal and had not slept much recently. He was wearing leather sandals and was dressed, as I had once been, as a Druid priest. But his white robes were filthy and torn. His beard, which was a genuine one, contained pieces of twig and earth.

"Well," he began, "I suppose I had better tell you what has

been happening."

I surveyed the room. It looked as if a bomb had hit it. As well as fragments of rubble, lath and plaster, the floor was covered with pieces of crystal and amber, feathers, statuettes, silk scarves and other tools of the mystic's trade. I cleared a space, so that Sidgwick could sit down. The others were in a trance, he explained, from which they would awake in due course. My aunt faced the prospect of a rather large repair bill; but had she not warned us that supernatural forces were not to be trifled with?

"What caused this?" I asked.

He looked at the wreckage as if it were entirely normal. "Oh, it was a little knock from the war club of the god Belenus, I should think. It was he who enabled me to come here."

"The god Belenus?"

"I know this will be hard for you to believe," said Sidgwick. I looked at him, wondering what he was about to tell me.

"Do you remember that evening in 1879 when you came to dinner and I showed you the chronospheres?"

I nodded.

"Well," said Sidgwick, "let me explain to you what happened next. The following day, I went into the stables, to make some final adjustments to the control system of the Daedalus. The machines were almost ready for their first journey, in which we would voyage to ancient Britain at the time of the ancient Romans and take up the noble cause of the Celts. I was to pilot the Daedlus. You were to travel with Lara in the Icarus."

"You did not tell me this!" I interjected. "Why did you not acquaint me with your plan?"

"I would have, Friedrich." Sidgwick looked evasive. "Honestly. But something happened that I had not foreseen. Who should I find in the stable but my servant, Snipe? He was behaving suspiciously. I should have realised long before that he was working for Nathaniel Vane, and that Vane was plotting against me."

"What happened?"

"I believe that Snipe, the cur, had already sabotaged the Icarus by re-setting its controls. He was now doing the same thing to the Daedlus. You see, he wanted both machines to become lost in the streams of Time and separated. With me eliminated from the scene, Vane could take sole control of our business. He is from bad stock. I should have known that he was a trickster!"

Should I tell Sidgwick that Vane had been identified as the Whitechapel murderer and that he was now buried in an unmarked grave in Wandsworth prison? I decided not to. These revelations could come later.

"I confronted Snipe," he continued. "He denied that he had been tampering with the chronospheres. But he began to sneer at me, calling me a dirty yid. This is very unpleasant, yes?"

I nodded. "It is unpardonable."

"I saw red, Friedrich. You will understand this. And there was a tussle. By a stroke of good fortune, Lara was outside, grooming her horse. She ran to my assistance. She leapt onto Snipe's back clawing at his head. She was like a lioness." He began to chuckle. "Snipe fell forwards. This, unfortunately, caused the Time Lever to be depressed. We shot off into the cosmos, Friedrich, like a cannon ball coming out of a musket." He smiled, happy with his analogy.

"What … I mean where?"

Sidgwick rubbed the back of his neck. I saw that his calves were filthy. His leather sandals had been specially made to his design. They had been copied from diagrams in the British museum.

"I am very thirsty, my boy," he said. "Do you think that there is anything to drink in this place?"

I rummaged in the kitchen. My aunt had a bottle of cooking sherry, but it would be hideously sweet. There was also a reasonable claret, stored in the scullery. The scene in the parlour was extraordinary. It had been devastated. Sidgwick sat impassively on the settee, in his white robes. On the other side of the room were six people, suspended in extraordinary postures, like a tableau in a waxworks. I tried not to look at Nuala. Pale and naked, she was like a toppled statue of Venus or Helen of Troy. Rogers' horns and tail suited him, I thought. His claw-like hand was placed lustfully on his wife's thigh. My aunt's wrinkled face was up-turned, towards the hole in her ceiling. She was going to be angry when she woke up. Alf and Mary, in their smart clothes, completed the picture, shocked and incongruous, like interlopers in a nightmare.

Sidgwick seemed grateful for his drink. "Thank you, my dear boy," he said. He wet his lips on the claret. "Now, where was I? Ah yes, I did not know it then, of course, but the Daedlus had landed us in the exact locality that I had intended and at the right time – AD 59."

"Where were you?"

"We were in the Clocaenog Forest, in the mountains of North Wales. I opened the door. It was grey and drizzly outside. It was impossible to tell the time of day. We heard a bird song – it was a curlew I think. That cheered us up. But Snipe was terrified. He was gibbering like a Barbary ape. I told him to pull himself together."

"What did you do next?"

"We put on the costumes that Lara had prepared. I, as you see, became a Druid; Lara adopted the guise of a first-century female Celt. Unfortunately, there were no clothes for Snipe. He had to remain in his dark suit and his bowler hat. To cut a long story short, Friedrich, we wandered around outside, in the rain. There was not much to see – just rocks and heather. We were on a hillside, close to a lake. At the top of the hill, fortuitously, was an encampment. Lara saw a boy. My heart leaped, for I knew that he was a young Celt. We followed him to the encampment. After some discussion we announced ourselves to the guards. They took us inside. They were surprised to see us, as you can imagine."

"What language did you speak?"

"Brythonic, of course. That is the tongue of the local tribe, the Ordovice. It is not difficult to learn, Friedrich, if you have a basic grasp of Indo-Germanic philology, as I do." Sidgwick looked down, modestly. "Snipe had become unintelligible. He was howling with indignation. But I managed to convince the guards that we had no evil intentions."

"And then?"

"We were led into the war hut of the Ordovice's leader, Caractacus."

"Who?"

"Caractacus, my boy, or King Caractacus, as he is sometimes known, son of Cunobelinus and great grandson of Cassivellaunus. Some people have maintained that Caractacus was the King Arthur of legend but I can assure you, Friedrich, this is not the case."

"What was he like?"

A look of distaste crossed his face.

"We did not like the man from outset, for he was a big head. He was vain about his curly blond locks and festooned with cheap-looking gold jewellery. He could not keep his eyes off Lara. He kept saying that she must be Blodwen, the goddess of the Western Isles of Paradise, much to her embarrassment."

"I see, but surely ..."

"You will remember from your Tacitus, Friedrich, that Caractacus had been taken to Rome in chains after his betrayal by Queen Cartimandua. He was shown the sights and paraded in front of Emperor Claudius. In my view, the experience ruined him. He became far too attached to hot baths and olive oil. When he returned to Britain, he was a pampered braggart."

Sidgwick looked across the room. He seemed to notice the motionless figures for the first time. When would they wake up, I wondered?

"I told Caractacus of my plan, which, I hoped, would ensure a victory for the Celtic nation against the Roman army."

"What did he say?"

"He wasn't interested. He brought in his second-in-command, Guidavius, who was his brother, and wandered off. Guidavius, was a good sort, not at all like his sibling. As I talked, I could hear Caracatacus boasting to Lara about his Roman connections. He kept calling her flower face."

"What was your plan?" I said.

"Well, I knew, you see, that the XXth legion would leave from its garrison in Chester the following year, led by their commander, Suetonius Paulinus. He wished to defeat the Celts in north Wales and to decimate the Druids on the island of Anglesey, or Mona, which was their spiritual centre. After this catastrophe, Celtic resistance would evaporate across Britain."

His eyes blazed with passion. "This must be stopped, Friedrich, at all costs!"

I touched his sleeve. He took a breath.

"I explained to Guidavius that Claudius had been poisoned by his second wife, Agrippa. The new emperor was Nero, a clown who had no interest whatsoever in the northern fringes of his empire and whose favourite occupation was talking to his horse.

"Here was an opportunity, I said. The Celtic tribes in southern England had capitulated to the Romans. But there were plenty of other tribes which could put up a good show – the Iceni in Norfolk, for example, led by Boudicca. The Celtic cause was far from lost, I said; it was just waiting for some leadership. As to defeating the XXth legion, there was an easy way to do it."

"Really?"

"Oh yes. I knew that to reach Anglesey the legion would have to cross the mouth of the Conwy, a broad tidal river. The Deceangli should plant lines of stakes on the other side, forcing the legion south, to find another crossing point. This you see, would divert the entire force beneath the Bodnant cliffs!" Sidgwick's face was glowing.

"The Ordovice could take them apart, simply by flinging boulders and javelins onto them from the cliffs. If anything was left of the legion after that – which would be unlikely – it could be finished off with a chariot attack. Can you imagine, a whole legion annihilated? Puff! The last time that happened, I told Guidavius, was on the 18th of July 390 BC, at the hands of the Gauls. In any case, if my scheme did not work, I had an alternative plan."

"Which was?"

"I cannot tell you, at the moment."

"I see. What did Guidavius think?"

"He was impressed. He was a good tactician. He even suggested a refinement – luring the Romans under the cliffs with a decoy attack. But do you know what Caractacus was doing? He was reciting obscene poetry to Lara – Catallus. Lara was as red as a tomato. After that, he tried to impress her with a conjuring trick, involving three goblets. Guidavius was disgusted but, of course, he could say nothing." Sidgwick sighed.

"What happened next?"

"That night, there was a feast. It was a jolly affair, with roast boar, tumbling, harp music, and so on. Caractacus made a speech. He was a good speaker. I understood then why he was the Ordovice's leader. Saying that he had carefully listened to my plan, he introduced me to the tribe as their saviour and Lara as a flower-faced goddess. The speech went down well and we were greeted as heroes.

"After that, things got out of hand. Everybody, including Caractacus, became very drunk. Fighting broke out and one of the huts caught on fire. Lara and I made our excuses. We were escorted to our accommodation at the edge of the encampment. Snipe was being held in a kind of pen nearby. The man had broken down completely, I am afraid. His clothes were covered in animal dung. Children were taunting him and prodding him with sticks. He was shrieking like a savage."

"And then?"

"We tried to rest. The festivities did not die down until just before daybreak. I think that I had just fallen asleep when something dreadful happened. There was a scream. I woke up to see a huge Ordovice tribesman manhandling Lara. He was hoisting her over his shoulder. There was nothing I could do, Friedrich, you understand." He looked at me sadly

"Of course not. It must have been awful."

"It was. The situation was appalling. I knew that Lara would be carried off to Carcactus's quarters, and, if that was the case …"

Sidgwick placed his wine glass on the floor. "I felt alone and afraid, Friedrich. I have not felt so bad since …"

His words trailed off. I knew that he must be troubled by some painful memory.

Chapter Eleven

The Rescue

"There was nothing I could do," Sidgwick continued. "Caractacus's hut was heavily defended by tattooed rough-necks. However, Belenus must have been smiling upon us, for, happily, Caractacus did not force Lara to submit to his lust that night. Perhaps he was too drunk."

"You must have been relieved," I said.

"I was. In the morning she was thrust back into the hut, where we were now held captive. Our situation was desperate, Friedrich. I heard mutterings outside. Caractactus was putting it about that Lara, the beautiful, was not Blodwen at all but a daughter of Macha, the Goddess of Death.

"It was almost Samhain, known to Christians as Halloween. I overheard that Lara was to be offered to the gods as a sacrifice, with Snipe. They were to be burned alive in the Samhain fires. I was not to be killed; Caractacus would not have dared to sacrifice a Druid."

"Of course not."

"I did not tell Lara what was afoot, but I decided that we must escape. It was not too difficult. We waited until dark. The skin of the hut was made from wattles. We could hear the guard snoring. We simply broke through. Unfortunately, the guard woke up and," he sniffed, "Lara was caught."

"What did you do?"

"I legged it, Friedrich, as your Cockneys say. There was nothing else for it. But I had a plan. I knew that close to the encampment must be a place where Ordovice's wise men lived – the Druids. If I made a plausible case to the Druids' leader he could intercede for us and demand the release of Lara and Snipe, directly to Caractacus. No rational chieftain, I thought, could ignore such a request. I stumbled into the forest. It was pitch dark. I had to feel my way between the trees. I was lucky because I heard voices quite soon. I decided to approach them. It was a group of bards, practising their poetry. Do you know, Friedrich, it can take up to fifteen years to master the arts of Druidry."

"Really?"

"Oh yes. Fortunately for me, they were most helpful. They said that they would take to me to see Brandon, who, happily, had not yet gone to bed."

"Brandon?"

"He was their leader – the Arch Druid."

"I see. What was he like?"

"He is a delightful man. He gave me some supper and we spoke for a considerable time. He explained to me that the Druids were to officiate at the sacrificial fires the following night. Of course, he asked me why Lara and Snipe should be spared."

"What did you say?"

"I argued that she was far too beautiful, and clever. Generally, it was only the lame and mentally deficient who were put to the flames, and enemies captured in battle. The Celts believed, and who could gainsay them, that without such practices their crops would not grow."

"What about Snipe?"

Sidgwick looked up. "I told Brandon that his ravings disguised the wisdom of a seer. He was far too useful to sacrifice."

"What did Brandon do?"

"He said that, the following morning, he would go and talk to Caractacus and argue that Lara and Snipe should be released." Sidgwick's eyes were shadowed by fatigue. "I passed an anxious night, Friedrich. The following morning, I saw that, close by, the Samhain fires were being constructed. At the top of each was a sculptural representation of the human form – a wicker man. The figures were made from wooden frames, with a skin of woven willow branches, threaded with rushes and grasses. To the side of each wicker man was a ladder. I knew, from the books that I had read, that, when the time came, the sacrificial victims would be pushed inside. The fires would be lit and they would be burnt alive."

I gulped. "Did Brandon meet with Caractacus?" I asked.

"Oh yes, just after noon."

"What did Caractacus say?"

"He refused the request. He said that Lara and Snipe were 'flame food' and that Brandon could … well, it was extremely rude, Friedrich, I shall not repeat it. Brandon told me that he was very sorry. But he suggested something."

"Which was?"

"He proposed that we offer a prayer to Belenus and seek his help. He is the Druids' Apollo, their god of fire, fertility and cattle."

"Did you?"

"Of course. I walked with Brandon into the most secluded part of the forest, to a sacred grove, or nemeton. It was a circular clearing, surrounded by venerable oaks. You will have read of such places in Frazer's *Golden Bough*. In the centre of the grove was a dolmen – a chamber of upright, roughly-hewn stones, roofed with a single huge slab – a doorway between the worlds of the living and dead. It was dark in there. Brandon lit a tallow candle. We dripped fresh chicken and goat blood into the earth and Brandon made an invocation using his magic cauldron."

"His what?"

"It was just an iron pot really, half filled with rain water. But it worked. To my amazement, the surface of the liquid became a shining mirror. Belenus's face materialised almost at once and we were able to talk to him, just as I am talking to you now. For the Druids, Friedrich, contacting the gods and goddesses is relatively easy – not a hit or miss affair, like Christian prayer. But you have to remember that their deities, unlike the Christian God, are not infallible. They cannot be relied upon, and they make mistakes."

"What did Belenus say?"

"He told me that, by coincidence, he had just received a message from your aunt Agnes, in Sevenoaks. Normally, of course, he would pay no heed to such crackpots. He simply ignored them. But he explained that the relative positions of the moon and the sun were propitious. For this reason, he would be able to send me to Kent in 1891, at least for a brief period, and that this would allow …"

Was it merely my imagination? Sidgwick's body seemed to be shimmering and growing translucent. I looked around. It also appeared that the six statues were coming to life.

Sidgwick assumed a worried expression. His face was vanishing before my eyes.

"Friedrich," he said, "there is something that I must ask you."

"What?"

"There is not much time. It is presumptuous of me, but I would like you to help me. Lara is in grave danger. If we do not rescue her, she will – He could not say the words. "Please, if you …"

My aunt's voice boomed across the room. She had seen the damage.

"What in the name of Nefertiti?"

I saw that she had returned to her previous self. She took a deep breath, her eyes bulging. Mrs Rogers was as pale as a ghost. Her husband, restored to human form, was ignoring her. The sight of Mary's face tugged at my heart. She seemed about to cry. Sidgwick had almost disappeared. He held out his arm. What was I to do? I hope that you will not reproach me for the decision that I made. Remember, I could have no inkling of subsequent events. I had no reason to believe that I would not be able to return to this scene, just as I had left it. Should I follow Sidgwick or attend to Mary? I am a man. I must live with the consequences of my choice. You should also know that it was made in a split second.

An instant before it was gone, I clutched Sidgwick's outstretched hand. At the same moment, I felt two arms grip my legs like a pincer. It was Alfred. He must have thought that I was being abducted. He had launched himself across the room, in another of his rugby-like manoeuvres.

"Don't worry, Mr ..."

I felt light-headed and a blackness engulfed me. I fainted once, at a wedding on a hot day. It was the same sensation.

I woke up sprawled on a hard floor, with two other people. Alf was still clutching my legs. I had become detached from Sigdwick, who was lying, indecorously, on his back. We were in a dark, clammy place. There was a stone roof above us. A bearded man in robes was seated nearby behind a metal pot. There was a complacent smile on his lips. I guessed that it was Brandon. We dusted ourselves off.

"Flipping heck," said Alf, "what was that?"

I realised that there was much to explain. Too much. At least Alf was out of the clutches of my aunt.

"We are in Wales," I said. He would have felt a surge of joy, on hearing the name of his native land. "It is AD 59."

"Oh." He said nothing.

"Welcome, Friedrich," said Sidgwick, standing. "And your companion is?"

"Alfred Thomas," formerly private Alfred Thomas of the Middlesex Regiment. He is my friend. I met him at the Battle of the Somme."

Sidgwick smiled. Alf was confused, suppressing his initial instinct, which was to salute, he did not know what to do.

"It is good to meet you. Very good," said Sidgwick. He took Alf's hand and shook it vigorously. Alf groaned, for his knuckles were sore.

"Gentlemen, this is Brandon. He is the chief Druid in these parts."

Brandon slid off his rock and greeted us. I would say that he was in his early thirties. He had shoulder length black hair and a moustache of the same colour. His brown eyes were soft and smiling.

"Very well," said Sidgwick, the formalities concluded. I could see that he had planned carefully what we were to do next.

Brandon offered us something to eat. Alfred and I were too excited to be hungry, but we accepted the victuals – blackberries and hazelnuts, with some coarse bread and water. After that, we walked through the forest. It must have been raining that morning. The delicious smell of wet vegetation reminded me of Doctor Wood's cottage. The aroma may have stirred happy memories for Alf, or perhaps he was merely relieved to have escaped from my aunt – he was still massaging the hand that she had crushed. He began to hum one of the songs of his forefathers.

Carrying a long staff and dressed in white, Sidgwick looked, I thought, like Moses at the head of his flock. He led us out of the wood and onto a hillside. It was warm for October. Clouds half covered the sky. They were veined silver by the sun, as if by streams of mercury. At the fringes of the wood were hawthorn trees. I saw that the grass had been close-cropped by grazing animals. Sidgwick stopped. He showed us something. A quarter of a mile off were two mounds of tree trunks and faggots. These were the Samhain fires, he said. At the top of each, in silhouette, was the shape of a person with outstretched arms. Sidgwick told us that these were wicker men and he explained their purpose.

"That's absolutely barbaric," said Alf.

I was surprised by his eloquence. Sidgwick explained that the ceremony would take place at midnight. The Celtic day, he said, began at sundown – the hours of darkness were just as important to these people as those of light. And they lived by the moon. When the moon was waxing, the Druids would perform positive magic and during the waning moon, binding or dark magic.

Samhain, he told us, which began the dark half of the year, was the Celts' New Year. The veil between the worlds was thinnest at this time. It was a time when the dead walked amongst the living and when other supernatural manifestations occurred. This, he said, would assist his plan.

"Which is?" I asked.

Sidgwick declined to answer.

"Come," he said.

We walked along a path fringed with lush ferns. Around a corner, beneath an outcrop of rocks, we saw it then – a large grey sphere, partially hidden by vegetation. It was the Daedlus! Two muscular Druids were guarding the precious machine. They were carrying heavy clubs. Sidgwick thanked them.

Next to the door were four small buttons. Sidgwick depressed them in a secret sequence. A short metal ladder retracted from the sphere. We climbed inside.

"Make yourselves comfortable," said Sidgwick.

Alf became grave. He must have been remembering the time when I had rescued him in France in the Icarus – the thunder of guns, the screams of his fallen comrades.

"Please, remove your jackets gentlemen."

We did so and placed them on the bed. Alf arranged himself, sighing, in one of the armchairs. I stood next to Sidgwick, at the bridge, behind what one would call a control panel. Sidgwick pushed a small white stud. There was a whirring sound, as a glass screen lowered into position at eye level. This panoptic, or viewing glass, he explained, afforded a one hundred and eighty degree view to the front of the chronosphere. He sat down on an organist's stool. Next to the Time Lever was a small brass rod – a joy-stick, if you like. Sidgwick pulled the rod back. Something curious happened. We heard no sound, but we felt and saw, from the panoptic, that the chronosphere was tilting skywards and lifting slowly, from the ground.

The chronosphere, Sidgwick explained, could defy gravity.

And he could control its movements. Using pedals beneath the control panel he was also able to swivel the machine on its central axis in either direction. He did, performing a full revolution. Sidgwick was grinning from ear to ear, like a child on Christmas morning. I had never seen him so happy. On the screen we saw a blur of grey rock and then the sky. We all felt dizzy. It was such fun!

We remained in the chronosphere for the rest of the day, flying around and partaking of brandy and chocolate. Of course, Sidgwick let both Alf and I "have a go". Alf was the best pilot, although I found that I could handle the chronosphere quite adequately. Unfortunately, the combination of the craft's motion and our sickly diet made Alf terribly seasick. He had turned almost green by the time we had finished and had emptied the contents of his stomach several times into a chamber pot.

Sidgwick's scheme was this. For the next few hours, we would duck and weave around the Ordovice encampment. We would carefully remain out of the warriors' reach. But in any case, said Sidgwick, even their most fearsome projectile could do us no harm. We would linger in front of Caractacus's hut, at least long enough for him to notice us. Then we would move on. Just before midnight, we would visit the scene of the human sacrifice. Sidgwick would then appear, in his full majesty, in the doorway of the chronosphere, the moonlight gleaming on its metallic skin. Faced with this incontrovertible proof of Sidgwick's celestial provenance, Caractacus would give in and grant Lara and Snipe their liberty.

We dipped and dived for the rest of the afternoon. It was easy to goad the warriors. We would position the chronosphere in front of a group of them, tempting them to hurl their javelins and stones. We would remain, provocatively, in the same position. Then, just as they drew back their arms, we would levitate the chronosphere to fifty feet or so, well out of their range, and cause it to spin in either direction. This movement caused repercussions for Alf's stomach, but it was highly effective.

While the light was still good, we gained an impression of perfect clarity of the Ordovice encampment and I should record here what we saw. The camp was fortified, but not so as to withstand a prolonged siege – a Roman legion, with its catapults and battering rams, would have made short work of its defences. Around the perimeter was a high wooden fence. It was tipped with sharp wooden stakes and surrounded by a deep ditch. At the southern side of the site, was the main entrance to the encampment. Here, were ramparts and walkways, where watches were stationed. Jutting out diagonally, on each side of the gate were long poles. At the end of these were dark objects.

Hovering just above them, we saw, to our mortification, that the shapes were human heads. Their wizened features, and the remains of beards and moustaches, were clearly recognisable. Sidgwick explained to me that the Celts were head-hunters. They believed, like many ancient peoples, that the soul resided in the head and they used these gory trophies both to appropriate their enemies' strength and to terrify them. Poor Alf. The sight of the impaled heads further intensified his nausea.

Within the stockade was the Celts' living accommodation. You should picture a group of large circular huts, with pointed roofs covered with thatch. The doorways of the huts faced south-east, the direction of the midwinter sunrise. I should imagine that each construction would hold several families and their animals. At the centre of the hut would be a fire, above which would be an iron cooking pot, hanging on a chain. We identified a large forge and several storage huts for agricultural produce. Goats were tethered in the encampment and there were pens containing sheep and pigs. Animal husbandry was vital to the settlement, Sidgwick explained, providing the clan with meat and milk and with wool for weaving. Around the perimeter of the encampment, were quite a few fields in cultivation. It was not possible to determine precisely what was being grown.

Presumably, one of the crops was spelt, an early form of wheat. I record these details because not many people have seen a first-century Celtic settlement, let alone lived in one, as I later did.

Darkness fell in a whisper of blood over the western hills. Our hearts skipped when we saw the moon – a full white disc skimming between the clouds. The sacrificial victims would be praying to their gods in their prison hut; the rest of the village would be eagerly anticipating the night's celebrations. It was a special occasion – a time for licence and festivity, as well as for the remembrance of the dead and communication with their spirits. When the sun rose, a new year would have begun.

We had done all we could. We landed the chronosphere in the forest, close to the Druids' camp and rested for a while. I helped Alf to clean himself up. Watching colour return to his face, I reassured him that there was only to be one more flight to be done that night. Sidgwick went to talk to Brandon. It was almost ten o'clock by Alf's gold watch – the timepiece that his platoon commander had given him during the battle of the Somme. Most of the clouds had gone. The moon's radiance was so bright that we could tell the time by it.

At half past eleven, Sigdwick returned. He had shared some mead with Brandon and was in good spirits. We saw that he had borrowed a head-piece, or diadem, from the Arch Druid, embellished with oak leaves of beaten iron. He was also carrying a curved horn. It was a cornu, an ancient Etruscan instrument, he explained, captured from the Romans in battle. Its shrill, plaintive sound would add to the drama of his appearance. Alf offered to blow it. He had been quite a fair trumpeter at one time, he said, and had played in the band of the United Grand Junction Temperance Association, in Brick Lane. It was arranged that Alf would also toss out a thunder flash during the rescue operation, while I would pilot the chronosphere.

The rest of the night went exactly according to plan. We took off and hovered above the hilltop where the Samhain fires were to be lit. Presently, we could see a snake of lights twisting its way towards us. The procession was led by Druids, in their white robes, carrying fire brands. Ordovice families followed them, with dogs snapping at their heels. To the rear, guarded by warriors with spears, the prisoners formed a miserable huddle, their hands tied together with thongs. Some had been gagged to stifle their cries.

The procession reached the hill. Now, some of its members began to point to the sky, because they could dimly make out the shape of the chronosphere. It must have seemed to them to mimic the moon, which was low in the northern sky. Soon the villagers were directly below us. We could hear their excited voices and the moans and wails of those who were to be sacrificed. As we watched, to our horror, the first victims were forced up the ladders into the wicker giants. The Arch Druid, Brandon, was to light one of the fires, while the High Priestess, Karlena, would ignite the other.

Brandon looked up and raised his staff. That was the signal he had agreed with Sidgwick. With butterflies in my stomach, I brought the chronosphere down, grazing the arm of one of the wicker figures. I then hovered, as Sidgwick had instructed me, equidistant between the fires.

"The door, Freidrich, the door!" exclaimed Sidgwick.

I fumbled for the control. For a moment I was all fingers and thumbs. It opened. Alf gave a long blast on the cornu. It was very effective. The arcane, spine-tingling sound, caused the crowd to fall silent. Everyone was looking up in the same direction.

"The thunder flash, Alf!" I said.

"Oh sorry, I forgot."

The bang was a disappointment. But it also produced a cloud of white smoke that billowed theatrically around the doorway. Sidgwick stepped into view.

"Why have my orders not been obeyed?" he bellowed, in

Brythonic. "The gods are displeased and I am very angry! Where is Carcactacus?"

There was a murmur. The Ordovice's leader appeared at the front of the crowd. His face was small and white below us. There was a gold bangle on one of his upper arms.

"Caractacus, spawn of the sea squid, do you dare to defy the gods! Did they not indicate to you, through their human intermediary, that the girl was to be spared?"

"Yes."

"Yes what?"

"Yes, Master," said Caractacus, reluctantly.

"That's better. So what are you going to do about it?"

He did not have much choice.

"Free the girl," he mumbled.

"Sorry?"

"Free the girl," Caractacus repeated, in a surly tone.

Lara was now detached from the prisoners, and I saw her. She was wearing a simple beige tunic. Her glorious hair was held with a copper clasp. Her face was filthy. But she looked calm and defiant.

"Bring her to me!"

Sidgwick's idea was that by entering the chronosphere and being removed in it, Lara would assume the status of a minor deity in the Ordovice's eyes and therefore be immune from further threats. He was right. She was lifted by a burly man into the welcome arms of her father. Tears were welling up in his eyes. But he managed to hide it. Gods don't cry. There was nothing further to do but close the door and beat a hasty retreat.

Sidgwick later suffered a profound sense of guilt because he had forgotten all about Snipe. It was not deliberate, he insisted; Snipe had simply vanished from his mind in the heat of the moment. We can only assume that the unfortunate man suffered the same awful fate as the other sacrificial victims. For, soon after we had departed, the fires were lit. And we never saw him again.

Chapter Twelve

The Tribal Gathering

As you can imagine, the aftermath of the rescue was taken up by tears, euphoria and explanations. After we picked up Lara, I flew the chronosphere back to the Druids' camp, using a fire that Sidgwick had lit there as a navigation aid. Gradually, Lara regained her vitality, as she came back to us from the safe, dark place to which she had retreated. Alf was singing, Men of Harlech, in his baritone voice. Sidgwick was deliriously happy; he was beaming as he stroked Lara's hair. He said that he had brought his fiddle and that, later, he would give us a tune on it. "Everything will be all right," he kept saying.

I landed the chronosphere. We climbed down the short ladder with joy in our hearts and stood by the fire. I hugged Lara – she was taller and thinner than I remembered – I looked into her face. It was just the same, except that the worry line on her brow had become a little more pronounced. I cannot easily describe how I felt. I was relieved and happy, certainly, but also nervous. Looking at Lara and hugging her, I felt that I was returning home after a long, arduous journey. Her smell was unfamiliar. She carried an aroma of smoke, grass and fresh air. My heart was beating like a humming bird's. I wanted to taste the perspiration under her arms. I wanted to drown in her eyes. I wanted to eat her.

"God, I can't believe it," I said, "I have missed you so much!"

"I have missed you too," she said.

"I love you." I clung to her, holding her fragile body as tightly as I could.

"And I love you." She began to cry.

Years had passed since I had gone to Spenhurst Hall to ask Lara to marry me, only to find that she was gone. But it could just as easily have been a few minutes. Looking at her now I felt the same emotions as on the day that she had first walked into my uncle's bookshop. It seemed to me that I had always known Lara; that our paths had crossed in many previous lifetimes, and that I had always loved her. She was a goddess – Isis and Astarte merged into one – exotic, but as familiar as my own reflection. There was nothing more wonderful than to look into her eyes. And our eyes would lock together, often communicating far more effectively than our mouths did.

"Lara," I said, "this is Alf. He is my best friend. I met him in France, in rather extraordinary circumstances."

"Hello, Miss Sidgwick," said Alf. If he had been wearing a cap, he would have doffed it.

Lara looked uncomfortable. Her cotton tunic reached down to just below her knees and her arms were bare. She was showing far more of her body than would have been considered seemly in Victorian England. Over the coming months, as she adapted to the ways of the Ordovice, Lara would wear short, sleeveless dresses of dyed goat's wool. She would decorate her body with bangles made from carved bones, shells and animal teeth. She would paint her nails red and darken her eye-lids with berry juice, just like the other women in the clan. Her limbs would be turned golden by the sun. Lara would become accustomed to her new appearance and it would seem perfectly natural to her.

She smiled, shyly.

"It's lovely to meet you, Miss," said Alf. "Mr Frater has told me a lot about you. He saved my life he did. Did he tell you? I was in a situation not unlike your own. They're flipping brilliant, these time machines, aren't they?"

We all laughed.

"I expect that everyone will be hungry and thirsty," said Sidgwick. "Please wait here."

He appeared from the shadows carrying food and drink. The meal consisted of roasted pork, speared on wooden skewers, freshly-baked bread and water poured from an earthenware jug.

"I am sorry that it is not claret," said Sidgwick, "but beggars cannot be choosing."

"Choosers, Papa," corrected Lara.

He lifted his beaker. "I would like to thank Friedrich from the bottom of my heart and to propose a vote of thanks to him. For without this young man, I think that Lara would not be here. To Friedrich," he said.

After the toast, Lara went to wash herself in a nearby pool. The Celts, surprisingly, used soap. It was a commodity whose secret they passed on to the Romans. She came back to dry herself and to brush her hair by the fire. The pork was delicious. We could hear laughter and shouting from a neighbouring hillside as the Ordovice enjoyed their Samhain celebrations. The revels would go on until dawn. The flames had, by now, eaten the wicker giants and the writhing humans inside them. Some of the ash from the fires would be raked into the soil and some would be stored. It was believed by the Ordovice to have magical properties. The warriors would rub it into their faces, to increase their bravery.

As we looked at our skewered meat, darkened by the flames, we were all thinking the same thing. But nobody articulated their mental image of the human sacrifice. Sidgwick told me later why he had not attempted to save all of the sacrificial victims. He said that rescuing Lara had been his primary task. The first rule of Time Travel, he informed me, was that one should intervene in human affairs as little as possible – for each interference, however small, set off a chain of repercussions; one literally changed history.

"So you live up at Spenhurst Hall then, Miss Sidgwick," said Alf, as we finished our meal.

"I do indeed," said Lara. "Do you know it?"

"Oh yes, Miss," said Alf. "Me and Mr Frater was up there once. We went to this costume ball and I got into a bit of bother, didn't I, Mr Frater?"

"Yes, Alf." I remembered the occasion. I recalled the trickle of blood dripping from Nathaniel Vane's mouth; the unbearable coldness of the night in the stable. I was about to tell the story, when I heard Alf say something that filled me with horror.

"Tell me, Miss Sidgwick, do you remember Mary?"

Insofar as silence could occur at a fireside on a Welsh mountainside, during a pagan celebration, it did. I looked at Lara. Her expression was non-committal.

"She was a maid up at the hall," continued Alf, chirpily. "You must do." He paused. "Well, she and Mr Frater …"

I nudged Alf's leg with my foot to shut him up. But Lara's face told me that she had divined at once that Mary and I had become lovers. Women have a curious, instinctive sense for such things. It also told me that she was furious. Sidgwick had removed his violin from its case, but he was not to play it that night. Laughter and shouting were still coming from the Samhain fires. However, a shadow seemed to have passed over our little gathering. I felt sick.

It was Sidgwick who proposed that we should go to bed, explaining that accommodation had been arranged for us by the Druids. He gestured towards some dark shapes, where trees mingled with rock and shadow.

The Druids, I should explain, had made their home amidst a collection of huge granite boulders, which seemed to have been scattered by an angry giant down a hill-side, next to the ancient forest. The Druids lived apart from the main Ordovice encampment in order to carry out their mystical and religious rites but close enough to seek protection within its protective walls, should danger approach. The caves' entrances were guarded by rowan and holly. These plants were thought by the Celts to repel their enemies and to ward off evil. The caves were surprisingly comfortable. One slept on a bed of bracken covered with fleeces. We cooked on a communal fire. At night, our homes were lit by tallow candles. When the weather was dry, the caves were extraordinarily comfortable.

Sidgwick hugged Lara as we bid each other goodnight. She looked extremely unhappy. I followed her meekly into the gloomy interior of her cave. When candles were lit, I could see her eyes. It is sometimes maintained by pedantic people, that eyes cannot flash, indicating emotion. But Lara's did.

"How could you?" she demanded. Her words formed a refrain that later tormented me. I wonder what the Ordovice would have made of our argument if they could have understood English. They would probably have recognised the familiar patterns and rituals of a domestic disagreement.

"Lara," I said, "I can explain."

She faced me full on. Her hands were on her hips.

"How could you, Frederick? I leave you for five minutes and what do you do? You sleep with the first woman who offers herself to you. It is contemptible." There was a steeliness in her face that I had never seen before.

"Lara, that is not the case," I protested. "It is simply not true!"

She turned away.

"Listen," I said, "I did not know where you and your father had gone and whether I would see you again. Remember, you have only been here for a few days, but, for me, it has been ten years. "

I touched her arm. She recoiled from me.

"When you told me that you loved me, in the boat house, did that mean nothing to you?"

"Lara, I do love you."

"You expect me to believe that now?"

"It is true! What am I supposed to say?"

"You are good with words, Frederick. You can twist them around to give the impression that almost anything you have done is the most natural thing in the world."

"You must understand, please. I have lost ten years of my

life!"

"How very careless of you!"

Her voice seemed to bounce from the roof of the cave. I was surprised by what happened next. She picked up a small rock, drew back her arm and flung it at me. Happily, her aim was imprecise.

"Get out of my cave!" she exclaimed.

"Lara, I ..."

"Get out!"

I went outside. The word sad does not adequately describe my emotions. Lara's anger seemed so unjust. What had I been supposed to do? Spend the rest of my life waiting, against the eventuality that she might turn up, like a piece of cosmic flotsam? I had to admit that I had, indeed, fallen in love with someone else. Could love be turned on and off then, like a bath tap? Was it merely a contingent phenomenon? Lara had said that I was too clever with words. Perhaps I was; I would, therefore, be able to justify my actions however cruel, deceitful and self-serving they were. But, if I was really such a bad person, how could I live with myself? The more these thoughts turned around in my head, the sicker I felt. How could you? I kept hearing those words in my mind, like a chorus. It was desperately cold. I huddled, shivering, next to the remains of the fire, occasionally seeking twigs and branches to feed its embers. For the first hour or two, I could hear Lara weeping. I think that I may, eventually, have drifted into a fitful sleep.

It was just after dawn. The birds were singing. The moon had been absorbed into the white sky and a faint warmth was raising the dew. I was awoken by a gentle voice.

"Freddy."

I turned around.

"Freddy ..."

Lara looked tired and sad. "I have missed you so much."

"I have missed you too," I said.

"I love you."

"And I love you."

Her eyes told me that I should stumble forwards, into the cave. I did. I would like to be able to describe the sweetness of our love-making on the bed of ferns. I think that there was a violence beneath it, a residue from our argument, which made it even more passionate. I must be honest and say that our reconciliation was more wonderful than I could ever have imagined, dreamed or hoped for and that, for the next few hours, I was in heaven.

That morning, life returned to normal for the Ordovice and the Druids, although most would have had hangovers and many would be regretting their indiscretions of the previous night. The sun was shining, which was thought to be a good omen on the day after Samhain, signalling that the gods were pleased with their offerings. Lara and I awoke at midday to a new world.

"Mr Frater, Mr Frater." I could hear Alf's voice from the mouth of the cave. "Are you all right?"

Was I all right? I was lying in the arms of a goddess, after one of the most blissful nights of my life.

Hearing no reply, Alf spoke again. "I've made you a cup of … well, I've made you a cup of hot water, but it's got honey in it."

"That is very kind of you, Alf." I yawned and stretched my limbs. Lara murmured, still drowsy. She would need a little longer to recover. I kissed her and crawled towards the light.

Alf was as bright as a button.

"Good grief," I said, "what on earth are you wearing?"

The Welshman was dressed in a woollen shirt, in a striped green and blue pattern; on top of this garment was a thicker, sleeveless, woollen jerkin, which was un-dyed. His trousers were made from a red, brown and blue fabric that one would almost describe as tartan, tied at the ankles with thongs, above sandals. He was wearing a leather belt with a bronze buckle and a neck ornament, or torc, of the same metal. These, more or less, were the clothes worn by the male Ordovice. In the winter they would also wear woollen cloaks, attached with broaches. They would go into battle equipped with a bronze or iron helmet, a spear, a javelin or two, a dagger and a sword. Luckier soldiers would be protected by an iron breastplate or a chain mail corselet, although, by tradition, Celtic horsemen and charioteers fought without helmets or body armour.

Alf liked uniforms. He looked particularly smart in this one.

"What do you think, Mr Frater?" he said. "Mr Sidgwick says that we must dress like the Ordovice and that we must think like them. We've got some clothes for you too. Would you like to try them on?"

The prospect did not enthrall me. Had I wanted to look like a clown, I would have joined a circus, I told Alf. On the other hand, there was at least a masculine quality to Alf's clothing that was lacking in the more effeminate garb of the Druids. Perhaps I would grow accustomed to the sleeveless jerkins and tartan trousers.

"I suppose that we shall have to speak like them in order to think like them," I said, rubbing my eyes.

"That's right, Mr Frater," said Alf, looking doubtful.

He had rekindled the fire in front of the caves and heated some water in an iron pot. As we talked, a noisy gaggle of Ordovice children collected around us in the mouth of the cave. Their skin was the colour of stewed tea and their white teeth flashed when they laughed, which was often. Intrigued by our pallid complexions and by our language, the children grew bolder. As they got to know her, they would become fascinated by Lara. Most of them believed the rumour that she was Blodwen, the flower goddess. A large group of children would trail in Lara's wake, from dawn until dusk.

"Would Miss Sidgwick also like a drink, do you think?" said Alf.

"I don't know, I'll see."

I went back into the cave. Lara was awake now, sitting

upright. When my sight was restored in the dimness, I saw that her upper body was naked. She was embarrassed and at first sought to cover herself. Then she changed her mind.

"Good morning, my love." The words felt uncomfortable, but they seemed right.

"Good morning."

Our eyes met.

I decided that the hot drink could wait. Lara and I did not see daylight until the following morning. I suppose that the next few hours were our honeymoon. I think that the next few months, during which Lara and I were rarely apart, were among the happiest in my life.

The forty or fifty clans that made up the Ordovice tribe, we were to discover, were scattered across Wales in fortified hill-top encampments. Their society and its customs had remained much the same since the Bronze Age. Money was unknown; barter was used as a means of exchange. Wealth, in so far as it existed, was measured in animals, which would be presented as marriage gifts and exchanged between clans in order to settle disputes.

The Ordovice were creative and resourceful. Nothing was wasted and they took joy in making things. As well as practising animal husbandry and growing crops, they cultivated hops, for beer, and kept bees for honey. They were skilled in blacksmithing and in making and dyeing cloth. Thinking ahead, which is a mark of civilisation, they would fill their grain stores when harvests were good, in preparation for leaner times. I suspect that the cattle raids that occasionally took place, served, as much as anything, to keep their attacking instincts well-honed for a people accustomed to warfare.

Relations between the tribe's clans were bound by precise rules that had been codified, over the centuries, into a quasi-legalistic structure. At set times the Druids would preside over meetings between clans, at which penalties or tributes would be decided. A tribute would be collected from every member of a clan whose member had transgressed and distributed to the wronged clan in the same way. Thus the Druids were lawmakers as well as priests, poets and magicians. They did not write anything down, for their mystique lay in their mastery of an oral tradition which took many years to acquire. Because of their lack of a written language, we only know of the Celts through the second-hand accounts of the Romans and from Saxon and medieval chronicles. That has distorted our view of them.

What the Ordovice loved best was getting drunk, telling stories and arguing and these activities would normally follow each other in close succession. Feuds could be quickly forgotten in times of collective danger, but they could also be re-kindled and would erupt in fresh outbreaks of verbal warfare, like family squabbles at a wedding.

For the next few months we would rise with the sun and take our breakfast of porridge or bread and curdled milk. Evening meals were eaten communally in the walled encampment. They frequently took the form of feasts, especially when visitors from other clans were present. On these occasions, Druids would recite poems or tell tales relating to the history of the tribe or how the world had come about. Brandon was the best story-teller – he was spell-binding.

The clan appeared to practice monogamy, apart from Caractacus, who took his pick of young ladies, belching his way through the feasts and displaying his female trophies, like a rock star's guitars. He would often eye Lara covetously but fearful of Sidgwick's magic, he never bothered her again. My moon wife, as I called her, took to this life naturally. We all did, especially after we had acquired something of the Ordovice's language. Lara taught the Ordovice children the art of portraiture with charcoal and of flower painting. She conducted experiments, using dyes made from plants, so that the little ones who followed her were soon attired in rainbow colours.

Inevitably, Alf became indispensable to the Ordovice for his skills in hut and chariot maintenance. I was useless at both, but I became Alf's translator, since I picked up Brythonic, whose grammar and vocabulary were relatively simple, far more quickly than he did. Sometimes, once we had been accepted by the clan, we went hunting wild boars, or pig sticking as Alf called it, in the depths of the forest. A tapestry of oak, birch, ash and lime, the forest was a vast, dark realm, full of magic and mystery. It sustained the tribe but they also feared it, for it was believed to be the home of the horned god, Cernunnos. Our trips sometimes lasted for several days. I found them extremely uncomfortable but Alf adapted easily to hunting and woodcraft.

The Ordovice's year was like a wheel with four spokes, corresponding to the phases of the moon. Samhain at the end of October was followed by the festival of Imbolc in February. Dedicated to the goddess Brigit, Imbolc celebrated growth and renewal. It was a time of cleansing and new-born lambs. Beltane came next, at the first full moon in Taurus, usually in May. This was a fertility festival – Christian societies adopted it as May day. Lugnassadh, at the first full moon in Leo, was a harvest festival, usually at the beginning of August, when the clan celebrated the marriage of the sun to the earth. We lived with the Ordovice for seven months. We had joined them at Samhain and were to leave just after Beltane the following year. I have never been happier. Our diet was healthy, our days were interesting and I was in love.

We did not see much of Sidgwick. After his *deus ex machina* performance in the chronosphere, he was feared and venerated by the Ordovice. In fact, he had become a deity. For they took to calling him, Lugh, the shining one – the god associated with the harvest festival, and with ravens and white stags. His staff was thought to be magic. It was said that the chronosphere was the sun and that Sidgwick could travel in it – which indeed he could. Sidgwick was somewhat embarrassed by his deification. He explained to us, modestly, that he had never expected to become a personification of Hercules, the sun god. On the other hand, he obtained for his staff a handle in the shape of a raven's head. His manner became rather grave. I think that he must have enjoyed being a god. Who wouldn't?

Sidgwick now spent most of his time in the company of Brandon. He delved deeply into Celtic cosmology, learning the nature of the energy flows, which were associated with the Celts' stone structures and their calendar, and studying the relationship between language and magic. Sometimes, we did not see him for weeks at a time. We suspected that he may be visiting other epochs in the future or the past, for what purpose we did not know. We all felt a slight sense of apprehension, I would not call it dread, for we knew that in AD 60 the ambitious governor of Britannia, Suetonius Paulinus, would embark upon his campaign. He would march his legion up Watling Street, in order to sack the sacred island of Anglesey.

However, this was an eventuality that was being planned for. In March, just after Imbolc, Caractacus called a war council. The largest circular hut in the stockade was converted into a meeting chamber for the occasion. Boughs of rowan were placed around the entrances and the floor was scattered with oak leaves to give the warriors strength. A rowan fire burned in the centre of the hut to summon spirits to assist the tribes in the coming battle. The chamber was lit with huge brands held by iron staves.

From Wales came the other clans of the Ordovice and representatives from other clans and tribes. From England, came the Brigantes, the Catuvellauni and from East Anglia, the Iceni, who were led by the famed flame-haired queen, Boudicca. Strictly speaking the Ordovice were feuding with the Catuvellauni, whose warriors spent the entire meeting with their hands on the hilts of their swords.

With regard to the Iceni, Sidgwick had pulled off something of a coup. Two of Boudicca's daughters had been raped by the Romans the previous year and she was itching to obtain her revenge. She had intended to attack the weakened Roman garrison in Colchester after the XXth legion had left for Wales. Through messages – or perhaps he travelled to the east of England in the chronosophere – Sidgwick persuaded Boudicca to forestall her scheme. Rather than carrying out a massacre of unprotected women and children, he said, why not take part in a larger, co-ordinated campaign, involving the entire Celtic nation? It would require more planning and patience but the potential rewards were far greater.

Boudicca reluctantly agreed. She sent, as an envoy to the meeting in Wales, her sister, Katia. A lithe but muscular woman, Katia had the copper-coloured hair of her mother, but a more guarded temperament. Druids and priestesses, bards and ovates from all over England and Wales were also in attendance, in their long robes. After greeting each other they stood around the perimeter. Some held rattles, in the shape of bull's testicles, which they would shake at climactic moments in the proceedings.

The Brigante's chieftain was the imposing Queen Zoatastra. She was the daughter of Cartimandua, who had betrayed Caractacus to the Romans seventeen years before. But the score seemed to have been settled. Zoatastra, a raven-haired amazon with emerald eyes, was utterly gorgeous; I could see that Caractacus was lusting after her. Lara noticed, of course, that I was carefully avoiding looking at Zoatastra, her rival in beauty, and this created a frisson between us. It is hard to please women; had I stared openly at Zoatastra, the result would have been exactly the same. By midnight, all of the clans and tribes were in place. The meeting was presided over by Caractacus. Its start was signalled by a long blast from an animal-headed war trumpet, known as a carnyx.

Caractacus, with his blond hair, his gold adornments and his complacent expression, was the strongest and sleekest of the chieftains. He was effusive in his welcome of the Ordovice's kinsmen, the Catuvellauni, who appeared uneasy. Occasionally, his eyes met those of Zoatastra. It sometimes appeared, from Caractacus's behaviour, that this whole occasion was merely a display of his manly prowess, arranged for her benefit. But she seemed unimpressed.

Caractacus first worked up the crowd by hurling abuse at the foreign invaders, the Romans. He said that they were laughing at the Celts, cosseted complacently in their garrisons and farmsteads and robbing the land of its bounty. Katia scowled, recalling the fate of her nieces. Caractacus derided the Celts of southern England as traitors. His audience hissed and spat. Finally, when the audience was primed, he introduced the next speaker, Sidgwick.

I have to say, the Polish doctor was impressive. He was now not only fluent in Brythonic, but also in several of its dialects, so that he could answer questions from all quarters convincingly. Grasping his raven-headed staff, he spoke authoritatively, with the air of a man who has reflected upon a problem for a long time. Caractacus smiled as Sidgwick spoke, flirting with Zoatastra. Guidavius nodded gravely, indicating his approval.

The XXth legion, Sidgwick said, was expected to begin its campaign in the next few weeks. He laid out a strategy which would ensure that this fighting force would be annihilated, as a precursor to expelling the Romans from Britain. Sidgwick's words were calm and measured. He held the audience in the palm of his hand. As soon as preparations for the Roman attack had been confirmed, a force of five hundred or so Silure warriors and a similar number of Demetae would make their way, on foot, to converge with their Ordovice comrades. The Ordovice, most of whom merely faced a day's march across the hills, would provide cavalry and chariots for the campaign; the Deceangli would fortify the western bank of the Conwy against a Roman river crossing.

Once the XXth legion had been destroyed and its silver eagle captured, word would be sent to England. A joint force would then be assembled with the Iceni, led by Boudicca. The weakened Romans would be attacked by a mighty army, first in Colchester, then in London and finally in Chester. They could not recover from such a blow, Sidgwick said. The Roman occupation would be over. The warriors raised their spears and roared their approval. The Druids twirled their rattles. It was as if the campaign had already been won.

The plan posed an obvious question. Who would be the leader of the unified Celtic tribes? Would it be Caractacus, the enigmatic Zoatastra or, the more obvious candidate, Boudicca? It was an important point. But it was not settled, or even discussed, that night. As dawn broke and the meeting ended, the victory had already occurred, as far as the participants were concerned. Catuvellauni warriors laughed and joked with Ordovice, forgetting their enmity. Sidgwick was carried triumphantly on the shoulders of a group of Silures, clockwise round the hut, in a lap of honour.

That night the mother of all feasts took place. Unprecedented quantities of pork, lamb and beef were consumed and oceans of beer and mead flowed through the warriors' bellies. The event was talked about for years. I only heard the proceedings – a cavalcade of crashing timbers, carousing warriors and stampeding animals – experiencing them at second hand. Lara claimed to have a headache. She was sulking, having convinced herself that I had amorous designs upon Zoatastra. I spent most of that night pleading with her that it was not the case. It is a pity that I missed the feast.

Sidgwick was lauded like a Roman emperor. As for Alf, as if stirred by a racial memory, he adopted the Silures, from south Wales, as his own tribe. They brawled and sang together as heartily as the members of a rugby club. When he was drunk, he claimed to be able to understand them. To Caractacus's dismay, Zoatastra left early, saying that one of her children was ill. Katia, Boudicca's sister, also made her excuses, on the grounds that she had a long journey home. She slipped out of the encampment with her retinue, guided by moonlight, long before the feast had finished.

Chapter Thirteen

The Battle

The scene is a hillside, somewhere in north Wales. There is a tang of brine in the air, for the sea is not very far away. A biting wind cuts the warmth of the midday sun. The hillside is scatted with yellow gorse bushes and goldfinches flit between them. Riding an air trapeze, a straight-winged red kite hangs motionless and then undulates down the valley. It diminishes to a dust-sized speck, although its wingspan is the length of a man. The grass is uncomfortably prickly. Far below, on the other side of the valley, we can see an array of small brown dots and specks. They are moving and we can hear, faintly, the whinnying of horses and the shouts of men. It is an army.

The distant warriors have grouped themselves into the largest offensive force that the Celts have ever assembled. We are too far away, here, to observe the detail of their equipment – the long, oval shields with their iron bosses, the baldrics, the polished bronze scabbards and the glistening helmets and spear tips – but we have a good impression of the shape of the army. At its northern end are foot soldiers with swords and spears, behind them are javelin throwers and bowmen; behind them is the cavalry and to the rear, waiting to race their way to the front at a decisive moment in the battle, are the Celts' most feared weapons, their chariots.

Caractacus, the Ordovice chieftain, waits impatiently at the rear. His light wooden vehicle is pulled by two horses, driven by a bare-chested charioteer. Caractacus's stomach is tight with fear. But he does not show it. Beside him, in another chariot, is his brother, Guidavius. Caractacus will inspire and lead his soldiers with his whooping war cries, while Guidavius will take stock of the situation and issue orders.

The combined army is waiting for the XXth legion to make its way along the valley, beneath the Bodnant cliffs. When that happens, death will fall on the legion in the form of javelins and boulders pushed from the cliff top. If all goes to plan, the legion will be destroyed, without the need for Caractacus's troops to engage it in battle. Soon, the soldiers' bodies will be stripped of their weapons and armour and their heads will be cut off and carried aloft on Celtic spears. Later, blood-sensing ravens will feast on their flesh.

"What an amazing sight, Mr Frater," said Alf. "I never thought I would see anything like this."

"I don't think that any of us did, Alf," I replied.

We were seated on a hilltop, perhaps a mile away from the army, on the other side of the valley. Alf despised "armchair generals". He would like to have fought with the Ordovice, but this had been ruled out by Sidgwick. Lara sat beside us. She was very quiet. She had been occupied for the past hour or so in making a daisy chain.

"It don't seem very brave, do it, Mr Frater, us being here, like?"

"I agree, Alf," I replied.

It seemed strange to be so close to an epoch-making battle, which would make an interesting paragraph in a history book, and yet to be so far away that it was merely a spectacle, like a play seen through opera glasses. We scanned the sky, expecting to see the chronosphere at any moment. Sidgwick had vanished a week before, in the Daedalus, but he had promised to return shortly before the battle. Our eyes flicked between the sky, the piebald shape of the army and the cliffs, beneath which we anticipated the XXth legion would appear.

In my recollection, the scene now became oddly still for a few seconds, like the calmness I had experienced on the Somme, just before the British attack. We heard a noise before we saw anything. It was a blood-curdling bellow from seven thousand throats. It was Alf who noticed that something was wrong. The XXth legion was not charging at the Celts from beneath the cliffs. It was attacking them from the other side, their unprotected rear.

In Alf's words, what we would witness in about two minutes, would be a "bleeding massacre". We came to the obvious conclusion that the Celts had been betrayed. We could not see, for it was too far away, a tiny chariot detaching itself from the Ordovice ranks, cutting a solitary path towards the advancing Romans. This was Caractacus, fleeing for the safety of his secret allies.

Time stopped. Soon, the Roman cavalry would engage with the Celts. Spears would penetrate shields and we would hear the first screams of the wounded. That did not happen. We now heard an amazing sound that made all the other noises seem like a whisper, as a herd of ten thousand cattle seemed to materialise from the clouds. It bore down on the Roman army in a terrifying stampede. The cattle were devil beasts. They were huge red, green and blue animals, with iron hooves and giant horns, as sharp as razors. The terrifying creatures made shorter work of the Romans than the boulders would have done. Within a few minutes, it was all over. More than five thousand men had been trampled into a pulp; the Roman siege engines and catapults had been shattered like matchsticks; the mercenaries and camp followers had fled in terror. The XXth legion no longer existed. The cattle vanished as suddenly as they had appeared. After a few seconds a tentative, ragged cheer came from the Celts. It swelled into a full-throated roar as it dawned upon the soldiers that they had won an amazing victory without even lifting a finger.

For a long time we were stunned. Above all, it was hard to take in the fact that the lives of thousands of men had just been extinguished. Alf had turned as white as a sheet – the battle had re-activated horrors from his past. We sat in silence for five or ten minutes. I do not know who noticed the chronosphere first. It was a black dot, then a small copper disc hovering over the scene of the battle and, finally, an imminent object, brushing the gorse and coming gently to rest in the long grass.

The door opened and a small ladder descended. Sidgwick looked grave.

It was Alf who spoke first. "What was that all about?"

Sidgwick regarded us with a look of incomprehension. "I should have thought that this was clear."

"How come the Romans came at them from behind?" Alf said.

"They were delivered into the hands of the Romans, Alfred, by their leader, Caractacus. Treachery is not unknown among the Celts."

"Did you know that it was going to happen?" I said.

Sidgwick's face gave nothing away. "Oh yes, I always knew that Caractacus was a bad egg."

"How did you ensure that the Celts would win?" I asked. A gust of wind flicked a goldfinch from a nearby bush like a scrap of yellow and red paper.

"I have made what you call a deal," said Sidgwick, slowly. "I knew that Caractacus would send a messenger to Suetonius Paulinus and give away the Celts' battle plan. Therefore, two nights ago, I spoke to Belenus using Brandon's cauldron and explained the situation to him. Belenus, by chance, was owed a favour by Dagda."

"Who is Dagda?"

"He is the head of the Irish gods, the Tuatha De Danann, the famed vanquisher of the Fir Bolg. Dagda agreed to lend Belenus his fairy cattle – those were the multi-coloured beasts that you saw." Sidgwick motioned towards the distant battlefield. We could now discern Celtic warriors, in their tartan clothes, picking their way between the Roman dead.

"The cattle stampeded the legion, yes?" said Alf.

"That is correct," Sidgwick replied.

"And they are all dead." Alf looked mortified.

"Alfred." Sidgwick spoke slowly. "These men were all warriors. They have perished in battle. Their souls are, therefore, in Elysium. Do you know of Elysium?"

"No, Doctor Sidgwick."

"Well, I shall describe it for you. It is a region of many wonders, where happiness is complete – a place of green bowers, delightful meadows and pleasant streams. The air is filled with the sound of bird song."

"It sounds very pleasant," said Alf.

"It is," said Sidgwick.

"What about their families, like?" said the Welshman. "Do they get to see them?"

"Oh yes, Alfred," Sidgwick assured him. "Their souls are also destined to reside in Elysium, in due course."

"Where is it?" said Alf.

"I wish that I could tell you. Some people say that it is in the Fortunate Islands, off the coast of Africa; other commentators place it close to the mouth of the Danube. But, according to Virgil, Elysium is in Italy."

"I've heard that Italy is very nice," said Alf.

"It is, Alfred."

Sidgwick's revelation that the Roman soldiers would live forever in paradise lightened our moods considerably.

On the other side of the valley, the Celts would be dispatching still twitching bodies with their swords and collecting heads. They would be seeking, particularly, the head of the traitor, Caractacus, on the assumption that he had suffered the same awful fate as the legion, and that of its commander, Suetonius Paulinus. The XXth legion's silver eagle, its sacred aquila, would become a prized trophy, stored in a secure place. The Celts would collect as much as they could of Roman war spoils and make a huge mound of it, close to the battlefield. This would be left to rot, as an offering to the gods. According to their custom, any person who was caught pilfering from the captured haul would be put to death.

We discovered, later, that Caractacus's body was never recovered. Some maintained that he had escaped from the battlefield in his chariot and gone into hiding. The corpse of Suetonius Paulinus, however, would have been easy to find. It would have been surrounded by the bodies of his tallest and strongest centurions and tribunes, the latter with highly polished armour and red-plumed helmets. The soldiers around him would have attempted to form a wall, or tortuga, with their shields, to resist the charging beasts. But the fairy cattle would have torn through these defences like paper. Now the soldiers and their weapons and armour would be mangled into a bloody sediment.

Suetonius Paulinus would have been found at the centre of the collapsed tortuga. He would still be wearing his wreath of gilded oak leaves and carrying his vine staff – his face frozen into a shape of terror. The warrior who recovered his head would go down in legend. I imagine that a grim struggle may have taken place as the Celts competed for possession of this valuable object.

"What are we going to do now?" said Alf, voicing all of our thoughts.

Sidgwick had clearly given this some consideration. He spoke carefully. "Our work here is finished. We have lived with the Ordovice and we have helped them to win their victory; I think that this is enough, yes?"

"Are we going back to the village?" asked Alf.

Sidgwick shook his head. His grey hair was now shoulder length. His beard almost reached his stomach.

"No, Alfred," said Sidgwick. "We are not going back. It is never a good idea. The only way for us to go is forwards."

"That is easy for you to say, Father," protested Lara. "I have formed attachments among the children."

"I know," said Sidgwick. "But you will forget them in time, and they will always carry you in their hearts."

"What about our possessions?" said Lara. She began to cry. I put my arms around her.

"These things do not matter," said Sidgwick, "they are merely illusions which have been given a material form by your attachment to them. I have explained this to you many times. You must release yourself."

"Yes, Papa," she said, faintly.

The wind's fingers ruffled Sidgwick's hair. His staff was planted in the grass, framing, with his arm and his body, the scene of the battle. From the valley we heard the beautiful song of a curlew as it traversed the muddy fringes of the river. The same river is still flowing today. There must be pieces of armour and men's bones buried in its silt; the leather articulations and the flesh, tendons and sinews long vanished. The curlew's song, the most lovely of any bird, seemed a message that we were motes of dust, pieces of light, swirling eddies of water.

"Wait here," said Sidgwick. "I have something for you."

He went into the chronosphere and returned with two bags tied with a leather thong. He handed one of them to Lara and the other to Alf.

In Lara's bag, were torcs made of gold and of electrum, which is an alloy of gold and silver, and a plain gold ring.

"I have been given these things by Brandon, to express his thanks," said Sidgwick. "They are extremely valuable. Alfred, you will have this." He gave Alfred the second bag. In it were freshly minted gold Roman coins, bearing the head of the Emperor Claudius. "With this, Alfred, I think that you can buy a new motor car."

"I could buy a flipping Rolls Royce with these," Alf said.

We protested, especially the Welshman, but Sidgwick was insistent. He explained that we would all need money, whatever happened to us. I placed the ring on Lara's finger and it fitted perfectly. When I realised that she had offered me her wedding finger, I was momentarily stunned.

"Look here, doctor," said Alf. "I would like you to have this." He pulled his gold watch from his pocket. "I ain't never going to find Mrs Dixon, I know that, and, well, you and Mr Frater have done so much for me, like, that I can never thank you."

"Alfred this is a marvellous present," said Sidgwick. He regarded the watch. It had stopped at precisely one minute to twelve, on the first of July, 1916.

"You may as well wind it up," said Alf. "I never did, like; it was a kind of superstition."

Sidgwick rolled the small knurled knob between his long fingers. Watches were once activated by clockwork, not miniscule batteries. The second hand flicked into motion. It seemed a good omen that the timepiece was working perfectly. And the watch appeared to have found the perfect owner. Sidgwick did not have a pocket. However, he solved this conundrum by looping its gold chain over his head.

"Now," he said. "I shall explain what we must do. Lara and Friedrich ..." He looked at us. "There is a time in human history that is extremely important in the progress of human affairs. It is the moment when the sun leaves Pisces and enters Aquarius and it occurs during the 1960s. It is the beginning of what has been called, the New Age. There are some places on the planet of extreme significance at this moment. They are where lines of power from the groves and sacred places converge, concentrating their energy. One, for example, is in Peru, close to Lake Titicaca. Another will be more familiar to you, it is in Camberwell, in south London."

"I was born near there," I said.

"I know, Friedrich," said Sidgwick. "You are a special one. That is why you have been chosen."

"Chosen by whom?" I asked.

Sidgwick looked evasive. He did not reply.

"So you want us to go to Camberwell," I said.

"Yes. In the twentieth century."

"Why?"

"I want you and Lara to live there. That is all. It will soon become apparent what you must do."

"Which is what?"

"I am afraid that I cannot tell you this. For if I told you what it was, it would appear to you to be impossible."

What could it be? Sidgwick was as stubborn as an ox. I knew that pressing the point would achieve nothing. However, we must make a decision. Lara clutched my hand, it was warm and I could feel the ring on her finger. Images of Spenhurst came into my mind – of the bicycle shop and my comfortable life there. Would I ever see the village again? I thought of Mary and of what our lives together may become.

I told myself that this was not a definitive decision. Once the task assigned to us by Sidgwick had been completed, I could return to Spenhurst. Once I had taken this mental step, the path seemed clearer. Of course, it was an assumption that I was not entitled to make. A reader of these lines may well reproach me for what I did. For, after all, I apparently abandoned Mary having won a place in her heart. But if I am guilty of any failing on this occasion, it is that of bad faith.

A harsh, urgent sound came from a wading bird on the estuary. Was it the sensation of the ring that sealed my fate, the cry of the sandpiper or the immutable expression in Sidgwick's grey eyes?

"Very well," I said. I had made up my mind. "I will do as you suggest."

Lara's smile told me that she approved of the decision. But what about Alf? A dilemma was written into his countenance. I knew that his natural instinct would be to accompany me. He owed his life to me and loyalty was deeply ingrained in his character. I told him that although I would be sad for us to part, his future must lie in Spenhurst, in the nineteenth century, where he would be able to resume his previous life. He needed a lot of convincing. But eventually, he came round. Sidgwick said nothing. His arms were folded across the top of his staff, his grey hair ruffled by the breeze.

On the other side of the valley, busy blobs swarmed, sifting the detritus of the battle, as British and German soldiers would have done after the battle of the Somme. I almost felt sorry for Suetonius Paulinus. His wife would be sitting in their Roman villa when she heard the news of his defeat. He would never be a senator now. His twisted lips would be pulled back from his white teeth, the blood around his mouth black and congealed. Soon, his head would be a valued specimen, displayed on the gatehouse of the Ordovice encampment. It was not a good idea to think of such things.

"We will be able to visit Alf, won't we?" I asked Sidgwick.

"Of course," he said. But there was little conviction in his words. "It is settled then. First, we shall take Alfred back to Spenhurst and then we shall go to Camberwell. Come." He led us towards the chronosphere. He stopped at the foot of the ladder and spoke.

I did not heed his words at the time. Perhaps I should have done, for they were significant.

"I must warn you," he said, "that our actions here will undoubtedly have had ramifications for human history and that certain things may be utterly different from what you are expecting." He paused as a faint smile played across his face. I know why now – Time Travel is not for the faint-hearted.

Lara turned in the doorway. She paused to make a final lingering examination of the distant river and the green and grey mountains. Her eyes were as sharp as an eagle's. I knew that she was recording the details. She may also have been thinking of the Ordovice children in their colourful tunics, hearing their voices and laughter in her mind.

"Hurry, my daughter." Sidgwick closed the door.

We sat down. He fiddled with the dials, muttering something

to himself. Then he pushed the Time Lever forwards. There was a noise of a roaring wind. I clasped Lara's fingers tightly. We squeezed our eyes shut. The chronosphere began to vibrate as a great weight pushed us back into our seats. I remember hearing a small moaning sound from Lara as darkness enveloped us like a voluminous velvet cloak.

Imagine bright light and sounds of clattering glasses and laughter. The noise was overwhelming. At first, I found it hard to unpick strands of conversation from the hubbub and to interpret them; partly because of the room's odd acoustics and partly because the accents were so peculiar. People were speaking a form of cockney English that was familiar and strange at the same time. It seemed uncouth and barbaric after the lilting language of the Ordovice. In any case, the loudness of the music, issuing from a garish machine in the corner of the room, made conversation extremely difficult. It did not sound like music, until we had become used to it, but merely a sequence of discordant notes. One could feel, as much as hear, its repetitive vibrations, which had the crude, relentless insistence of a blacksmith's hammer. And the curious intonations of the singer made the words of the song hard to understand. Lara and I sat bewildered at a small circular table, in a corner of the public house.

Only minutes before, it seemed, we had set Alf down in Spenhurst High Street. The year was 1891, Sidgwick told him, just before Christmas. It was cold and foggy. Alf clasped my hand. He looked into my eyes. "I shall never forget what you have done for me," he said.

"Don't be stupid, Alf," I replied. "You have done just as much for me – and Lara."

He sniffed. We embraced each other awkwardly and said our farewells, wanting to get them over with. Alf had changed back into his normal clothes – his civvies. My last sight of him was climbing down the ladder and disappearing into the fog. I sank into an armchair next to Lara. The chronosphere resumed its journey.

I shall not describe in detail, the fear and disorientation that we had felt after Sidgwick set us down at the end of Wren Road, close to Camberwell Green, in London. Camberwell had always been a busy place but it seemed to have been transformed since Victorian times into an annex of hell. I recall the horrifying effect of the horseless carriages, sleek metal boxes that seemed to rush towards us, only inches away from the pavement; the huge red motor omnibuses, lurching like crimson dinosaurs along Denmark Hill; the strange accents and clothes of the people who jostled us; the profusion of strident messages and signs competing for our attention. We were surprised to see a horse and cart threading its way through the motorised traffic, controlled by a shabby old man and laden with items of furniture. It seemed like a vision from a previous era. We were also surprised to see the different hues of people's faces – there were black, yellow and brown ones, as well as beige and white.

We spent several minutes simply gazing into the window of a chemist's shop. We could not believe the variety and profusion of what was on sale, marvelling that the premises were emblazoned with electric light, although it was the middle of the morning. Our eyes could not always interpret what they were seeing. Another shop window had been filled with wooden boxes. Framed in each box was the image of a man's head in shades of grey. Each picture moved identically as the man's jaws mouthed silent words. He had thin black hair covering a bald pate in slimy strands. He seemed to be talking from the corner of his mouth. We turned the corner into Camberwell Church Street. My father had walked along here each morning in his black frock coat and silk top hat to catch the omnibus into the city. He had stood beneath the plane trees, which were then barely more than saplings, fringing the green. Now the trees had become friendly giants with feathery fingers and thick piebald trunks.

It was Lara who suggested going into a public house, the Hermit's Cave, for a drink; for we needed something to steady our nerves. With its frosted glass windows, its brown-varnished interior and the creased, careworn faces of its patrons, it had appeared, at least at first, comfortingly familiar. The English tend to favour, for their pubs, the homely decor of a Victorian living room. This moment in history, the summer of 1968, was a period, Sidgwick had told us, when social conventions had been somewhat loosened by planetary influences. But it is fair to say that our entrance had turned heads. I should explain that I was wearing a sleeveless sheepskin jerkin and loose crimson trousers tied at the ankles with twine. My hair, which had not been cut for more than a year, reached below my shoulders; I had also grown a straggly moustache and beard. Lara was wearing a thin blue dress and multiple bangles and beads that jangled as she walked. Her hair had been tinted to a rich hue, somewhere between teak and mahogany, and cascaded far down her back. Our appearance had caused a minor sensation.

"Bloody hippies," I heard someone say at the bar, disapprovingly. I did not have the slightest idea what this meant. The pub was crowded. We made our way, uncertainly, to the edge of the room.

"I like the gear, man."

"Sorry?"

"I like your clothes."

The speaker was sitting at the next table. He was a well-built young man with blond curly hair. By coincidence, he was also wearing a sleeveless sheepskin jerkin, but his tanned arms were far more muscular than mine; one would have described him as brawny. His trousers were of a dark blue velvet, with an exaggerated flare, like a sailor's bell-bottoms. His name was Sid, he said.

Next to him, a taller, thinner youth was rolling a cigarette. Sid's companion had unkempt brown hair, partially slicked back with oil and had neglected to shave for a few days. He was wearing a black suit waistcoat over a white linen shirt with no collar, and a single earring. He was a kind of dandy, one would have said, a beau fallen on hard times.

"Hi, my name's Dean. Dean Jenkins." He extended his hand. His fingers were long and nicotine stained, the nails cut short. He smiled at Lara, acknowledging her with the polite, attentive manner that he adopted naturally with all women. "This is my chick, Sandy."

Sandy was a female version of Dean. Her clothes were almost identical to his and she unconsciously copied his physical mannerisms, including the way he invariably tapped the end of his cigarettes on the table before he lit them. She did not say much. It was Dean who talked. But he was also a very good listener. Dean was a brilliant mimic; I think that this ability explained his extraordinary musical ability.

"We're in a band," explained Sid. "I'm on drums and Dean plays guitar."

Dean blew a thin jet of smoke between his lips. Everything he did, I realised, was for effect.

"A band. What, like brass band?" I said.

Sid and Dean laughed.

"No, man. It's a ... oh, never mind. Where have you guys come from?"

"My name is Frederick and this is Lara. We have been living in Wales, recently, but I am actually from Camberwell. I was born in Havil Street"

"Cool," said Sid. "We live in a squat around the corner." He sniffed. Sid sniffed a lot. Later, I would discover that his nostrils were the favoured entry routes for certain white powders that he took. "We've just moved in. This is the only pub around here which will serve us. But it's not exactly friendly."

I could see what Sid meant. Camberwell's population had changed surprisingly little since the 1870s – men in cheap suits courted faded women with crimped hair and floral dresses. Anxiously guarding their damosels and their pints of bitter, the men would be easily roused to violence. Our little group in the corner did not look like them. We were aliens.

"Oh wow, do you like this?" said Sid."

Music, with a loud repetitive rhythm, was issuing from the machine in the corner. To my ears it was deafening. Sid tapped in time with his fingers, on the table. Dean accompanied the song in a falsetto voice, causing people nearby to stare at us. We all listened, trapped in the song's magic, until it ended. After a short interval, another one began.

"Have you got any bread?" said Sid.

"Bread?"

"Do you have any money?"

I realised at that moment that we had become so unused to money that we had entirely forgotten about it. Even the concept seemed alien – pieces of metal and paper used to buy things.

"No we don't," I said. "But we do have some rather valuable pieces of jewellery."

I looked at Lara. Her expression was eloquent. I don't have them, said her eyes. I thought you had them.

Have you ever sustained a loss so serious that it causes you, momentarily, to lose your reason? That is what happened to Lara and me. We interrogated each other for half an hour, going over all of our recent movements, over and over again. The upshot of it was that the torcs were gone and that we had no idea where they were. Lara was wearing her gold ring, which was a consolation, but this hardly equated to a lifetime's financial security.

To use an expression favoured by Alf, we were buggered. We had no means of support, nowhere to live and only the ring and the clothes that we stood up in. We had no idea when we would see Sidgwick again. What on earth were we going to do?

"Don't worry," said Sid. "I'll buy you a drink."

Chapter Fourteen

Dazed and Confused

I suppose that being drunk provided some compensation for having lost everything. After we left the pub, the five of us made our way merrily along Camberwell Church Street. Dean walked or rather, weaved in front, singing, as he played an imaginary guitar. This road existed on the threshold of my memory, for my family had left Camberwell when I was a small boy. I had a dream-like sensation of being surrounded by a familiar but fragile landscape, like the reflection on the surface of a soap bubble. In my memories, were hansom cabs and horse-driven buses, women in black dresses, umbrellas pushed against the rain.

Around us was a summer evening, perfumed by pollen and dust. The candle-like blossoms of the horse chestnuts and the scabby trunks of the plane trees had not changed since Victorian times; nor had Camberwell's narrow-shouldered houses and its dark little shops, their pigeon-soured cornices layered with soot and grime. I knew that if we continued to walk down Church Street we would reach the union workhouse at the end of Havil Street and St. Giles church – at least if they were still there. Cars passed us, their impassive drivers scanning the road ahead. Lara and I had already grown used to them. Our ears and eyes had become tolerant to London's new rhythms.

Dean and Sandy walked ahead. Dean's guitar playing was causing passers-by to look away anxiously. Sid, Lara and I followed behind. Sid was not wearing any shoes. This was also viewed, by those who noticed, as a dangerous, almost revolutionary act. We felt protected and invulnerable. I remembered Sidgwick's words: "You are a special one. That is why you have been chosen." It seemed that we had always made up this eccentric little group, walking through south London in a golden light.

We stopped at the corner of Camberwell Grove. I do not know if you have ever been there. A tree-lined avenue of substantial houses, it rises steeply from Church Street to the brow of Dog Kennel Hill. From here, on a clear day, you can see the North Downs. In Victorian times, those who lived in the Grove owned carriages and held balls in their drawing rooms.

"Our house is up here," said Sid. "I'll race you." He began to run up the hill, overtaking Dean, who had just lit a cigarette. I took Lara's hand and we followed, as fast as we could.

It took us a long time to reach number one hundred and eighty-six. It was a grand and imposing dwelling – part of a Regency terrace. On the ground floor were sash windows with curved heads; above them, a balcony with an iron railing crossed the width of the house. There were three more storeys above. Small, square windows protruded from the roof. There was also a whitewashed basement, reached by steps from the front door. It is not only because I was born there that I like Camberwell. I have always thought that its dappled plane trees and its terraces of London brick form a congenial urban environment. It is a shady backwater, its calm tributaries feeding the city's turbulent waters.

"Come in," said Sid.

The front door was pink.

"You see that?" he said, pointing to where a piece of plywood had replaced a pane of broken glass to the right of the front door. "That's how we got in."

It was easy to imagine this small act of vandalism, effected by a nonchalant Sid, while Dean stood by, tugging on a cigarette.

"Who owns the house?" I said.

"An old lady. She lives in Ashford. She's totally cool about us living here."

"If she is cool about it," I said, "then surely you will have to move?"

I had not yet discovered that cool had reversed its adjectival meaning. It now, in the argot of the young, connoted something that was good or favourable.

"You're a laugh," he said. "The way you talk ..."

He led us through the hallway. The carpet was long gone and there were fragments of rubble on the floor. One wall had been painted lime green, with a mural of colourful flowers and the word, Love, picked out in bright yellow leaves. I guessed that this was the work of the present occupants.

"We tend to live upstairs," said Dean. "We hang out down here sometimes, but it's a bit dark. Our gear is set up in the basement. We use it as a rehearsal room."

Through a doorway I glimpsed the ruins of a dining room. Light from the back garden filtered through its dusty, ivy-framed windows. It was empty, except for ghosts. At the end of the hall was a kitchen. Sid did not encourage us to linger there, perhaps because the sink was scattered with the remains of many previous meals and the stove was thickly encrusted with grease.

On the first floor, a substantial room, which was the width of the house, had been carpeted with rugs and made comfortable. A huge, battered settee, salvaged from the street, was the main item of furniture. It was soft and yielding but redolent of tomcats. Guitars and other instruments were scattered around, along with large cushions that took the place of chairs. The bookshelves were not lined with the drab, leather-bound artefacts I would have recognised as books, but colourful, decorative objects with pictures on their spines and interesting, variegated typography.

Someone had begun a naive but confident mural around the fireplace. Half-finished orang-utans dangled from the dado rail and tigers stalked through creepers on either side of the chimney breast. The jungle would never be completed and its artist was rarely mentioned. It had been a previous girlfriend of Dean's, a student at Camberwell Art College.

Later, when we were wealthy, we would inhabit even more spacious rooms. But they would always resemble this one, being aligned towards the activities of lounging, strumming on guitars and reading, in a position as close to the horizontal as possible. They would always seem transient. I think it was the impermanent quality of the house that made Lara and me feel immediately at home there.

Dean placed himself on a cushion, lit a cigarette and began playing an acoustic guitar. He was replicating, exactly, a song that we had just heard in the Hermit's Cave, adding baroque variations of his own invention. Dean's intuitive and untrained facility for music applied to any instrument; he could probably have picked up a tennis racket and played it. Sandy sat watching him in awe until he asked her to make him a cup of tea.

"You can crash out here if you like," said Sid.

"I beg your pardon."

"You can stay here. We've got so many rooms we get lost sometimes. There's a really nice one upstairs. I can show you."

I looked at Lara. She smiled, cautiously.

"That would be marvellous, Sid. It is most kind of you to accommodate us."

"That's okay." Sid had removed his jerkin. He was wearing what looked like a black vest – a garment that revealed his powerful shoulders and thick biceps.

The second-floor landing was hung with colourful fabrics from the Indian sub-continent. It smelled of incense. For an uncomfortable moment my mind was carried back to Aunt Agnes and to our bruising encounter with the spirit world in her parlour. Our bedroom had no door, merely a piece of purple cloth, printed with swirling red mandalas. Its windows overlooked the back garden. This was shady and overgrown. There was a long lawn but any garden plants had long since been swamped by weeds. At the foot of the garden was a magnificent horse chestnut tree.

There was no bed. Beds were bourgeois, Dean would have argued. And, besides, they were expensive. A double mattress of uncertain provenance lay on the floor. An ancient damask curtain served as a coverlet. One would not have wished to inquire too closely what bedding was beneath it – sheets and blankets were still used in those days. But to Lara and me, uprooted and inebriated as we were, the mattress was blissful. Sid left us. We lay in each other's arms, too tired to speak. Within a few minutes, we were fast asleep.

"Let me make sure that I have understood you correctly," I said to Dean, the following afternoon. "It is not a crime for you to live here. You are provided by public authorities with water, gas and electricity. But you do not pay for them. You also pay no rent. You are under no obligation to work and, every week, you receive money from the Government."

"Yeh," said Dean, laconically. "That's about the size of it."

This was the land of the Lotus eaters, I thought. "Does everybody live like this?" I asked.

Dean, as usual, picked up his guitar. "No they don't."

"Why not?"

"I don't know. Because they're straight I suppose."

"Straight?"

"Conformists."

Dean had been enrolled at a London university until the previous year, when music had taken over from his studies. He was highly intelligent and extremely knowledgeable about politics. To account for my curiosity, I had explained to Dean that I had suffered from a rare neurological illness and had lost my memories of historical events. It was an unlikely tale but he believed it – many of his friends, he said, suffered from a similar affliction.

"Does anyone disagree?"

"With what?" he asked.

"With the fact that it is possible to live outside society's normal rules and yet to benefit from its advantages."

"Of course they do," said Dean, tuning his guitar. "A lot of people think we need a good war to sort this country out."

"You mean like the Great War?" I said.

"The what?" Dean looked puzzled.

He appeared to be unfamiliar with the apocalyptic conflict from which I had rescued Alf.

I persisted. "The Great War, between Britain and Germany. It began in 1914, following the assassination of Archduke Ferdinand of Austria. The front line extended from Switzerland to the North Sea. The armies were dug into trenches. There were huge battles."

He looked at me blankly, tuning his guitar.

"It was not just about Britain and Germany," I continued. "The colonies were also involved – India, Australia, Canada."

He played a minor chord. "India, in 1914?"

"Yes."

"But India achieved independence," said Dean, "in 1913."

I computed the new fact. "Did it? Was Randolph Churchill still the Prime Minister?"

"Nah. He was dead by then. Of a brain disease, so they said."

"So who was the Prime Minister?" I said.

Dean frowned, making a minor adjustment to one of his strings. "Er ... Joseph Chamberlain, I think."

"How did that come about? I thought he ..."

"Jesus," said Dean. "This is like a history lesson."

I explained that I needed to fill in some gaps. Because of my condition, large areas of knowledge were missing. Dean kept me waiting. He played a rapid intricate sequence combining full chords and arpeggios. His virtuosity was startling. He stopped.

"Let me see if I can remember this. Chamberlain won in '06, on a pro-Empire ticket. However, he could only remain in office with the backing of the Labour party, led by Ramsey MacDonald. Chamberlain did a U-turn. Ireland became independent. But the main thing he did was to remove the power from the House of Lords."

"Are you sure?" I said. "I mean wasn't that ..."

"Controversial. Yes, it was. But he had to do that to get his budget through and to remain in power. Labour won in 1911, I think."

"Labour?"

"The Labour party. Surely ..." He looked at me. "You do know who the current Prime Minister is don't you?"

It was my turn to look blank.

"It's Warburton. Nicholas Warbuton, the MP for New Malden. He pretends to be a Cockney, but really he's quite posh." Dean imitated the man's accent. I laughed even though I was not familiar with the original.

At this moment, Lara came into the living room. She was wearing a long man's nightshirt. Her hair was tangled, her face pale. We both knew that she was not interested in politics so we changed the topic of the conversation.

It was a hot day. I remember making bacon sandwiches as Dean and Lara talked in the garden, where the cat, a ginger tom, was sunning himself. For Lara, this was something of an ordeal. Dean was an inquisitive person and she was rather shy. She could hardly reveal that she had been born in 1863. I could see that she was struggling as I carried out the sandwiches and mugs of tea.

"Do you know anything about the Druids?" I asked Dean. It was the first thing that came into my head.

He thought for a moment, his brow furrowed in concentration. "Are they a group?"

We laughed. Like most people, Dean had a vague conception of Druids as men in white robes, harvesting mistletoe by the light of the moon. I appraised him of some of the facts. It was a near perfect evening and a long summer stretched ahead of us. The back garden was a sun-trap and we enjoyed it in much the same way as the cat did. We had few things to worry about – only to look out for each other and feed and clothe ourselves. The fact that we had no worldly possessions no longer seemed important.

Sid obtained bicycles for us – modern ones, that were far more comfortable than the bone shakers of the Victorian era. We did not inquire too closely where he had got them from. It was good to cycle again, although Camberwell Grove has a steep gradient. Most of our expeditions were purely local, foraging for food, but once we travelled as far north as the exotic fastness of Camden Town. We were isolated – the first squatters in the locality – but I soon discovered that there were groups of people like us all over London. They formed a single, inter-connected community, with a shared language and culture. All tended to be interested in artistic activities and music making. I now called Lara the Camberwell Beauty, after a variety of butterfly that had been associated with the locality.

Our immediate neighbours had no animosity towards us. The old lady next door had not talked to anyone for years and soon adopted us as her family. She even said that she liked the racket we made. She was deaf and it was the first music that she had heard for decades.

At the end of the afternoon Sid came back from a gardening job, full of earth and sun. He rolled an enormous hemp cigarette. It was my first experience of the drug. The sweet smoke enhanced all of my senses, including taste. Remaining outside, we ate a delicious meal of vegetables and rice and drank a bottle of cider. Sid told us about his new girlfriend, who, he said, was a Brazilian of staggering beauty and athletic physique.

At different periods in my life Sundays have been depressing days, but only, on reflection, because I have been forced to go to church in order to be fanned by the flames of hell, or have faced the prospect of drudgery in an etiolated workplace the following morning. I now know that Sunday's pall of gloom was a social construction. It was created by hymn writers and factory owners.

That evening, Dean and Sid took me down to the basement and I picked up a guitar for the first time in my life.

"One, two, three, four …" Sid's shoulder twitched as he began to create a complicated rhythm with his bass drum and hi-hat. It was two weeks after my first music lesson and we were having a late night jamming session.

Just as Dean was predestined by his physique and attitudes to be a lead guitarist, Sid was a natural drummer. First of all, he was physically strong; secondly, he was an intuitive rather than intellectual person. Let us be honest, there was an element of madness in his personality. He was by far the most reckless person of the three of us – that is what made him a good drummer. You could tell that by the way he drove his ancient, over-powered sports car. I was his passenger once, on a suicidal journey down the Walworth Road. The experience was so terrifying that I never repeated it.

"Rubbish!" said Dean. "Start again."

He had been developing a tricky guitar riff for the past week. Much imitated by other guitarists, it can be heard on the final track of our first LP. The riff was synchronised perfectly with Sid's beat but it played games with the time signature. I could hear Dean cursing under his breath when it got away from his fingers. His amplifier was close to maximum volume. It made a beautiful sound, full of lovely harmonics and half-crazed distortions that only made sense when Dean was playing. We started again. Having completed eight bars, each more confident than the last, Dean nodded in my direction. That was the signal for the bass to come in.

The bass line for that song was so simple that a child of six could have played it. Unfortunately, I was not in the right key and my timing was woeful. A wrong note boomed through the basement. I love the bass. It is an instrument that you should feel in your diaphragm rather than hear, the heartbeat of a song. Playing it suits people who have low-key personalities, rather than show-offs.

"For God's sake!" Dean exploded. "That was horrible! Try to get it right!"

He was in a bad mood that day, probably because he had argued with Sandy. Dean snorted and paced over to me. With difficulty he controlled his temper, placing his left hand on my fret board, to show me the correct fingering.

We practiced, Dean demonstrating the riff on an acoustic guitar. After about half an hour I had mastered it. I think it was the first song I learned. As usual, it was in the key of E major, with a middle section that saw Dean playing impossibly fast passages of notes. We called it Henge Bender, or Freddie's Freakout, on account of its lobotomising bass line and we used it as our end-of-set show stopper. Like most of our first songs, it had only a few rudimentary words.

"One, two, three ..." We started again. I was spot on this time, give or take a semi-quaver. We enjoyed five minutes of near perfection that would have put Edie, next door, into raptures. Then Sid started doing something peculiar.

"Stop!" Dean was close to exasperation. The palms of his hands always turned red when he was like that. "What the hell was that?"

"It was a samba rhythm," explained our drummer. He gave a further demonstration with the snare and high hat. Sid claimed to have learned it from his girlfriend. Whether this was from her record collection or the motions of her body while love making, we never found out.

"This is not ballroom bloody dancing," said Dean.

"No listen." Sid tapped out the rhythm again. A light went on in Dean's brain as he realised that it had potential. He showed me how the bass should drag the beat and was almost as astonished as I was when I discovered that I could do it, creating a subtle interplay with Sid's sticks. Like explorers at the edge of a new continent, we played around with the rhythm for the next six hours.

As dawn rose over Camberwell Grove, Dean said that we were tight and that the new song was "brilliant". Our eyes were wide and our teeth chewed on nothing. The roofs of our mouths were as dry as the Gobi desert. You see, Sid had acquired some small white pills from his mate at the Hermit's Cave. While they lacked the hallucinatory properties of Doctor Sidgwick's patent remedy, the pills speeded up considerably one's biological and mental processes. Camberwell Grove was now awake and so were we, for the next two days. Another problem with the pills was the ghastly, nauseating experience of "coming down". It was like descending slowly into a dark cellar. We turned off our hot amps, put the guitars into their battered cases and went into the kitchen to consume large quantities of tea. We felt incredibly pleased with ourselves, knowing that we were now a band.

Lara and I lay in bed at the end of June. Our morning ritual was to drink a pot of tea and eat cream cakes from the local shop. Often, we did not get up until midday. June, when that purple marvel, the mallow, is in flower, is my favourite month. My birthday, on the first, had been superb. It consisted of making love, consuming tea and cakes, having a long discussion with Dean on the latest, most modish form of French philosophy, strolling down to Camberwell Church Street for a drink in the Hermit's Cave, lounging on Camberwell Green and, that evening, meeting, in our back garden, an incredible group of Brazilian percussionists from South Norwood.

We set up our instruments outside. The Brazilians' English was rudimentary but they played their instruments with the poetry of Diaghilev's dance troupe. There was delicious food and a punch that was mildly narcotic. Sid was in nirvana and Dean and I were close. I was never more than adequate as a bass player but I think that Dean's power, finesse and rhythmical acuity on the guitar approached genius. It was not just that he played louder and faster than anyone else – of course, he did – there was a sweetness and lyricism in his playing that could almost make you cry.

Nobody in the Grove complained about the sounds that we made, possibly because they were heavenly. I would guess that their like had never been heard before in England. We played, ate, laughed and drank until it was light. Afterwards, Lara and I took a walk to the green, long before the commuters, the buses and car drivers had arrived on their trajectories of frustration. We sat on the dewy grass, talking. Finally, we had a swim in the ornate Victorian public baths at the end of Artichoke Place. It was one of the best days of my life.

Lara rose and stretched and I tried to discourage her from getting up, ending our in-bed pleasures. The night-shirt draped from her pale shoulders. I adored her body. I had always felt that it was utterly perfect.

There was a writing pad on my knees, on which I had been scribbling. On Saturday our group would have its first concert, in the crypt beneath St. Giles Church on Camberwell Church Street. As principal lyricist I had been assigned the difficult task of choosing a name. Some of my attempts had been fatuous – The Sun Worshippers, Stoned Henge, Heaven. Others were so puerile that I cannot bear to remember them. I had now narrowed the field to two contenders. The Druids seemed a possible name, but the thought of making, and wearing, white robes again was a deterrent. My pen hovered over the words it had just written like a diviner's twig.

"The Chosen," I said. "How about, The Chosen?"

Lara contemplated the three syllables. She did not reply.

"Do you think that your father would like our music?"

"No … I don't know. It is very loud, isn't it? He is quite open minded, so perhaps he would."

"Maybe he could play with us on his violin?"

Lara considered the proposition. She laughed.

"Do you think that The Chosen is a good name?"

There was a pause. "Yes, I do."

"That's it then."

Sid was indifferent to my proposal. We could have been called, The Cornflakes, as far as he was concerned – a name he actually suggested. Dean hated The Chosen as a moniker. However, he was not able to offer a viable alternative.

"Listen, Dean," I said, "it's The Chosen, or nothing."

"That's a good name," said Sid, "Nothing. I like it."

"Shut up!" I threw a cushion at him.

Dean was adamant. It was only the evening before the concert that he finally gave in. So that our guitarist could not change his mind, I instructed Sid to paint the name on his bass drum in large silver letters. Unfortunately, Sid's formal education had ended at an early age with his dismissal from school. His writing was hard to decipher; also, he was under the influence of exotic chemicals when he performed this relatively simple task. It was for this reason, as you can see if you study the photographs carefully, that we played our first ever gig as The Cousin.

Chapter Fifteen

The Meaning of Life

The electric light in the crypt was horribly bright. The walls were a shade of yellow that hurt the eyes and scattered with patronising posters. Our gear was set up on a small platform serving as a stage. The rest of the crypt, newly swept, was our auditorium and "freak-out space". But at the moment, an audience was lacking and the only person freaking out was Dean. Later, we became familiar with Dean's strange pre-gig moods as a normal pattern of behaviour. It was just the same when we played for forty thousand people in Buckingham Palace Park in the summer of '69. But that was ahead of us. Dean's thin legs swung from the edge of the table he was sitting on. He always wore narrow trousers, not flares like Sid and me. They suited him.

"I told him not to touch my amp. It was him." He tossed his head contemptuously in the direction of the vicar. The vicar's beaming face protruded, teeth first, through a serving hatch.

"Is everything all right, gentlemen?" he inquired, anxiously.

"Yeh, fine," I said.

Our concert was the apotheosis of the vicar's campaign to reach the kids, as he put it, of Camberwell. He had arranged cups of orange and lemon squash in the serving hatch and hung some paper chains around the crypt. Sid had already availed himself of the squash, to wash down various pills. I don't know what was in them. They were probably barbiturates, which would have made him drowsy but for the amphetamine sulphate he had hoovered up his nose through a rolled up bank-note. Sid's pupils were like large black tadpoles. He would soon sweat out the drugs as he pounded on his drums.

"Oh Christ, look out," said Dean, "he's coming this way."

The vicar was bearing down on us. He was a tall ginger-haired man. He seemed to have copied the essential elements of Dean's hairstyle but, in his case, it looked ridiculous. He was almost as agitated as Dean was.

"Are you nervous, gentlemen?" he asked. "I know that this is your first er ... engagement. May I?" He reached towards Dean's guitar, a battered red Electra with six pick-ups. We all knew that he secretly wanted to play it. Dean glared at him so fiercely that he withdrew his hand as if from a hotplate.

"Well, er, everything seems ready. I suppose that all we can do now is to wait for our congregation. Ahum!" He gave a nervous laugh. "Did you see my posters?" We had. They were embarrassing. "Oh dear!"

The vicar's surprise was caused by the fact that the crypt had been plunged into total darkness but for the tiny lights on the amps and the glowing tip of Dean's cigarette. Our sound and lighting man, Cyril, was up to his usual tricks. Cyril was a genius. He was just as responsible for the success of The Chosen as anyone else. We had found him in the back room of a guitar shop in Denmark Street – a small, gnome-like creature in a threadbare tweed jacket, with a soldering iron permanently protruding from his pocket. It was hard to understand what Cyril was saying most of the time but we knew, at once, that he had been given to us by a higher agency.

Cyril, without us even asking him, had constructed for us the most powerful PA system in south London and a primitive mixing desk. Even in the early days his lighting effects and back projections were far ahead of their time; they became even more so as we were able to afford more elaborate equipment. A pinprick of magenta light cut through the darkness and expanded into a pulsating disc on the back wall. It began to spin like a Catherine wheel, flicking out red and yellow flames.

"Gosh," said the vicar. It was a Dante's Inferno-type thing – an eschatological dead zone, poised halfway between heaven and hell. A low frequency drone began to ooze from the speakers. It was aboriginal music recorded by an anthropologist. Cyril increased the volume imperceptibly, adding percussive effects from a tape machine and swishing noises, like passing lorries on a rainy motorway.

On later gigs, when we had a dressing room, Sid, Dean and I would share a spliff as Cyril twiddled with his knobs, building up expectation. This was our pre-performance gin and tonic. Sid and I would creep onto the stage in total darkness. A soft bass line would begin, accompanied by the hiss of a snare drum. The bass line formed an envelope for Dean's improvisations. Dean came in with a whisper, in a white spotlight. He didn't need effects pedals. A curious alchemy took place between his brain and his fingertips so that he could make the guitar do whatever he wanted. Just as the bass line became too insistent, like an irritating stranger, Sid would flick his cymbal and kick the bass drum.

Having sketched the outline of the song with a few chords, Dean would colour the spaces in between, like an old master painting a mural. Almost imperceptibly the bass would become faster. Gradually, we would work up the audience into a frenzy, so that it writhed like a crazed, many-tentacled sea creature. But sometimes, we played simple, melodic tunes that you could waltz around the room to. Or we would slip into a time signature that was so obscure and complicated that not even Dean knew what it was, and we wondered whether Sid had grown another foot.

I kept the set list for our first gig for several years. It was written in ballpoint, in the dark, on a piece of crumpled paper. The running order was – Celestial Vibrations (you can probably imagine what that sounded like), The Cave of Artemis – part one, Little White Pills (that one was Sid's), The Cave of Artemis – parts two and three and, finally, Henge Bender. Our songs sounded spontaneous but actually, Dean had carefully drilled us through every bar, in between impatient drags on his cigarette. He would not tolerate anything less than complete concentration from Sid and me. He needed that, just as Michelangelo depended upon well-constructed scaffolding while painting his ceilings. We would always leave the stage with the audience wanting more, and then give it to them, after a leisurely post-gig spliff, neatly rolled by Cyril.

The vicar was stunned by our performance that evening. For him it was a theological as much as an aesthetic experience. It made him quiet and thoughtful for several days. "The kids" began to drift in halfway through the first song. It was not the constituency the vicar had intended – most of them had been loitering on the pavement in front of the Hermit's Cave drinking cocktails of cider and vodka in the evening sun and smoking dope.

As word spread back along Camberwell Church Street that something weird was happening in the crypt they began to replicate themselves, like amoebae. There were girls in black duffel coats with hooped tights, strange, thin youths with wispy beards and roll-your-own cigarettes; bikers in oil-encrusted denim with death's head insignia on their jackets. Soon the crypt was sweating and dancing wall to wall and my bass was rocking the foundations of St Giles church. Cyril's light show was brilliant. It was a thing of beauty – the vicar later said. Freaks from the art college and shadow boxing alcoholics who lived beneath underpasses formed the nucleus of our following. They were our apostles. Having found us, they spread the word.

I think that Lara drifted in about halfway through. I saw her dancing in a melee of whirling dervishes. I remember feeling that I was in a bright bubble of light as my fingers skipped over the strings, playing hide and seek with Sid's beats, and that I had always been here. The bass lines moved through people's stomachs and pulled at their feet. Our music was a love generator, a joyous head bang. That night I was as happy as I have ever been. Cheers, Sid, I thought.

We walked up the Grove, arm in arm in arm. Dean had been

reconciled with Sandy (for one night only, as it turned out), Sid had split up with the Brazilian. He was with a woman he had met that night. We had left our gear in the crypt. The gig had finally ended when public health inspectors had arrived just before dawn, with sound-measuring equipment, accompanied by the police. They asked who was in charge and the vicar stepped forward. He seemed to be suffering from shell-shock. It had ended in confusion, our ears still ringing. But we knew that something magic had happened. Cyril curled up under the sound desk and fell asleep. It was talked about for years, that first gig in the crypt. It was rumoured that there was a bootleg tape, but we were never able to get hold of a copy.

The Grove was growing lighter. I remembered watching dawn come up in Wales, my arm around Lara's waist. Half an hour before, in between numbers, Sid had given me a small brown pill. Actually, it looked more like a chess piece than a tablet. It was, I recall, a crooked miniature pawn, with a globular head. I had gulped it down without thinking. It was LSD. When I realised what was happening to me, about halfway up the hill, I felt a rush of excitement as the sensory effects hit me. Looking down, I perceived that the pavement was made out of glass. Fallen leaves had been carefully sculpted by craftsmen from precious materials. The most scary thing was that I could see into Dean's soul – a conflation of anxiety and genius – I could see into everyone's soul; I knew exactly what they were thinking. I could not express it in words, for the Truth was ineffable. But I had become omniscient. I was God! Seeing sounds, hearing colours, and so forth was only a part of it. Each spectrum was laid out before me. I merely had to choose how far I wanted my senses to reach into the secret, internal realities of Things and their molecules and vibrations.

Something very strange had happened to Time. The second hand on my watch was moving with agonising slowness, if at all. I may have looked at it for seconds or hours, I had no way of knowing because, just as there was no essential difference between tininess and bigness, there was no distinction between short and long. Had you asked me "what is the time?" I would merely have laughed and echoed the phrase back to you, as if you had said, "what is Time?" It is a butterfly's wink, I would have said; a footprint in the desert; a man crying in a hotel bathroom.

A car sped down the road (this was long before Camberwell Grove was obstructed by speed humps). Its sound was attenuated; it trailed behind the vehicle in shimmering fragments like the tail of a shooting star. I was walking, unsteadily, on a tight rope of eternity, whose ends were joined together. I could change the colours around me at will and I did. I could also extend my hand – this was really strange – and stretch it as far as I wanted, like a rubber attachment. Oh my God, I thought, I'm having a Trip. The realisation hit me fully as we approached the front door, which, by the way, had become a pulsating coral reef.

By the time we were on the doorstep I was giggling helplessly, like a man breathing pure laughing gas, and three people were holding me up. Sid was tripping too. But he was an old hand and he knew how to handle it. Dean had not taken any LSD, only some speed, so he was lucid. The experience I had that night was awe-inspiring. The second time I took LSD the effects were not nearly as powerful and the third time even less so. Perhaps you can only have one true epiphany per lifetime. The speciallydesigned drugs that we later had made for us were just happiness pills. They were shandy, not bitter.

Lara had not taken anything – she was always wary of drugs. I did not need to look at her to know what she was thinking. I had felt the essence of her pulsing through her hand, coming up the Grove. Did I really want to look into her soul? Of course I did. I always do what I should not; for I am reckless. I realised immediately, from her face, that she was the White Goddess, the triple deity of ecstasy, fertility and death, merged into one being.

I had always known. I had merely denied the knowledge.

Lara was frightened by my behaviour. It was Dean who took me inside. He understood. He sat me down on the kitchen floor, where I listened to a tap dripping for eight hours. I heard the meaning of life in that tap. I wish I could explain it to you. Unfortunately, it could not be described in words, even if I could remember what it was. The meaning of life is whatever one chooses it to be. The point is, there is no meaning.

A month later, Dean and I walked down a greasy London backstreet, smelling of rancid Chinese food and hastily relieved bladders. We found an anonymous building in a canyon-like road off Shaftesbury Avenue and surveyed a list of names next to multiple electric bells. After we had filtered out the prostitutes and the obscure film production companies, we discovered what we were looking for – R. Simlick, neatly printed on a scrap of card. Dean was very keen. Making an appointment with an agent had been his idea. The name and address had come from a friend of his father's, who was a novelty act, a crooner in the working mens' clubs. I was doubtful of the whole idea. We had travelled to the West End on a big red bus from Camberwell Green, got off at Whitehall and walked through Trafalgar Square with its square-topped obelisk where Nelson's column had once been. (The Fenians had blown up the wretched statue just before Irish independence.)

From Charing Cross Road we cut through into Soho. One of the main things that struck me was how little the area had changed since the 1870s when I had first known it. The air was less smoky and chemical-laced and the ubiquitous horse dung was gone. But there was still an aura of furtive copulations and of crime and revolution in its dense streets. The address we sought was in Windmill Street.

"I don't think that this is a good idea, Dean," I said.

"Listen, man, it's cool," he reassured me. "You don't have to say anything. This bloke is the real thing, okay? Just go with it."

Although it was August, and warm, Dean was wearing what he thought was a stylish topcoat. It was long and beige, with a fur collar. I thought it made him look like a second-hand furniture dealer in one of the minor suburbs.

Dean pressed the bell. Soon we heard descending footsteps. We followed a girl's bottom as it wiggled up the stairs, barely covered by a tiny blue skirt. It was Sharon, a secretary. That evening I would hear Dean energetically having sex with her through the thin wall of my bedroom. At the top of the stairs was a door with gilt lettering on frosted glass. Reuben J. Simlick, it said, Theatrical Agent.

The smiling girl led us through and returned to filing her nails. We studied black and white photographs on the walls. It was a gallery of jaunty aspiration matched against abject failure – comedians who weren't funny, plate spinners, dog acts, warbling singers who were decades out of date and whistling ventriloquists. On each photograph was an unnaturally large signature and an insincere message.

"That's my dad's mate," said Dean. The picture was of a stunted-looking man, slapping a thin thigh and grinning. He looked as if he was about to cry. The inscription said, "To my pal Reuben, love Franky XXX."

A door opened, bringing a waft of cigar smoke followed by a man. All impresarios combine essentially the same ingredients. They have shiny bald heads, with rolls of fat around the chin and tufts of grey hear sprouting from their ears and nostrils. They favour gold cufflinks, ostentatiously large signet rings and brands of after-shave that make your eyes water. Reuben Simlick fitted the bill. He hugged us and clasped our hands, like long lost members of his family.

"Sharon," he enthused, "this is Dean, Franky's boy."

"I'm not actually Franky's …"

"Please, come in, come in."

"Sharon love, no calls please."

Reuben never actually listened to what anyone else said; he just picked up enough of it to get a general meaning and then interrupted them. He sat us down. We declined cigars. In Reueben's office were more photographs, with even larger signatures. One of them was recognisable – it was an old-time thespian whose career had recently revived in a television series. The series was about Time Travel, strangely enough.

"That's dear old Eric," said Reuben, "he's like a son to me is Eric. Do you know, I first met him in 1937. Have you seen his Corialanus?" He winked and leered at us. It was ghastly.

Now then, Reuben's expression said, we've had our fun, let's get down to business.

"As you can see, boys, I have a number of clients. You probably know some of them. There's Vera Sidebottom, the singing seamstress; Alfie Higgs and his magic harmonium; Tommie Treacle ... I could go on. They all have one thing in common and that is this, staying power. What do I mean by that? I mean that, while they may not be consistently at the top of the bill like old Eric here, they all make a damn good living. And that's largely thanks to me. Take little Tommie. Found him in Deptford. Now he's starring in his own musical. Okay then." There was a pause, which he exploited to unburden the end of his cigar. "Think carefully. What is it that you can offer me that little Tommie can't?"

"A pair of balls," said Dean, softly.

Reuben did not hear him. "You see, the thing is, your kind of music may be very popular – now. From what Franky tells me you're very good. But what's going to happen in a few years time? Now, if you had some kind of animal in your act, or a pretty little girl, things would be different. There would always be work for you, and, of course, I would be happy to find it for you. As it is, I'll be perfectly honest boys. What you do is probably just a flash in the pan."

"You haven't even heard us," said Dean.

"But I am prepared to do this." The end dropped off his cigar. "My son, Nigel, has just started in the business. He's a good boy and I trust his judgments. He's going to take over the younger acts for me. I'll send him down to see you. If he likes you, well, we'll take it from there. I can't say fairer than that now, can I?"

Reuben extended an arm, exposing a starched cuff, and we shook. That was it, the verbal contract that launched us on our brief journey of fame and glory.

"Give your address to Sharon and she'll sort you out. It was lovely meeting you er ... Give me regards to your dad."

"He's not my ..."

"Goodbye." Smiling, he pushed us out of the door.

Dean established firm eye contact with Sharon as he wrote our address on a piece of paper and the place and time of our next gig. She smiled at him sweetly. He arranged to meet her later that evening in Soho. That was why he was in a buoyant mood as we bounded down the stairs, not because of Nigel. We both expected Reuben's son to be a tasteless dim-wit like his father, a complete moron. How wrong we were.

Much to our surprise, Nigel Simlick came to our gig that weekend in Streatham. We were the headline act in a venue that also served as a bingo hall, with the Angels, a folk duo, and a band called the Road Warriors. We had now acquired a van for our equipment and a driver and roady. This was necessary because Cyril was as weak as a kitten and a useless driver. I had a new bass amp for that gig and we were using a keyboard player, a white-haired student from the Royal College of Music.

The routine for our early gigs was always the same – checking the screen-printed posters around the venue, the sound-check, a period of boredom in the afternoon, waiting to go on after the other acts had finished (longer and longer as we became more successful) and, finally, crossing the stage as the crowd chanted and stamped.

Our long sideburns and the black frock coats and stove pipe hats that we wore on stage had been Lara's idea. You see, our unique selling point was that we were a Victorian rock band. They were not real frock coats but lightweight imitations and my sideburns were stuck on with glue. That night, most of the audience was there for us. The word had gone out that the Chosen were the coming thing – we were cool. The audience ridiculed the Angels, giving them a slow hand-clap, and were indifferent to the Road Warriors. But we were a triumph. It was the best gig we had ever done. We came off stage feeling like kings.

In the dressing room, a tall man in a lilac shirt and blue corduroy trousers was waiting to see us. He was wiping his face with a handkerchief. Nigel Simlock was polite and quietly spoken, the opposite of his father. He said that he loved our music and wanted to talk to us. He offered to give me, Lara and Sid a lift back to Camberwell Grove in his car. We did not see Dean that night. He could have slept with a dozen barely-clothed women who had clustered around him after the gig like iron filings around a magnet.

Nigel had been privately educated and was used to money. Already, he possessed the kind of car that has fawn leather seats, a polished wooden dashboard and a cigar lighter. Sid sat in the front, Lara and I in the back. Nigel drove with quiet, economical efficiency. Occasionally he glanced at Lara and me in the rear view mirror. Unlike his father, he listened to what people said. Sid rolled a joint. Nigel declined it and so did I. I was still buzzing from the gig. The roads were empty. We had never been in a car like this before. It was like riding on a magic carpet.

The streets of south London were almost deserted and would have been quiet but for the singing in our ears – a mild form of tinnitus. We glided through Streatham and took the South Circular road to Tulse Hill. Nigel said that he knew the area, because he had been to school near here – Dulwich College.

"The big posh school where you have to pay?" said Sid

"That's right."

Our drummer blew out a lung-full of smoke. It filled the car.

"You know what," said Nigel. "You're bloody amazing."

"Who is?" said Sid.

"You are. I love the way you play the drums. I've never seen anything like that. You are a crazy man."

"What about him?" Sid poked his thumb towards the back seat.

"Who? Freddy? Put it this way, I've heard worse. I always think that if you notice the bass player in a band there's something wrong and that's the best compliment I can pay. As for the guitarist, he's fucking marvellous. Who is he?"

"He's called Dean Jenkins," I said.

"Where does he come from?"

"Croydon. He used to be a milk man."

"Well, he can deliver my Gold Top any time," said Nigel. "I think he's the best musician I've ever heard … really."

"Better than Vera Sidebottom?"

"No. But he has a nicer arse."

We had stopped at the traffic lights in Herne Hill, at the end of Half Moon Lane.

"Where do you get the inspiration for your songs from?" said Nigel.

"Various places," I said. "Greek and Celtic mythology, magic …"

"What about the name, The Chosen?"

I looked at Lara. Should I tell him?

"We're called that because we've been chosen by a higher agency to advance the spiritual destiny of the human race."

Nigel looked at me blankly."Who chose you?" he said.

"I could tell you, but I would have to kill you."

Sid blew out another cloud of toxic smoke. He started to giggle.

"Well, anyway," said Nigel. "I think what you are is brilliant. I like the Victorian thing that you do. I know that I can get you bigger gigs. And do you know what?" He paused for effect. "I think I can get you a recording contract."

He depressed a switch. There was a whirring sound as a window at the front of the car smoothly descended a couple of inches.

"My friend, Simon, runs a company called Divine Records out of Fulham and he's looking to sign up new acts. Different ones."

Nigel put his hand on Sid's knee, as he turned back at Lara and me on the back seat, smiling. Sid looked concerned.

"Let's not get too excited though, shall we. No promises."

I knew then that it would happen. However, there was something in his expression that I did not like.

"Okay. Whatever."

I had picked up a non-committal way of talking from Dean. It was the style of the time.

Nigel lived miles away, up at Holland Park. He dropped off the three of us in Camberwell Grove and his big white car disappeared into the darkness. My ears were still ringing.

Chapter Sixteen

Up the Revolution

Achieving success in one's adopted sphere, whether it is baking tarts or playing football, is a pleasant and gratifying experience. Normally, the recognition of one's family or peers is followed by a gradual process of wider acknowledgement, culminating, eventually, in a piece of silverware or a public honour. But the success of The Chosen was so rapid and comprehensive that it seemed supernatural. Perhaps it was. Sidgwick had said that the planetary conjunctions ushering in the New Age would become manifest at this time. Events moved quickly after Nigel Simlick had witnessed our gig in Streatham. Our progress was like that of a clockwork toy rattling across a table. On that night Nigel, rarely for a member of his family, was telling the truth. He did like our music and he did have a school friend who owned a record label. Nigel's contact came to our next gig, at a club in Charing Cross Road. The following week, we signed a recording contract.

The result was an advance on royalties of the dizzying sum of £5,000. The money translated into a van that was not a death trap and a mountain of new guitars, drums and amplifiers. It also paid for a PA system of awesome power and a month-long drugs binge that made a significant impact on the economy of south London. Increasingly we were now being written about by a tribe of frighteningly serious young men and women, who worked for what was known as the music press. They wanted to know our opinions on a range of subjects and they had pages of space to fill.

Sid was the band's idiot savant, Dean was its Delphic Oracle and I was its eager mouthpiece. To those who would listen, I expounded upon Theosophical concepts, such as the illusory nature of physical reality and the transmigration of souls. I explained, having stumbled upon the theory one drunken night in the Hermit's Cave, that Sid, Dean and I were more than a mere rock group; we were the avatars of a higher form of consciousness, which I described as Atlantean; the conduits of a lost system of vibrations. The A-waves in our music, I said, promoted love and harmony. As our music was more widely played, peace would reign on earth. The journalists smiled as their pens skidded across their pads. I was good copy.

I felt in disseminating these ideas, that I was realising the destiny that had been promised by Sidgwick. I believed that my prophecies would become self-fulfilling; this justified the fact that I was making them up as I went along. We were not special as human beings, I said, we were merely lightning conductors. But I knew, in my bones, that no-one believed me. I came to realise that rock stars were the deities of a latter-day Mount Olympus, their fame and excesses compensating for the pain and banality of the human condition. Magazines pictured their marble-tiled bathrooms, their fast cars and their swimming pools. Every so often, a new mortal would be plucked from the mud to join them, to demonstrate that theirs was a democratic pantheon. When one of their number crashed a brand new car into a tree, or choked on vomit between silk sheets, there was a sense of schadenfreude – people were reassured that being a god or goddess had its drawbacks.

We signed our recording contract in November 1968. By the following year, we had progressed from bars and small clubs to large concert halls. Our first LP was released in June. By that stage it was eagerly awaited. We were more successful than Vera Sidebottom, the biggest star on his father's roster, according to Nigel, who now had his own offices in Soho Square.

About an hour of music could be held on a so-called long player or LP. A 12-inch wide vinyl disc, it was an advance on the wax cylinder, but only just. The main advantage of LPs was that they came in cardboard slip-cases which were a convenient size for rolling joints on. There would often be what were called sleeve notes on the back, whose literary style was that of the school swot, showing off. Our album, which was called Gladstone's Bag, broke the mould. We did not want our picture on the front, that would have been far too literal, and there were no sleeve notes.

The front of the record was decorated with an abstract, swirling, mandala-like pattern, in colours so bright that they hurt your eyes. The back carried one picture of the band playing live, luridly lit by Cyril, and another of Druids celebrating the midsummer solstice. For a brief moment Gladstone's Bag was the thing to have if you were one of those people who was remotely aware of what was going on. It was more than a record; it was a cultural artefact. We knew from our social contacts that it was more popular with hippies and other non-conformists than any other record. Only a sick or desperate person would have rolled their joint across the matronly breasts of Vera Sidebottom, the singing seamstress.

It was trippy but also, in the words of Dean, it rocked. Side one was our basic set, culminating in the stomping Henge Bender. You will notice if you ever hear Gladstone's Bag – which is unlikely, I know – that there is a short bass solo on Henge Bender. I blush to admit that this was actually played by Dean, although I did play bass on the rest of the tracks. I tried to get the solo right for a day and half, in the Divine Records studio in Fulham. In the end Dean lost patience. He cracked it out in about ten minutes.

Side two, which was most popular with marijuana users, consisted of one extended piece of music called Voyage to Ecotopia. The track was created using over-dubbing, thanks to the production wizardry of Cyril. There were some strange sounds and instruments on it – echoing pipe organs, hunting horns, dawn choruses, blue whales mating, chanting football crowds, and so on. Like a London bus, it took you round the houses. You were relieved and slightly traumatised when you got to the end.

The second side of the album led to thousands of people asking whether Ecotopia existed. There was a box number to which they could write and I made sure they received replies. This was excellent. Sidgwick had asked me to save the planet and, hey presto, I had unwittingly stumbled upon a means of instant communication with disaffected people in duffel coats all over the planet. I opened a bank account – we all did. Soon, absurdly large amounts of money were flowing into them. Lara and I had travelled from penury to riches in less than two years.

August 1969 was a high-point – a well-publicised outdoor gig at Buckingham Palace Park. On that gloriously hot day we were the coolest people in London (Dean wore a dress). But we weren't different from the audience; they were us. Pictures of the gig made the front page of virtually every newspaper. Now outrage was turning to acceptance. I could see that we were becoming part of the establishment.

Shortly afterwards I was invited onto a television show broadcast during the Sunday evening God slot. I was very stoned at the time. My pupils were huge. A bishop interrogated me. He said that our music was a threat to morality. I countered that religion was the main threat to morality. I said that human spirituality had little to do with hymns and churches, arguing that churches had obliterated older pagan energies – in many cases literally, for churches often squat on the remains of pre-Christian worship sites.

I said that I would rather see God in a leaf than in a vicar and had often done so. Spirituality, I said, was a journey into the self. It required no architectural or human mediator. I asked the bishop whether he had ever been into the interior of an ancient forest where a canopy of high boughs knits together over a still green space. That to me was a church. I asked him whether he had ever smelled hawthorn blossom. That was what made headlines in the following day's newspapers – "Sniff flowers says pop man". It was great publicity.

December. Camberwell. It is a grey Sunday afternoon. Nigel sits in the kitchen in the Grove with Lara, Sid and me. Dean sometimes lives here. But he has a pad in central London. He is incapable of staying in one place, or with one woman, for very long. Most of the time, we do not see him. Sid is too dependent upon the Hermit's Cave for his pharmaceutical supplies and social contacts to leave the Grove. At least once a week we rehearse in a warehouse in Purley, where we keep our growing mountain of gear.

The papers are spread out on the table with the breakfast things, now collecting ash from Nigel's cigar and Sid's joint. In the crumpled papers are snippets of gossip about us. Nigel says that we must go easy on the drugs, especially Sid (try telling a fish not to swim). He also says that there are nasty rumours in the underground press that we are hypocritical bread heads, living rent-free when we are as wealthy as King Midas. We are growing too famous for the Grove. People know where we live – the plod especially – and that is bad.

As we eat breakfast Nigel suggests that it is time we bought a country mansion. Nothing too grand – four or five bedrooms he suggests, large grounds with stables for a studio, maybe a lake.

"A fucking lake," says Sid.

"Okay, not a lake," says Nigel. "It's too pretentious, but definitely a swimming pool."

I can foresee a problem. Swimming pools and people high on drugs do not go together – the combination invites tragedy. But I say nothing.

"Look," says Nigel, "have a shufti at these." He produces from his briefcase some glossy magazines. They are a specialised kind of pornography – publications depicting country mansions for extremely rich people.

"You know what I want," says Sid. "Our own helicopter pad."

I pick up one of the magazines. It is nauseating but fascinating. In the front pages are photographs of aristocrats, their equine faces moulded by years of in-breeding – Lady Arabella Snotgrove announces her loveless marriage to Lt. Col Rupert Dimwit of the Coldstream Guards, you know the kind of thing. Nigel has thoughtfully ringed what he feels are suitable properties. It has to be no more than an hour's drive from south London. It has to be old and tasteful and surrounded by lots of greenery to ensure that we don't disturb the neighbours. That narrows our search down to the Home Counties. Our price range is up to a quarter of a million pounds.

There are few suitable properties in the magazine Lara and I look at. Most are not in the right price bracket or are situated in the wrong place.

"Hang about," says Sid, "here's one." He reads the description beneath a small black and white photograph.

"Spenhurst Hall. Weald of Kent. Tudor manor house. Twelve bedrooms, banqueting hall, many beautiful features. Surrounded by twenty acres of parkland, with stables and boathouse."

"Yeh, I like that one," says Nigel.

I look at Lara. A chill passes through our bodies.

A week later, we drove out to Kent in Nigel's car. Dean was not with us. He had just taken up with a Japanese girl. Lara and I did not say that we knew Spenhurst as we drove into the village from London. I had been deeply shocked by the landscape around it. There were still hops and oast houses, but instead of the small-hedged fields of my youth it was a countryside of large green prairies and lonely clumps of trees. I was even more shocked when, the following summer, flowers failed to appear in the cornfields and meadows. The fields, I learned, had been doused liberally with poisonous cocktails of herbicides and pesticides. I mourned for the poppy, the corn cockle and the wild pansy; I missed the hare, the shrew and the red admiral butterfly. Even the farmers said that the countryside was not what it had once been. But that flat statement does not convey the horror of what they had done. They had taken a vibrant, teeming landscape and turned it into a wasteland. Farmers were practical people. To them fields were factories and colours and smells were superfluous.

Nigel's words brought my attention back into the car.

"I think we're here, guys," he said with a touch of irritation, implying that it had been a bad idea to give Sid the map. "This is Spenhurst."

"We can see that," said Sid, sarcastically.

Of course, Lara and I, who were sitting in the back, knew exactly where the hall was and how to get to it. We were trying to hide our mounting excitement. We allowed Nigel to drive the length of the high street, past where he should have turned off. The Celtic market cross was still there and the village green. There was the Green Man pub. It had changed little as far as I could see.

"Do you think we can get a newspaper?" said Nigel.

"Nah," said Sid, "it's the sticks. They can't even read around here."

It was Sunday lunchtime and the village was asleep. Gardens were neatly-trimmed, in their dormant winter state. Milk bottles waited obediently to be collected on door-steps. Outside the car would be a delicious aroma of a thousand Sunday lunches. In the twentieth century people could afford to eat meat every day. But the Sunday roast was still regarded as special.

We drove east towards the bridge at the edge of the village. It felt bizarre passing my uncle's old shop and remembering the winter's day when I had stood outside with Alf and discovered that Edward was dead. Today, too, the shop looked abandoned.

"Are you all right, Freddy?" said Nigel. "Is this place freaking you out?"

"No," I said, "I just remembered something."

"So did I," said Nigel. "To phone my accountant."

"What a dump," said Sid. "Holy cow, look at her."

There was an old lady on the other side of the road. She was wearing a fawn overcoat and gloves. Her hair was white. She must be coming back from church. She glanced in our direction and looked away. I realised then how incongruous and exotic we must seem. If we wound down the window the car would be fogged with cigar smoke, patchouli oil and dope.

"We could ask her directions," suggested Nigel.

"Are you joking?" said Sid.

"I'll do it," said Lara, calmly.

Nigel stopped the car – a basking shark in the tepid waters of an English village. Lara got out. Her dress, beneath a white alpaca jacket, was a sheath of aquamarine silk, with red, fish like, decorations. She was pencil thin. Her hair, tinted orange, was tied up with her copper clasp. The old lady looked at her impassively. We watched the dumb show of the directions.

"Back to the market cross and turn left," said Lara. "Then it's the first turning on the left, down a twisting drive." She smiled and a conspiratorial look passed between us. We held hands.

"Right then." Nigel restarted the purring engine with a twist of his fingers. We moved off, towards our destiny.

We could not see Spenhurst Hall properly from the road from the village. It was screened behind a laurel hedge that had consisted of little more than twigs when I had seen it last. Sid got out of the car to open the wrought iron gates at the end of the drive. Nigel slowed to a funeral cortege pace and as we turned a final corner, we saw the hall. Its stone was more weathered than I recalled; the ivy covering the walls had grown thicker. The afternoon sun at our back was sinking into the Weald, causing the hall's Tudor casements to glitter like gemstones. The venerable yew tree shadowing its north side had changed little; a century is merely the blink of an eye for a yew. But the elm on the other side of the house was battered and stooped. It was dying.

I could not remember seeing anything more beautiful.

"Jesus," said Nigel, "how much is it again?"

Sid read from the advertisement we had brought from London. "One hundred and eighty seven thousand pounds."

"We can afford that," said Nigel, "with money left over. There's the estate agent."

He was waiting for us by the front door, a dark-haired man in grey slacks and a double-breasted blazer. His handshake was limp, his smile was painted on.

"So you're the pop group then," he said. "Haven't heard of you myself but my daughter has all your records."

"We've only made one record," said Nigel, deftly parrying the estate agent's first lie.

"I suppose you would like the grand tour," the man offered. "House first, then grounds, I suggest, if that would suit. Ladies first."

He gestured Lara through the open door. His smile was unctuous. I saw a strange expression on her face. She had first arrived here with her father in the summer of 1879. Her father would have reflected upon the strange fate that had brought a penniless Polish refugee to the threshold of an English manor house. Now her face looked blank. She touched the wall in the hallway, as if to establish that it was real.

"Who lived here?" asked Sid.

"Many people," said the salesman, "as you can imagine. It was built in 1561. One of the owners, in Victorian times, was quite famous. His name was Sidgwick. He was a pill maker, I think. His associate," he lowered his voice, conspiratorially, "was Nathaniel Vane, better known as one Jack the Ripper." He smirked. "However, I don't want to frighten you." There's nothing like a good story to sell a property, he must have been thinking.

He explained that the hall had been empty for a long time. It had previously been leased to the army, to use as a training school.

"The extraordinary thing is," he said, with a greasy smile, "there's no dry-rot, very little infestation, and hardly any damp. You could move in more or less straight away."

We followed him up the staircase. Lara tried to look nonchalant. She must have been biting her tongue.

"You see this lovely Jacobean panelling. And look at these newel posts. They're original. Now, if you'll just …"

We were close to the top of the stairs. Something was waiting for us on the landing, a large grey rat. Its beady eyes swivelled from person to person. When it had finished, it scuttled off into a small hole in the wainscot.

The estate agent showed us the bedrooms and bathrooms on the first floor and the servants' quarters. Lara did not revisit her old room. He kept the ground floor drawing room, the former banqueting hall, until last. This was where Sidgwick had sat with me and told me of his life, a century before. It had known many forms of decoration since the peacock feathers and black-lacquered furniture of that era. Now the room, with its hammer-beamed ceiling, was an echoing shell. I could imagine Dean playing his electric guitar up in the minstrel's gallery. In fact, we could get the whole band up there.

Nigel was far too shrewd to tell the estate agent that we loved the house, wanted it and could pay by cash. He engaged him in at least an hour's worth of detailed negotiations, taking in drains, structural guarantees and water rates. Meanwhile, Lara, Sid and I inspected the ruins of the walled garden and marvelled at the size of the deer-park. Sid soon grew tired and his silver-painted boots were not conducive to walking very far.

We met up again at the front of the house.

"That's it then," said Nigel. "We're the lords and lady of the manor. We can move in as soon as we want."

The estate agent sped away, like a rodent, in his little red car.

"Let's get something to eat," said Sid, "I'm starving."

Dean was silent as we enthused about Spenhurst Hall the following weekend, in the kitchen at the Grove. It was unusual for him to be with us on a Sunday. We had recorded a live TV show the evening before in north London and had been driven back to the house in a small fleet of sleek black cars.

Our guitarist looked dishevelled. He always looked the worse for wear, that was his trademark. But this morning his straggly, greasy hair, shadowed eyes, chin stubble and sad expression combined to produce a woeful impression. Dean's relationship with his girlfriend was unsettling him. She had planted some seeds in his mind. He was preoccupied by images of single hands clapping, of naked people painting their rooms white with flowers and of clowns in pin-striped suits, trapped in invisible cages. But he loved playing his guitar, so he was confused.

"It's got twelve bedrooms, a deer park, stables, Jacobean panelling, a minstrel's gallery ..." Sid repeated the estate agent's list of wonders over breakfast.

"I don't want to live in a fucking stately home!" Dean jabbed out his cigarette in the remains of a fried egg.

We were all shocked.

"What is this?" Dean's eyes moved around the table. "I mean what are we? Chartered accountants? We get some money, so we scuttle off into some little bolt-hole in the green belt, next to a golf course. I hate people like that; I despise them."

"I'm a chartered accountant," said Nigel.

"Okay." Dean gesticulated with an unlit cigarette. "But that doesn't take away from what I'm saying. I mean, what're we actually doing? Next thing, we'll be sending our kids to private schools and investing in the arms trade. Well it stinks."

I could see what Dean meant. Not long before, when he was a student, he had demonstrated at embassies and jostled the police on picket lines in front of drab factories in west London. It was because of Dean's previous activities that revolutionary socialists came to our gigs. In their sober, rational minds, they thought that our music was bourgeois; it was far too frivolous to indulge in while the proletariat continued its struggle. On the other hand, they got off on it, particularly Dean's guitar playing which echoed the agonies in the soul of a Bolivian coal miner. The revolutionary socialists stuck with us from the early gigs, forming a stony-faced vanguard – an unofficial security cordon. But Dean no longer went to their meetings.

"Dean, I do understand you," I said. "But there are other factors here. First of all, it's not having money that's a crime, but what you do with it. If we bought our castle and pulled up the drawbridge, that would be really bad. But we don't have to do that. The way I see it, we can share our wealth."

"How?" Dean looked angry.

"Well. This mansion, right, it won't just be ours. It will be everybody's. Anyone will be able to stay there. And we'll have meetings." He liked that idea, I could see. "We'll use the gardens to grow things, which we'll sell. We'll also do experiments in alternative technology. All that land … just think what we can do with it. We'll be able to have festivals there, for Christ's sake. If the ownership thing really bothers you we can set up a co-operative."

Nigel looked sceptical but I could see that I could win him round. There was a non-conformist side to our manager. He had refused to join the army cadets at Dulwich College and had eventually been thrown out for "taking drugs". Sid would go along with whatever we decided. Playing the drums was what he loved; everything else was just a sideshow. Dean would disagree with me vehemently, just as he had over the name of the group. But, like most people on the left, he could be won over by logic. Eventually I would batter down his resistance and he would give in, without ever admitting it. That was the dynamic of our relationship.

I said that just because you were a revolutionary, you did not have to be bored and miserable like the down-trodden masses in some awful factory. I said that the revolution we were promoting was not just about money; that was far too materialistic an objective. It was about the way everybody lived and what they did with their time, instead of being anaesthetised by television and drugs. Drugs were good, Sid chipped in. Well, yes. I conceded the point. Our revolution, I said, was also about what you did in your front room. What was the point of promoting a new way of living, I said, if you did not live it yourself?

Dean regarded me blankly. It was hard to read any meaning in his haggard face. He stabbed another cigarette into the toxic remains of his egg.

"I'm going to bed," he said.

Chapter Seventeen

Falling Petals

The Hit Factory was the biggest music show on television in those days. It was broadcast in the early evening on Thursdays, a time when mums and dads, and their kids, would be watching. Like all successful television programmes it was based on a simple and unchanging formula. The performers were supposed to generate outrage in adults as they peered through their long fringes, dressed in outlandish costumes. "Is that a girl or a boy?" asked a million fathers. A million teenagers snorted derisively at their out-of-date parents, making a mental note of the clothes and physical movements of their heroes. Every so often a performer was allowed on the show who would appeal to the parents' or grand parents' generation – it would often be an orange-faced man in a wig, warbling a sentimental ballad; Vera Sidebottom, to Reuben Simlick's delight, was on several times.

The presenters were rotated, like crops, but the most popular was called Brendan Fowler, a faux Cockney with shoulder-length bleached hair and over-large glasses. On-screen Brendan was heterosexual – an important feature of the show was its low-angle camera shots, up girls' short skirts, as they jiggled in their Saturday night finery. Off-screen, he was of the opposite sexual orientation and a ruthless sexual predator. That was why he was known, in the business, as Brenda. The strength of Brendan's sexual interest was in inverse proportion to the age of his quarry. His career ended ignominiously, with a blanket over his head on the steps of Bow Street police station. But that is another story.

We appeared on the Hit Factory for the first time in January 1970, just after we had moved into Spenhurst Hall. It happened because a four-minute version of Henge Bender had been released as a single just before Christmas. Singles were seven-inch diameter records, played at 45 revolutions per minute – they were the offspring of LPs. The record sold like hot cakes. Dean loathed the Hit Factory and despised Brendan Fowler. But Nigel insisted that we go on. He said that our audience would understand that we viewed the proceedings with ironic detachment, particularly if we mimed badly and looked disinterested.

Of course, that simply made us more shocking to parents and more appealing to their children. Henge Bender, which had a sickly song on its B-side, played by Dean on an accoustic guitar, sold more copies than any other record – ever. There was a riot in Smethwick, apparently, when copies were slightly delayed in reaching the shops. To Dean's disgust, we were obliged, by showbiz tradition, to appear on the Hit Factory until people grew tired of us, or until a new band appeared that was even more shocking. That is what happened. We were on five times.

Backstage, February. A small cramped room in television centre, Acton. It smells of sweat and talcum powder. Coloured light bulbs frame the mirrors that line the room. Dean takes his guitar out of its case and tunes it, not that he needs to. We will be miming to a tape of our song. Brendan Fowler's head appears around the door and he totters towards us on platform shoes. Dean is wearing a white silk one-piece suit, with sequins, about one size too small. He had bought it from a stage shop in the Commercial Road, the same establishment that was patronised by his Uncle Franky. Brendan was educated at a famous public school, where he was bullied mercilessly, then at Cambridge University. But he talks, for professional and psychological reasons, like a pantomime cockney.

"Wotcher, Dean, me old China," he says with a leer. Make-up is plastered thick on his face. Beads of sweat are breaking through the beige membrane, thanks to the combined effects of hot lights and vodka.

"You know, I love your music, mate, love it to pieces. It's far better than all this kiddy crap I have to play." He winks, distorting one side of his face grotesquely. He is getting uncomfortably close to Dean, who has just lit a cigarette and clamped it onto the machine head of his guitar like an unwholesome joss stick. Soon his sickly breath will be on Dean's face. Brendan's sexual technique works through its shock value and incongruity, like a commando raid.

I observe the scene play out with a horrified fascination. I know exactly what is going to happen.

"That's a lovely whistle," says Brendon.

"What?" Dean's deep frown speaks clearly.

Brendan chooses not to pick up the signal. "Whistle and flute, suit. It looks gorgeous. Is it silk?" The Lothario's fingers brush against Dean's thigh. Dean is uncompromisingly heterosexual – we have had abundant proof of that over the past two years – and he is from Croydon. These two facts, combined with the position of Brendan's hand on his body, can only produce one result, like a chemical reaction.

"Fuck off! You wanker!" The verbal assault silences the room, like an eclipse. "Don't you EVER, EVER come fucking near me again, do you understand?"

Brendan makes a noise – it is a small, frightened gargle. He seems to shrink in size.

"Now FUCK OFF you little prick and leave me alone or I'll tear you in fucking half." The final third of the sentence is gratuitous, but elegant embellishment is Dean's thing. Even without it Brendan would have been traumatised. His face goes pale and he backs out of the room, muttering. The following day we received, by special delivery, a letter from his solicitor. But nothing ever came of it.

We are on in five minutes. That gives us just enough time to recover our composure and to see the funny side. We are giggling as we walk onto the stage, a small raised platform surrounded by cameras, shop girls and hipsters. We try hard to look moody.

A camera is on Brendan. His eyes are cold and hard through the mask of slap. A fake bonhomie, as natural to him as breathing, hides his fury. "They're here, they're hot, they're the henge men and it's still number one. Ladies n' gennelmen ... The Chosen." The second the red camera light goes off, Brendan pushes his way through the audience, demanding to see the floor manager. But now the spotlight of fame is on us. Fourteen million people watched us that night.

Later, we saw a tape of the performance. Dean disregarded health and safety laws by smoking whilst playing, or, in this case, pretending to play – he had perfected this difficult art over many years, in Croydon's snooker halls. Dean's body movements were economical but eye-catching. His expression reflected, with rapture, the showers of notes cascading from his fingers. I stood still, my long hair held in check by a top hat. I always wore black and adopted the menacing stare of a sociopath. That was my trademark.

Sid looked more stupid on the tape than he actually was. He had a head of thick blond curls, like a cherub. While playing his jaws rotated on chewing gum. His party trick, in the middle of the song, was to throw one of his sticks up in the air and catch it. We all knew that one day he would drop it on live TV. But tonight the four minutes had gone perfectly. All I had to do for the bass solo was to wiggle my fingers up and down the fret-board vaguely convincingly – the majority of our audience did not know what a bass guitar was and that it was different from what Dean was playing. There was a final mimed crash on Sid's cymbal, taped to muffle it. Then it was all over. We had done our duty and offended public morals. Fathers were shaking their heads: "That's a girl, that is. I'll bet he's never done an honest day's work in his life." Bishops were composing letters to The Times, accusing us of promoting wickedness.

The story of Brendan Fowler's humiliation by Dean in the dressing room made a small paragraph in one of the Sunday papers. But it rampaged through the music business like a forest fire. Brendan said that we were finished in the business. On the other hand, he was too greedy for vicarious success and too much of a hypocrite to make anything of it. He never made eye contact with any of us again, even when we appeared on his radio show. What a nasty man.

We always felt elated after TV gigs, but unfulfilled. On this night, Dean and Sid put on dark glasses to make them look conspicuous and we went to a club in Fulham. It was a pounding place, full of bare flesh, hair and sweat. We took speed and mescaline. The weird thing was, we were dancing to our own music. It was like hearing an echo in a canyon. Lara had watched the Hit Factory on her own at Spenhurst Hall, tingling with pride and excitement. But her mood turned to bitterness when I did not come home. I knew that I should phone her; I ignored a persistent signal coming from the back of my mind all night.

I returned to Spenhurst the following morning in a deserted railway carriage smelling of fish and took a minicab from Tonbridge station. As I pressed the doorbell I was moist and bedraggled from the night before. I was still wearing my stage clothes, minus the top hat – a white, collarless shirt, black jacket and black velvet trousers with an extravagant flare. I felt sheepish.

Lara avoided looking at me as she opened the door and turned away.

"Wait!" I put my hand on her shoulder.

Her face conveyed both suspicion and disappointment.

"Listen. We went to this brilliant club. They were playing our music. It was amazing." I realised how lame I must be sounding.

"Did you!"

"Lara, you could have come. I forgot to phone you. I was going to, honestly."

She moved closer and, I swear, sniffed me. Whatever she detected confirmed her suspicions.

"You bastard!"

"Lara, I haven't, I mean, I didn't!"

It was true. I had not actually had sex with anyone. But three women had followed me down a dark alley behind the club. In that situation, what would you have done? I mean, if you were a man?

"I knew this was going to happen." Her mouth was trembling. "You're despicable, Freddy. I knew that I couldn't trust you; I feel so stupid. I wish I had never let you back into my life."

"But I love you."

"If you did, how could you copulate with some cheap tart?"

"I didn't!"

I think that Lara realised that my defence was merely semantic.

"Go away! Just leave me alone."

I followed her across the hallway. She entered the kitchen.

"I said, leave me alone!"

"But Lara …"

There was something in her right hand. It was a carriage clock. She drew back her arm. The timepiece, bought from an antiques market in Tunbridge Wells, missed my head but took a lump of plaster out of the wall. It was the first of many similar arguments. I should have kept a list of the projectiles that Lara hurled at me. They included a display case containing a stuffed bird, a telephone and an electric toaster. We made up after two days. It was enough time, to my great relief, for the love bites on my neck to disappear.

In retrospect, the summer of 1970 was the heyday of The Chosen, our golden time. It was a brief, glorious flowering, like that of a field poppy, also signalling that the end would soon come. We did a UK tour that spring. Reading, Birmingham, Leeds, Glasgow, Bristol, Cardiff – the itinerary sounds like a list of dreary railway stations. We made up new songs on the tour bus and put them straight into our set. A second LP, contracted to be produced by the autumn, was starting to coalesce. We made preparations for a world tour and there was talk of a live album. If things had turned out differently we would have crossed the Atlantic and had a crack at America, no doubt offending the sensibilities of the Bible belt. But that was not to happen.

My ideas for the second LP were more metaphysical and abstract than those of the first. I wanted to explore, musically, the influences of non-monotheistic religions, including pantheism, on human consciousness. The record should be called, I thought, Free at Last. Dean was going in an even stranger direction. He was starting to wear white clothes off stage and to stare into the middle distance. He adopted spectacles with round lenses, even though he did not need them and a strange beard. Dean's guitar playing became more minimalist as his talent matured; he used to say that what he left out was more important than what he put in. He said that he would like to make an LP consisting of a single sustained note, over two sides. It would have an all-white slipcase, with no writing. I protested that people would not know what to ask for in the shop; Dean said that was the whole point. He then had a further brainwave – the record should not have a hole in the middle. Sid said, why not just release a hole, without an album?

Although Dean had his own wing at Spenhurst Hall we did not often see him there. Sid had bought a brand new Italian sports car. When he was not hurtling it around country lanes it sat ostentatiously on the drive in front of the hall. It was bright yellow. Furnishing and decorating Spenhurst Hall was a delight because we did not want for money. As before, Lara masterminded the process. Amazingly, she was able to use the same shop that had attracted her custom a hundred years earlier, Liberty, off Regent Street. Daily, pantechnicons arrived from London, loaded with Persian carpets, William Morris fabrics and wallpapers (his designs had proved extremely durable), pieces of furniture in rare, embossed woods, cushions, throws, mirrors, curtains and lamp shades. We spent so much money in Liberty that we virtually emptied it. We were treated with the fawning politeness that is normally reserved for Arab princes.

The drawing room, now called a lounge, was where we spent most of our time. We furnished it more simply than the other rooms. There was a thick cream carpet (this alone cost as much as a small house) and white leather armchairs and settees. They were so comfortable and free of tomcat smells that you never wished to leave them. As you can imagine, we bought the most sophisticated and expensive audio equipment available. It came from Scandinavia and its sparse design fitted the mood of the room. Our television set was a white plastic bubble. It was wired to hidden quadrophonic speakers devised by Cyril. One could press buttons and make the television rotate and levitate – rather like a chronoshere. The walls were also white, complementing the room's dark wooden beams and its icons, mirrors and paintings.

That summer, which was hot, the French windows were always open, even at night. I remember smells of jasmine and honeysuckle coming from the walled garden; the cat sunning himself; the warmth that radiated from the ancient flagstones; red and yellow petals showering from the climbing roses. I had wanted Spenhurst Hall to become a commune. But it did not happen. We did not keep animals or feed ourselves from the gardens. There was no time; we lived in the hall for less than a year, much of which was taken up by touring. I did grow some runner beans and lettuces but you could hardly have kept a mouse alive on them, let alone feed the poor.

At first, Lara blossomed in the house and loved living there. She was much occupied with painting, weaving and dyeing. She converted one of the stables into a studio and encouraged young artists to join her. For the village children, the studio and deer park were a marvellous playground. We heard their laughter all summer and the sound of electric guitars as fledgling Deans tried to copy his riffs in the stable we had made into a music room. We made plans for an outdoor music festival, the following summer.

The political meetings I had promised Dean did take place after a fashion, not that he was around very much. For the advocates of various causes – the legalisation of cannabis, sex with animals, contact with extra-terrestrials – made their way assiduously to the hall. These wild-eyed lunatics wanted The Chosen to sign their manifestos, to play at their events and to fund and publicise their crusades. In many cases the supplicants believed that what was ours was theirs. It was a democratic form of hero worship. I did not mind sharing. But I did take exception to items of jewellery and furniture, as well as guitars, disappearing from the house. One day Lara and I returned to our bedroom to find a couple making love on our four-poster bed. They looked at us, at first guiltily and then lasciviously. Lara screamed and fled. I behaved much as Uncle Edward would have done in these circumstances – like a shocked prude. It was an awful moment. After that we were more circumspect about allowing people to stay.

Our income grew even larger – the spring tour had swelled our coffers considerably. Nigel started to talk about "punitive tax rates" and to dilate upon the advantages of offshore bank accounts. A fierce stare from Dean usually stopped him in his tracks. But we had to do something with the money. Then, stoned one night with Sid, I had an idea. Why not buy my uncle's old shop in the village, and the one next door, and start a business? So we did.

The Good Vibrations Tea Rooms served a clientele of hippies and puzzled villagers. Attached to the cafe was a "head shop", where you could buy beads, joss sticks, crystals, clothes and records – preferably ours. Like a latter-day evangelist, I wrote a pamphlet for the shop in order to promote our way of life. It contained my own interpretation of Eastern mysticism.

Ecotopianism, I argued, was a new version of an old form of consciousness. The music of the Chosen would help peace and harmony to spread across the world.

The tea rooms were a sensation – nothing like them had ever been seen in Kent. Newspaper reporters, then film crews, came to do stories about the colourful invasion of Spenhurst as dusty, tie-dyed customers flocked in from farther and farther afield. Overcrowding eventually forced us to abandon our open house policy. Reluctantly we locked the gates of Spenhurst Hall, allowing only the most convincing and persistent of our visitors to get through – and those with ladders.

Spenhurst was full of bicycles again and the smell of marijuana wafted across the village green. Locals, led by the vicar, started to mutter that "the character of the village" was being lost. But they were also proud of Spenhurst's connection with a world famous rock band and they were only too happy to reap the financial benefits. Even the post office began to sell joss sticks.

We found a couple to run the tea rooms, a hippy from nearby Sidcup called Simon and his girlfriend, Emily. Nigel had gone to school with Simon – who was a softly-spoken ginger-haired man with blond eyelashes. He said that beneath Simon's easy-going nature (he smoked dope all the time) was a "business brain". Those words proved to be prophetic. Simon and Emily moved into the cramped accommodation that I had shared with my uncle aeons before and later with Alf.

September. It had been a weird and contradictory gig – at first. First of all, the sound quality was awful. The venue was a toilet and, as for the support act, let's just say that Alfie Higgs and his magic harmonioum would have been more entertaining than a bunch of brutes who communicated by grunting. In theory, it should have been a triumph. We were playing the largest theatre in Croydon. It was Dean's home town and we were at the height of our popularity. The concert had been sold out for weeks.

In practice, a large contingent of the audience was there to bury Dean, not to praise him. They were local jack the lads; it was, quite simply, a matter of sexual jealousy. The reception of our first song, Atlantis Survives, was cold, bordering on hostile. We then made the mistake of playing one of our newest songs. Croydon was not ready for it. Coins, followed by tentative beer cans and bottles began to rain down on the stage. A Neanderthal youth on the first row was fixing Dean with a look of pure hatred. The words "poof" and "wanker" emerged periodically from his cupped hands. Dean was furious. Finally, he unplugged his guitar and flung down the lead. Reversing his normal function, a security man had to restrain Dean from leaving the stage.

"Fuck it," said Dean. As the fusillade of coins and wolf whistles grew fiercer, he chopped out the opening chords of Little White Pills. That song made the hairs on the back of your neck stand on end. Followed by a spotlight Dean crossed the stage in time to the riff, moving jerkily, like an automaton. It was electrifying. Those who were bent on violence were confused, their support melting away. Whistles turned to cheers as the crowd realised that Dean was an authentic guitar hero. He would have been proud to learn that £10,000 worth of damage was done to the auditorium that night. There were three arrests.

The hall shook to its foundations. The crowd was fused by sweat and motion into a stomping, cheering beast. This caused us to play louder and faster, like feedback. We segued from Little White Pills into Henge Bender. The song built from a simple bass riff and drum pattern into a resounding affirmation that we were the best band on the planet, or at least in Croydon, that night. After we had finished, the audience would not let us go off! If we had, there would have been a riot.

We could see the theatre manager gesticulating wildly as he argued with Nigel Simlick at the side of the stage. Soon they started to wrestle with each other. The plush seats were in shreds;

the stage was sticky with beer. Dean looked at Sid and me and made an agreed signal with his thumb and forefinger. He played the intro to the Cave of Artemis. In this song he constructed a spacious melody from a funky riff; he knew that it would gently wind the crowd down from its euphoria, allowing us to finish the set. After the gig, Dean was carried off the stage on the shoulders of the same youths who had mocked him. His small, white form bobbed up and down on the dense crowd – like a footballer on cup final day. That was the last time I was to see him. Sid and I quietly made our way to the dressing room.

I drove to London Bridge station with Nigel, in his Bentley, to catch a train. Sid was to join Dean at a hotel near Croydon where a whole floor had been booked for us. There was to be a post-gig party for the band and its entourage.

Spenhurst Hall was dark and silent. I let myself in and made my way to the kitchen to put the kettle on. My body was still tingling with adrenaline. I was feeling smug. I had proved to Lara, definitively, that I could avoid the temptation presented by dozens of hysterical women flinging themselves at me. If Dean was unavailable for sex, the bass player, according to rock protocol, was an acceptable alternative, a minor achievement, like scoring a half-century in cricket. I turned on the switch filling the room with painful white light. The first thing I saw was a note on the table.

Dear Freddy,

I have left you. It is a difficult decision because I love you so much, but I know that it is for the best. I do not think that you have been aware of me for the past year. Of course, I am glad that you have been a success. But did you ever think how it would make me feel? You never listen to me anymore; you never seem to notice what I do. At night, I long for you and I cry for you. I want to feel you; I want you to hold your big strong body against me. But you are not there; you have not been there for a long time. I miss you, Freddy. I do not

think that you realise how much I want you and how sad I am. That is why I am going away. It is not an easy decision. But it is what I feel that I must do. I hope that, one day, you will understand.
With love, Lara.

PS Papa told me in Wales where the second chronosphere, the Icarus, was hidden; it was not destroyed by Nathaniel Vane. I have gone to another time and place. Please do not try to follow me.

One of Lara's tears had left a small indentation, like a pock-mark, at the bottom of the paper. Soon I noticed that things were missing from the kitchen. Her things. Lara had removed all of them, down to the tiniest objects. That was when I realised that she was not coming back. I began to howl like an animal. I drank half a bottle of whisky. Later I took a knife from the dresser and made small deep cuts on my left forearm. The marks are still there – a row of faint white scarifications, like the indentations on a hillside, marking an ancient tumulus.

Chapter Eighteen

A Journey to Heaven

I spent a sleepless night, sweating with terror. Lying in our bed, I could not accept the fact that Lara was gone. My brain tormented itself with re-enactments of past events. What would have happened if I had done this, or that, differently? But it kept short-circuiting. All of my thoughts led back to one ineluctable conclusion. The fact that I may never see her again and, even worse, never touch her face, never share her bed. At dawn, I was still awake, wishing that I had gone to sleep and never woken up. It was midday, I remember looking at the clock, when a noise summoned me from the depths of my despair. It was the telephone. I stumbled downstairs.

I heard Nigel Simlick's voice, calm and measured. "Is that Freddy?"

"Yeh."

"I have some bad news for you." There was a silence. Did he know about Lara?

"Yeh, what?"

"It's very bad. I'm afraid that Dean is dead."

"What?"

I felt like a punch-drunk man being hit on the side of the head.

"What are you talking about? We were with him, last night at the gig. I mean, he was in the audience. He was on their shoulders."

"Listen." Nigel's emotions were always controlled. "I'm just telling you because it's going to be all over tomorrow's papers. You need to know what happened. And there's something else. Sid has had a car accident."

"Sorry."

"He was driving from the gig to see Dean and he crashed. But don't worry he's still alive."

That's good news, I thought. Sid is still alive. "Where is he?"

"At St. Helier's Hospital." He paused. "There's a problem though."

"What's that?"

"He's lost one of his arms."

"What?"

I expected Nigel to giggle and tell me that it was all a joke. But he didn't.

"Don't go anywhere," he said. "I'm coming over." He hung up.

I sat in the lounge drinking until Nigel arrived. My head felt as if it were stuffed with wadding. Other people called me and I was able to piece together what had happened. Dean had suffered heart failure, probably caused by a drugs overdose, in his hotel room. Sid was critical but hanging on. However, his right arm had been amputated. That was all I knew by the time Nigel rang on the doorbell.

A legend gradually accreted around Dean's death, based on lurid stories in the newspapers and the facts that came out at the inquest. It was reported that unfeasibly large quantities of drugs were found in his bloodstream, as well as a prescription medicine for asthma. It was said that he had drunk up to fourteen double vodkas in the bar of the hotel before going upstairs. A half-consumed bottle of the same spirit was found in his room. That, at least, I knew would be true. It was rumoured that there had been seven women in Dean's room, of four different nationalities. There were some lewd variations of the story, involving an ice bucket and a python.

These appear to have been pure invention but they acquired the status of facts. The newspapers recorded that only one woman was present when room service was called at four o'clock in the morning as Dean fought for breath in the bathroom. An ambulance was called and took him to hospital. He died on the way there. As for Sid, driving far too fast, he had skidded on leaves at a sharp bend at Carshalton Beeches and had crashed into a wall. His right arm had been smashed.

Dean's last rites were held at a crematorium in Thornton Heath. Apart from press photographers and reporters, his father was there, me, Nigel, Sid and his Uncle Franky, a wizened man, bent with arthritis. Sid was as pale as a ghost. A sleeve of his charcoal grey suit was pinned poignantly to his jacket. They played a track from Gladstone's bag, as the coffin slid into the furnace. It sounded weak and tinny, but it still made us cry. Dean's dad said some words about how Dean was free at last; his soul had left the prison of his body. My eyes gushed like fire hydrants. We all went back to a dark little house in Croydon and ate sausage rolls.

"Hi, Freddy?" Nigel phoned me at Spenhurst Hall, a week later. "I've something to tell you."

I had not bounced back and had no energy. Even my hair was listless. Oh God, I thought, here we go.

"I really don't want you to worry about this, because it may never happen. But I do feel that I have to keep you informed."

"What?"

"Well, you know we're being sued over that gig in Croydon. I've spoken to our solicitor, and I think we'll have to settle out of court. Also, you'll be aware that we're in dispute with that American promoter. And that we have to pay the record company its advance back."

"So?"

"After all that, I'm going to have real problems paying the mortgage on Spenhurst Hall – especially as we've lost Dean and our drummer only has one arm. Basically, we're broke."

"How can we be?" I said. "What about the tea rooms?"

"That's what I was going to tell you. You know Simon and Emily? Well, I've found out that they've been defrauding us, on a large scale. I've checked the account and there's absolutely nothing in it. In fact, there's an overdraft."

"Don't be ridiculous. Haven't you spoken to them?"

"Can't"

"Why not?"

"Because they've gone. They've fucked off."

"There's the stock, though."

"What do you mean?"

"The stuff in the shop. That must be worth something."

Nigel was silent for a moment. "There's nothing in there, Freddy mate, I went over on Tuesday to have a look. It's as clean as a whistle."

I pictured the interior of the shop – cobwebs, sun-curled posters, sad letters on an unswept floor.

"But you knew Simon," I said. "You went to school with him."

"Yeh, well I was wrong about him. Look, we really need to talk about the mortgage."

His mind had already dismissed the problem and flicked to something else. I saw him, suddenly, as a snake oil salesman, a vendor of ice to Eskimos, a glib, expensively-educated version of his father. After two years the spell that had made our relationship possible was broken. A hard, cold feeling came over me.

"I don't want to talk at the moment," I said, "I'm really tired."

"Look Freddy, we've got to ..."

"Sorry, I can't deal with this now." I put down the receiver.

He called back a couple of times, but I did not answer.

The little world that we had created disappeared quite quickly. Spenhurst Hall was repossessed in January 1971. Bailiffs had stripped it long before then. It was empty and hollow on the day I moved out, with my bass guitar and a few clothes. Everything the bailiffs didn't want I left there – photographs, books, Lara's dresses. I also left my heart. I was a broken man, living on tranquilizers and strong lager. I had even fallen out with Sid. A while later, he joined a country and western band called The Lucky Seven, based in Balham. They were quite successful. There were lots of articles about him in magazines – "One-armed drummer's brave battle", you know the kind of thing.

Although I had a little money left in the bank I hitch-hiked lifts into London, on the Sevenoaks road, one cold December morning. Hitching, as it was known, was begging rides from cars at the side of the road, with one's destination written forlornly on a piece of cardboard. It was a bit like playing Russian roulette. I was wearing Dean's old coat, with the fur collar.

A builder's van took me through Greenwich into New Cross. New Cross is a cold, gritty place, where an arctic wind is always blowing. The driver took pity on me and offered me a job labouring. I declined. He set me down in the Old Kent Road. It was raining heavily. All of the colour had washed from the people and the sky. I caught a bus to Camberwell.

I was fortunate because our old squat in Camberwell Grove was empty. Its ground floor windows were covered with sheets of plywood; it was not too difficult to prise one of them off and climb through. I thought of Sid breaking in and of the golden, inebriated day when we had arrived – me, Lara, Sid and Dean.

One morning I was awoken from a horrible dream of snakes and scorpions by a loud hammering coming from downstairs. Only bailiffs and policemen bashed on doors like that. I don't know why I responded as I did; normally I would have rolled over and gone back to sleep. Something impelled me to wrap a stained sheet about my shoulders, make my way to the landing window and investigate. I looked and felt terrible. My hair was mostly gone – I had hacked it off into bristling, savage clumps, with blunt scissors. I had been wearing the same clothes for days and my diet of beer and pizzas was oozing through my skin like a greasy shadow. The sour taste in my mouth was now permanent.

You don't bother to brush your teeth if you are as depressed as I was.

Sighing, I pulled back a soot-blackened curtain to see what was going on. A large, rich person's car was parked on the kerb. It was predominantly silver, with long, curving wings and a pale blue roof and bonnet. Nigel Simlick, I immediately thought. Fuck him. I was about to turn away when I saw a man standing by the front gate, peering anxiously upwards. He was wearing a neat grey suit. What made him look unusual were his long, flowing locks of white hair. It was the hair of a shaman. Sidgwick.

I was feeling so negative that I almost did not go downstairs to let him in. My first preference was to sit on the stairs stewing in my own juices, blaming Sidgwick, along with everyone else I had ever known, for what had happened. Look at me, my tortured soul declaimed; look how messed up I am. The problem with this strategy was that nobody could see me. I went downstairs.

"Friedrich, my dear boy!"

He appraised me, like a man examining a horse. "What on earth has happened to you?"

I looked into his face. Hair now covered most of it. His grey eyes were clear and steady – Lara's eyes. A convulsion racked through my body and I began to sob as if I was vomiting despair. My soul left my body. This allowed me to see myself for the first time since Lara had left me – a crumpled, dishevelled victim, standing on the doorstep. Because we love, we also despair. If we could wipe our minds clean, like computer discs, there would be no problem.

Sidgwick hugged me for a long time. He brushed his hand across my shaved scalp. "Don't worry," he kept saying, "I am here now. Everything will be alright." I realised then that I actually loved him. I started to sob even harder.

"Dear oh dear." His English was better now; it was less idiomatic. He was wearing a well-pressed white shirt with a blue paisley tie and smelt faintly of liniment. Beneath his grey jacket was a waistcoat. Looped from pocket to pocket was a gold chain. It was Alf's old fob watch."You have certainly been through the wars, my boy."

Sidgwick studied my face. Did he know about Lara? He must do? A shaft of unhappiness impaled me.

"Come, I have something to show you." He led me down the path.

I glanced back at the house. I was never to return there.

"Do you like it?" asked Sidgwick. He placed a fatherly hand on the bonnet of the car. Our eyes were drawn at the same time to the well-polished mascot at the top of the vertical, chromium-plated radiator, the silver lady. "It's a Rolls Royce Silver Cloud, mark one."

Sidgwick looked proud; not because he owned the car, but because the human race had produced such a wonderful artefact. Its large silver wings swept back in a graceful arc. The car's impeccable styling – the narrow door pillars, the carefully-defined wheel arches – hid its enormous size and power. It was regal. The Silver Cloud's six-cylinder engine and its four-speed automatic gearbox had added up to a miracle of power and smoothness when it first came off the production line in April 1955. Fewer than three thousand of this model were made. Sidgwick's had been only the seventh to leave the factory in Crewe, he told me proudly.

When he opened the passenger door a smell of leather wafted out of the car. That smell and the yielding stiffness of the front seat; the sense of being cocooned inside something immensely strong, acted like a sedative on my nerves. Sidgwick positioned himself in the driver seat. His eyes moved slowly along the mahogany dashboard.

"Are you comfortable?"

I nodded.

"Good. Would you like to hear some music?" He turned the

ignition key. You could barely hear the engine – it was more like being in a boat than a car. The opening bars from Voyage to Ecopotia slid silkily into our ears; the song began deceptively softly.

"I have come to see you, because I have something to show you."

"How did you know where I was?"

"This was not difficult, Friedrich. You are famous, you know."

"I was famous."

The song reached a passage of impossibly rapid notes played by Dean. It sounded like Handel.

"Your music is very good."

"Thank you."

I had not heard Gladstone's Bag, since going to a club in Fulham with Dean and Sid, after we appeared on the Hit Machine. I had been so happy that night, before a deep, dark precipice had opened up beneath me.

"You have done well to become successful so quickly," said Sidgwick. "You have offered people, in your music, a glimpse of an earthly paradise."

"We were off our heads all the time."

"That is why your music is so good. There is a danger in it. There is darkness as well as light."

Dean's guitar began to soar through the car. His playing was like being on speed but it squeezed your heart with its beauty.

"I can't believe he's dead." I had spoken my thoughts aloud.

"I know, Friedrich." Sidgwick looked at me.

"Is he dead?"

He looked away. "I have not come here to talk about metaphysics. I have come to take you somewhere."

Croydon? Biggin Hill? The Downs of West Sussex? My mind reviewed the possibilities. I pictured a therapeutic pint of bitter in a fire-lit pub.

"I have made some modifications to the Silver Cloud," he

continued. "The vehicle is ideally suited to the purpose of Time Travel. I think that through this I may have invalidated the car's service contract, but that is a small price to pay. You will find that this machine is a lot more comfortable than the Daedalus and the Icarus were."

I remembered our bone-jarring journeys in the chronospheres and the headaches and nausea that had accompanied them.

"Where are we going?" I asked.

"To heaven."

Sidgwick did not wait for my reaction. His long fingers moved busily, setting the parameters of our destination. He activated a control, which, I guessed, converted the gear stick to the more extraordinary function of Time Lever. He pushed it forwards. The car windows turned green, then purple, then black. Sparks of light showered from the silver lady's head as she breasted us through Time. For a few moments we were buffeted and jostled, like wind-blown seeds, as our tiniest sub-atomic particles expanded to fill the universe. There was a long, rumbling explosion. Time tossed us down, finally, like a sun-bleached bone. The roar died back to a hum. The windows lightened. I was surprised, because I did not feel sick or light-headed.

Sidgwick looked at me reassuringly. "Welcome to heaven," Friedrich, he said. "Or ecotopia, as we should call it."

It looked like the south coast of Kent to me. A grey road ribboned through smooth green fields edged by white cliffs, as if a giant had truncated the chalk hills with a cleaver. The sun was shining. The sky was perfectly blue.

"The weather's nice," I said. It was banal but it was the first thing that came into my head.

"It always is, Friedrich. Shall we proceed?"

His bony hand reached for the dashboard. With the purr of the engine came the sound of Voyage to Ecotopia – a slow passage containing the sound of bird song and a church organ.

"Where are we going now?"

"To the Acacia Hotel. It is not very far. You will be able to ask me questions on the way."

Sidgwick slipped the car into drive. The vehicle moved forwards sedately, like a big cat. I did not say anything at first, lost in my own thoughts. Thousands of feet below us were tiny black dots on chrome yellow beaches. Holiday makers.

"What became of the Ordovice?" I asked.

Sidgwick chuckled.

"Oh them. It is such a long time ago. Let me see now. Well, Caractacus was not trampled by the fairy cattle of the Tuatha de Danann. He escaped and made his way, crawling through ditches, to the Roman headquarters in Colchester. The Ordovice were jubilant after their victory. They accepted Caractactus's brother, Guidavius, as their leader. There was a meeting of the tribes at which it was decided that Queen Zoatastra of the Brigantes would be leader of all the Celts. But Boudicca was jealous and attempted to have Zoatrastra poisoned – that re-opened a feud between the Brigantes and the Iceni. The Roman IXth legion picked off what was left of the Iceni in a huge battle in a place called Honor Oak, south of the Thames."

"What happend to Caractacus?"

Sidgwick smiled. "That is the only good part of the story. He went to Rome but the emperor Nero did not take to him as Claudius had done. He was fed to the lions in the Coliseum, in AD 64." He chuckled to himself.

"So the Celts were beaten?"

"Yes. But that was always going to happen. My main task had been to innovate a written language for them so that their magnificent achievements would be recorded by history. We remember the Romans as civilised and their enemies as crude barbarians, Friedrich, because we read only Roman books. But the Celts were just as advanced. They were the first Europeans to build stone circles and tombs for their chieftains. They understood ship building and solar time long before the Mediterranean peoples. They lived with nature. They did not fight it."

"Did you succeed in your project?"

"I did not. The Druids did not want to lose their mastery of a secret lore, for their power was based on it, and they turned against me. The night before the Iceni's final battle Boudicca's sister, Katia, told me that I was to be killed. I was forced to flee, to lick my wounds. My hopes then centred on you, Freddy, and your music, to save the planet."

"That was a mistake," I said.

Sidgwick turned in his seat. The car crested a hill. It began a long descent to a bright emerald bay.

"On the contrary, my dear boy. Your successes have been remarkable. I am well pleased with you."

"What successes?" I felt depressed; my self-esteem was extremely low.

"Well, you prevented the First World War from happening."

"What?" I was aghast.

"You may not have meant to, but after you had rescued Alfred from the trenches, your thought patterns, and his, shaped events through their subtle influence upon the people around you. Because of you, the world was saved from a colossal conflagration that would have decimated an entire generation."

"Really?"

"That is not all that you achieved, Friedrich." He slowed the car fractionally, steering it expertly through a bend. "The British constitution was also modernised by the energies that you liberated. The House of Lords was reformed and a democratic Socialist party attained a strong hold on power."

"It was still essentially a bourgeois state," I said. "Marx would not have regarded that as an achievement."

"Marx was wrong," said Sidgwick. "He did not like the idea of democracy because it would have threatened his own power and that of his friends. The man was a bully."

"But if the world had followed his ideas …" I began.

"The results would have been appalling. The egotism of his followers was over-whelming. The pretenders to his crown would have butchered each other. Whole races would have been sacrificed in the name of a crude dogma."

"But …"

"There are no buts, Friedrich. Democracy is a good thing. That is one lesson that I have learnt from history."

I was hungry, for my mind, released from its former torpor, was imposing demands upon my body. Sidgwick proposed that we stop at an inn, the Sea Spray, where they served a fine ploughman's lunch. I was surprised that people ate in heaven. Sidgwick replied what could be more of a treat than English bitter and cheddar cheese?

The pub was at the mouth of a valley cut by a small languid river through the chalk. We ate at a wooden bench outside. The tang of sea air and the sparkling eyes of the barmaid increased my appetite. The blonde-haired girl noticed the Rolls Royce and smiled. She did not say anything. The food was delicious but we did not linger. To my surprise, Sidgwick did not pay for the meal with a bank note but with a small rectangle of plastic.

It contained, he explained, on a thin strip, a record of his worldly goods. Money, he said, no longer distorted people's pockets. And work, in the old sense, was no longer necessary since the advent of totally automated factories. Those who wished to be were still busy and people still made things, but purely for their pleasure – they no longer exchanged their labour for what he described as magic numbers. Soon, he said, these numbers would not be required at all and the plastic cards would fade away just as surely as bank notes and coins had done. That was the ultimate sign of a truly advanced society – not the end of capitalism, but the end of money. It was simple. When want and the need for rationing were abolished, and when men and women were at peace with themselves, money was redundant. Sidgwick encouraged me to finish my beer and to stop looking at the barmaid's smiling face and at her small round breasts. She had vaguely aroused my libido, a welcome sign that my depression was ending.

The road ran at sea level by a coastal lagoon before turning inland. A sharp breeze was blowing off the sea. Leaving the wetland area of reeds and wagtails we climbed into a valley. It was early summer. The hillsides were splashed with poppies, like gouts of blood. Larks were singing – more larks than I had heard since the nineteenth century. I asked Sidgwick what year it was – the question had not occurred to me before.

He said that it did not matter. The year did not need to be recorded anymore. Time, in that sense, had stopped. But if I really wanted to know, it was the first of June, 2058. That was strange, I told Sidgwick. It was my birthday. I was exactly two hundred years old!

Sidgwick said that I did not look it. We would crack a bottle of Dom Perignon, as soon as we got to the Acacia Hotel.

"What is it like in 2058?" I asked.

Sidgwick gave me a curious look. "It is ecotopia, Friedrich; the state of grace that you and I have worked towards."

"Meaning?"

"No wars, a population in balance with its environment, stable ecosystems."

"But how …"

Sidgwick answered the question before I had completed it "For a long time it was touch and go. In the second half of the twentieth-century the competitiveness and madness of the human race reached new heights. In the 1940s, a super weapon was developed that could destroy all life upon the planet. States tussled for global domination as stocks of oil, the basis of their wealth, were depleted. They greedily ravaged the environment. We thought that we were so strong. But our strength was that of an emasculated and alienated man; it was really weakness. Weak, pathetic men make by far the worst tyrants, Friedrich. This is something else that I have learned."

"I see."

"Because of our delusions, the seas were poisoned, the ice caps melted, the forests were desecrated. Do you know that more than half the species contained in the forests were lost in the twentieth-century alone, while the human population approached nine billion. In Britain, we slewed the countryside with chemicals to produce food that we did not need. We stripped the landscape of our native plants and animal species." There was spittle on his lips.

"We destroyed our natural environment, Friedrich, like a child with a chainsaw. We gobbled down chemically-produced food and we drowned in plastic waste, which we buried in holes in the ground. We gave so-called farmers huge subsidies to dig up hedges and to keep animals in concrete prisons, dosed with growth promoters and antibiotics."

A long straight road was taking us through a heath nibbled by sheep.

"Well, something good must have happened," I said. "I mean, look at the landscape now. It's full of flowers and birds. How did that happen?"

"It was science, Friedrich. I know that this is a paradox. It took me a long time to understand. But that which destroys can also be a force for good."

"What do you mean?"

He sighed. "Humans evolved slowly. But their machines did not. And they solved many of our problems, as they had always done. Take this car. Like the chronospheres it is powered by anti-matter. It removes nothing from the environment and it adds nothing, unlike a crude rocket that sucks ozone from the sky."

"But surely science is the villain of the piece," I protested. "Look at ..."

"No, Friedrich," said Sidgwick. "Let me explain it to you. Science and magic are not opposites, they are complementary, like the two sides of a coin. Science is magic; it is the magic that we understand. Do not fall for the Frankenstein myth – the idea that tampering with nature will bring down a curse upon humanity. It is nonsense. For God's sake, we have been interfering with nature since the Stone Age!"

At that moment, by an extraordinary coincidence, the car passed a giant etched from chalk on a hillside. It had been drawn in the Neolithic period with a few neat, sinuous lines.

"The problem was not science, *per se*. The key to our success was working sympathetically with nature, not against it, as we had done when we had poisoned the seas and cut down the trees. The key lay in our realising that the earth is rare, Friedrich. It is an exceptional, beautiful and precious place. We are lucky to have it. We are blessed."

He lowered his voice. "I am so sorry. I did not mean to make a speech."

"No, no," I said. "I don't mind."

"For example, look at surveillance technology," he continued. "Cameras tracking us all the time, so that we are watched everywhere. And computers reading our minds and anticipating our needs. You would think that these things are bad?"

"Perhaps." I shrugged.

"Well, you are wrong. They are actually good things."

"How do you mean?"

He shifted in his seat. "Let me ask you a question. Would you mind your movements being constantly monitored by cameras, Friedrich, if it made you completely safe? Safe from being attacked and robbed. Safe from any harm, in fact."

I thought for a moment. "Of course not."

"Nobody would, apart from a few idiots and crackpots. There was an idea that surveillance would inevitably lead to a tyranny of 'us' by 'them'. It took a long time for the human race to realise that there was no 'us' or 'them'; there was only 'we'. Opposition to scientific advances were based upon the Frankenstein myth or a sense of guilt – a feeling that the human race is inherently sinful, that it has fallen." He smiled. "Feudal landowners opposed progress the most because they had the most to lose. Marxists were also terrified by scientific ingenuity and the progress that it brought because it challenged their control. Once a genie is out of the bottle it cannot be put back in."

He continued. "Once all of our actions were observed all the time, how could we commit crimes? This was omniscience – one of the characteristics of godliness. We were now watching over us. People could give complete strangers lifts in their cars quite safely, and welcome them into their homes. There was no need for taxis or buses clogging up the streets. People talked to each other without fear." He stopped and pursed his lips. "What are the other characteristics of godliness, Friedrich?"

"Let me see." I reflected. "Omnipotence and eternal life?"

"Thank you. Well, we have now achieved all three of the characteristics. Or we are very close. In other words, we human beings, have become gods. The gods of our own heaven."

"But surely ..."

There were naturally many questions in my mind. But there was no time to ask them. The car slowed. We had rounded a final corner, revealing, to our right, the Acacia Hotel.

Chapter Nineteen

The Music Hall Riots

The hotel was a white, flat-roofed building, on top of a hill. There was something health-promoting in the clean, square lines defined by its windows and roof terraces, which were feathered by trailing plants. The building was surrounded by tall Douglas firs. It commanded a fine view of the sea. Sidgwick seemed about to speak when a chirruping sound came from his jacket.

"Excuse me," he said, reaching into his pocket. He pulled out a rectangular object about the size of a small hip flask and clipped it onto the dashboard. The device had a round-cornered screen, like a miniature television. A man's face looked out from it, smooth and beardless. His pin-prick eyes met mine then turned away to face the driver. Sidgwick spoke with an edge in his voice. He was almost curt, I thought.

"I cannot talk now. I am in the car."

The tiny lips moved. "When can you …"

"I do not know. Perhaps when I have washed and changed. I will tell you when I am ready. Good-bye."

It was the first time I had ever heard him sound cross. "What was that?"

"It was nothing, Friedrich, merely a business matter."

"No, I mean the machine."

"Oh I see." Sidgwick seemed relieved that my query was merely technical. "It is an amos – an advanced mobile operating system."

"What is that?"

"You would recognise in it elements of a telephone, a television and a computer, but it is also a diagnostic device and a navigation system. It monitors my bodily function. It also indicates exactly where I am at any time, with the aid of a satellite orbiting the earth."

"May I see?"

"Of course." Sidgwick unclipped the device from the dashboard. It moulded itself to one's hand, featureless except for its blank screen and a little green eye that winked. Sidgwick explained that the amos responded to verbal commands. He demonstrated this by asking it the time. The device replied, in a neutral southern English voice, that it was three-thirty pm on the first of June. The device then asked him why he was in bad mood. Sidgwick sighed heavily and turned it off.

"You can talk to it?" I said.

"In a sense, Friedrich. It is programmed to pick up cues from one's voice and to make appropriate responses, rather like a psychoanalyst. Initially, its conversational range is limited to a few pre-programmed topics – astrophysics, bee keeping, coin collecting. Of course, it can learn from its interlocutions and build up a store of useful knowledge. In this respect, it is different from a psychoanalyst." He chuckled.

It occurred to me that such a brainbox must be incredibly expensive. Sigdwick said that, on the contrary, only slightly less sophisticated devices were given away as prizes in Christmas crackers.

We turned into a gravel drive leading to a car park. It now struck me, for the first time, that I was wearing a stained tee shirt and a pair of frayed, filthy trousers. I was not dressed for a country hotel. Sidgwick seemed to read my mind.

"Do not worry about your appearance, Friedrich. There will be clothes for you in your room. In any case, you will be meeting old friends. There is no reason to be nervous."

"Will Lara be there?"

He looked at me strangely but said nothing.

We stopped. Three other vehicles were parked nearby – a green open-topped Bugati, a three-litre Lagonda and a beautiful Hispano-Suiza. It was bright but not too hot. A cool breeze caressed the fir trees. My nostrils detected brine, pine needles and suntan lotion, an exciting, stomach-tightening aroma. Sidgwick removed a brown leather suitcase and a Panama hat from the boot of the car.

"Do not worry that you have no luggage, Friedrich," he said, answering my concern. "You will find that all is ready for you."

A blue-uniformed porter took Sidgwick's bag. We followed him into a marble-tiled lobby and stood at the reception desk. A languid ceiling fan pushed shadows across the floor; there were parlour palms and Chinese vases. Sidgwick checked us in.

He turned round. "Friedrich, it is an indulgence, but there is something I would like you to do for me, if you would be so kind. Can you meet me here in half an hour's time? I would like you to help with one small task." He smiled winningly.

How could I resist? "Of course."

"Very good." He looked at Alf's pocket watch. "I will meet you here at four o'clock? When we have finished our little job, we shall return here. Six o'clock is the hour of cocktails."

A porter insisted on accompanying me to my room. In the room, neatly prepared, were a white linen suit and some pale blue, well-ironed shirts. Everything fitted perfectly. My safety razor, or one exactly like it, had been placed on the glass shelf in the bathroom, with a fresh blade. There was a rattan chair by the bed and a washstand, although this was entirely decorative. A door led to a balcony overlooking the sea. I took off my clothes, had a bath and put on a fresh skin. Suddenly, I realised that something felt different – I was happy! Sidgwick had told me that a change of scenery would do me good.

I stood on the balcony feeling the soft sea breeze on my face. Inland, beyond the downs was a patchwork quilt of fields and woodlands. Further along the coast I could see lines of houses following the contours of hills and a sparkling bay. I had been in this vicinity years before. It was one of my favourite places, Hastings. I observed tiny specks moving in the water and the colourful triangles of sails. Above the town was a forest of slowly-moving white propellers, like sycamore seeds. I guessed that this was a wind farm. In the previous century some misguided conservators of the countryside had claimed that wind farms were ugly and opposed them on aesthetic grounds. Actually, they were beautiful.

Occasionally a flying machine wheeled over the cliff tops. They were small, light craft with buzzing engines and fabric wings, like the biplanes of the Edwardian era. Sidgwick had told me that speed was not worshipped or fetishized in 2058. Now that human beings could travel as fast as they had ever desired, they had rediscovered the aesthetic and sensual pleasures of earlier forms of transport. Inland, canal barges moved slowly through the shires. For international journeys, airships were often used. A lovely silver-skinned craft with a long, cigar-shaped gondola, left for India each week from a mooring mast near Bexhill-on-Sea. It was called the Karina. It took three days to make the journey to Bombay, stopping overnight in Algiers and then in Cairo, with a morning detour over the pyramids.

I breathed in the sea and the sky. My head filled with light and I thought that it would explode. We've made it, I thought; this was paradise. To be honest, I began to blub. I did not know if my tears were from joy or sadness. At length, I stepped in from the balcony. I love hotels and have always wanted to live in one – imagine never having to wash your clothes or tidy up.

I decided to distract myself before meeting Sidgwick in the lobby. There was no television in the room. But, looped on a hook above the headboard was a helmet, incorporating headphones and a pull-down visor. Sidgwick had told me something of virtual reality during the car journey. He said this technology now made it possible to live in one's dreams or memories, or other people's. One could also interact with phantasmagoric landscapes that were entirely imaginary. Or were they? Virtual reality had created its own ontology. It was the melting pot of dream, memory and fantasy.

Have you ever felt the coarse grass of the African savannah between your toes? Have you sniffed the rancid aroma of a gorilla's lair, high in the trees, gazed across the immensity of the Antarctic, or stood upon a Himalayan peak, giddy in the thin air? I did. And that was only the demonstration programme of the voice-activated virtual reality helmet. I could become a character in any film ever made; I could revisit the events of my childhood, out on the lonely ice-pack of memory; I could create an entirely new landscape, and live in it, evoked from my imagination, or from an adventure story I had read in my uncle's bookshop years before.

Sidgwick had told me that the initial thrill of virtual reality wore of, particularly once the erotic possibilities had been plundered. But it was not merely a toy. It gave each gender access to the sensory experiences of the other. And this had changed the relationship between the sexes; old conflicts, based upon prejudices and misconceptions, had dissolved. It also allowed people to go to battle without killing others, offering a vicarious outlet for their destructiveness. My own explorations were voluntarily curtailed on this occasion. I dragged myself from the deserts of Mars, realising that I had to meet Sidgwick in only ten minutes. Feeling slightly apprehensive, I went into the bathroom. I shaved carefully and brushed what was left of my hair.

Sidgwick was waiting for me. He glanced at his pocket watch. "You're late Friedrich," he said, tersely. "Come with me."

We strode across the lobby. He had left the Rolls unlocked. Without saying anything he inserted the ignition key. The engine began to purr.

"Where are we going?"

Sidgwick turned in his seat. "I shall tell you when we get there. Are you strapped in?"

I nodded.

"Good." He pushed the Time Lever forwards. I shut my eyes, not particularly wishing to witness a pyrotechnic display around the car. After only a few moments I could tell that we had arrived at our destination. There was stillness around the car. My ears could detect a faint sound of birdsong. I opened my eyes. We were surrounded by closely-shaved grass. The car was parked between London plane trees, at the edge of what looked like a park. There was no-one about. I guessed that it was early morning.

"Where are we?"

"We are in Finsbury Park." He turned off the ignition.

"Now, you must listen to my instructions and you must follow them exactly, even if they seem strange to you."

I murmured my assent.

"The date is the 30th of April, 1907, and we are in north London." He paused. "Tonight, close to here, in an obscure church, an extremely important event is set to take place, the Fifth Congress of the Russian Social Democratic Labour party."

"The fifth what?"

"It is a meeting, that is all you need to know, a meeting that is set to shape the future of literally millions of people. More than 300 delegates have travelled especially to London for the congress. They are principally Russians, Poles, Latvians and Lithuanians. The majority of them are Bolsheviks."

"Bolsheviks?"

"Followers of Karl Marx."

Sidgwick explained to me that among the delegates to the congress would be some of the most celebrated characters of the twentieth-century. They would include Maxim Gorky, the writer, Lenin, Leon Trotsky and Rosa Luxemburg. One of the delegates would be a young Georgian, known as Ivanov. He would not play much part in the proceedings, other than observing them, and nobody would notice him. Later, the world will know him by a different title – Joseph Stalin.

I shrugged.

"Believe me," Sidgwick said, "he was one of the colossi of the twentieth-century – a truly wicked tyrant. Or, at least," he smiled, "he would have been. I hope that through our efforts, that may be changed."

"How?"

"The plan is this."

As Sidgwick spoke, the sun peeped through the clouds. Through railings a long way off I saw a lady in a white dress pushing a perambulator. She glanced in our direction, but did not appear to see us.

Sidgwick instructed me to take an electric tram down to Essex Road. From there, he said, I should strike eastwards, on foot. My goal – he gave me a map, sketched in pencil – was the Brotherhood Church in Southgate Road. This was where the famous fifth congress was to take place. It would be a meeting between Bolsheviks, whose leading figure was Lenin, and more moderate Mensheviks, led by Martov. The Bolsheviks believed in pursuing the objective of a proletarian revolution, led by an inner core of full-time revolutionaries; the Mensheviks favoured a more gradual approach, relying upon existing liberal institutions. The congress would mark the first meeting between Lenin and Trotsky; it would sow the seeds for the October Revolution of 1917. Or at least it would have done.

"Are you ready?"

I nodded.

"I would like you to put on some special clothes."

"I beg your pardon?"

From the boot of the car, Sidgwick produced my "costume". It consisted of a battered felt hat and a loud check jacket, with a wilting flower in its lapel. There was also a pair of brown, baggy trousers, with a length of twine serving as a belt.

"What on earth?"

There was a mischievous expression in his eyes. "I want you

to adopt the role of a cheeky cockney chappie, of the kind who walks the boards. A comedian. Do you think that you can do that?"

I was struck dumb.

"Don't worry," said the Pole, "you won't have to tell any jokes. But I do want you to distribute these outside the church."

He waved a handbill in front of my face. The cream sheet was headed Music Hall War! Beneath, in dense type, was a list of complicated demands – to be paid full union rates, to be reimbursed for extra performances, and so on. I squinted at the piece of paper.

"Does this have anything to do with Bolshevism?"

Sidgwick laughed. "Nothing whatever."

"Then what on earth?"

"I have recently been in communication with a gentleman called Joe Elvin. Mr Elvin treads the boards. He is a music hall entertainer. He also represents, although you will not have heard of it, the Variety Artistes Federation. Mr Elvin's members are concerned that a small number of music hall managers are imposing restrictive conditions upon performers. Earlier this year they embarked upon a strike. The strike has the backing of some of the most celebrated music hall performers in the country. Admittedly, their demands do not have the weight of those of the Russian proletariat. However, they feel passionate about their cause."

"I don't understand ..."

He smiled. "Through the auspices of Mr Elvin, I have arranged for a mass meeting of the Variety Artistes Federation to take place this afternoon, in the Brotherhood church."

"You mean at the same time as the ..."

"Precisely. There will be jugglers, plate spinners, ventriloquists, clog dancers, sword swallowers, trapeze artists, living statues, descriptive singers, lion tamers ... they are converging as we speak, from the four corners of Great Britain. It will be interesting to see if the artistes make common cause with the Bolsheviks and Mensheviks, particularly those who speak English. Perhaps," he stroked his chin, "they will storm Downing Street together – they have been instructed to come in costume by the way – bolstered by the revolutionary theories of Lenin and Trotsky. Who knows what forces will be unleashed by our intervention."

"Indeed." I was holding the bundle of clothes awkwardly. "All I have to do is to give out leaflets?"

Sidgwick reassured me. He told me that all of the ingredients for the experiment were in place. We merely need to give the beaker a little stir. I put on my new clothes, hiding behind a tree. Sidgwick gave me a handful of coins for the day's expenses and five hundred handbills, wrapped in brown paper. He told me that I should have a leisurely breakfast in a workman's café and then make my way to the Brotherhood Church. The music hall artistes would begin to assemble, with their banners and placards, from midday. Most of the revolutionaries were staying in doss houses and lodgings in the East End. They would arrive a little later. We arranged to meet at precisely the same spot, at midnight.

It was one of those ill-defined days that characterises an English spring, dull but with glimmers of sunlight. The soles of my battered boots were flapping. The grass was still moist from dew or rain; this meant that I would have to spend the day with wet feet. As I squelched across the park I heard the engine of Sidgwick's Rolls flick into life. I turned and looked back. Before my eyes, the silver vehicle became translucent, like a dragonfly's wing. It shimmered briefly, then vanished. Only an observant person would have noticed the car dissolving into the shadows.

I hoped fervently that Sidgwick would be there to pick me up at the appointed time. He had not thought to provide me with a coat and I was already shivering. I was cut adrift from my own time with only two shillings and sixpence in my pocket. At that moment I felt more like a tramp than a comedian. However, a fried breakfast and two mugs of sweet, steaming tea cheered me up considerably.

They were an odd bunch, the music hall artistes. Some were in their performing clothes – leotards, evening dress or theatrical rags. Even those in their normal mufti had the look of performers. Their faces had a waxy sheen; their eyes blinked, as if unaccustomed to the daylight. Their accents formed a gazetteer of the United Kingdom and traversed the social divide from the public to the saloon bar. Kaufmann's Cycling Beauties were seven, sloe-eyed, dark-haired girls in tight-fitting, short-legged pantaloons. Through them, I met Hatsley the Boy Wonder. Hatsley's astonishing specialism was to play a trombone while riding a unicycle on a high-wire. His friend, Miss Victorina, could swallow light bulbs so that they glowed through her flesh.

A frisson passed through the crowd when a true "star" arrived, the coquettish Miss Lottie Collins. She was famous for her skirt dance – a kind of can-can that showed her bloomers – and a risqué song, Ta-ra-ra-boom-der-ray. To Kaufmann's Cycling Beauties she was minor royalty. I learnt a lot from my brief conversations. Astonishingly, some artistes – the brightest stars – earned more than £100 a week. Those lower down the bill risked life and limb for far more modest sums. They were treated like chattel. I thrust my leaflets into the hands of passers-by. Some mistook me for Gus Elen, the coster comedian – "'ere, you're that bloke ain't you!" – which was flattering.

At two o'clock the first bemused Bolsheviks and Mensheviks begin to filter into the edges of the crowd. They were all of a type – thin men in their twenties, with haunted eyes and unshaven faces. Sidgwick had told me that many congress delegates would have been imprisoned or sent into exile – east Siberia was a popular destination. The first to arrive had no idea what was going on. They just stood and gawped. Perhaps they thought that the thespians represented the British contingent of international

Bolshevism.

At first, the mood was good-natured. Little by little, annoyance developed because the way to the church was barred, especially when important-looking officials arrived with a trestle table and bundles of documents. Heated discussions now took place. The revolutionaries kept on coming – wave after wave, filling the road like a football crowd. Soon, jostling started. The artistes were carrying home-made placards – pieces of hardboard on wooden staves. I did not see the first one crashing onto someone's head. But I heard a sickening thud.

Close to me, a man in a silk-lapelled dinner jacket and a top hat lurched his way to the kerb. His face was a caricature of hatred. He was a diminutive creature – no more than four feet high. The chap was twirling a wooden stave menacingly around his head. I looked down. Black tights revealed short, stunted legs. Everything was out of proportion. The bloated face, the tiny top hat. And his boots. They must have been three feet long! They were unfeasibly narrow and curved slightly at the toes like chili peppers. "Little Tich", for that was his sobriquet, advanced towards an uncomprehending Latvian. The preceding events must have triggered an irrational hatred of foreigners from the depths of his psyche. He began to snarl some vile insults. But his absurd footwear restricted his movements.

The Latvian, a giant with a black beard, howled with laughter. This enraged the large-footed dwarf. Saliva and obscenities showered from Little Tich's lips. The Latvian placed a huge hand, like a ham, on the performer's head and held him off, as his arms flayed. Tich was screaming with rage. It was hilarious. In other parts of the crowd, fists were flying. I now became aware that a motor car was slowly breasting its way through the crowd. It was an open-topped Rolls Royce. Marie Lloyd, the Queen of the Halls, had arrived!

I could not make out much of her – principally a white hat, plumed by an extravagant arrangement of feathers, and a fur boa. It is quite possible that some of the Russian delegates believed that a real monarch or a czarina had appeared amongst them. Many of them had been involved in a demonstration at the czar's winter palace in 2005. Hundreds of men, women and children had been shot down. Their reaction is understandable. They advanced towards the car.

Marie Lloyd was far from an aristocrat. She was from Hoxton. Her main claim to fame were her suggestive songs – She'd never had her ticket punched before, Oh Mr Porter and Whacky whack whack. She was ill-equipped to defend herself, although she soon began to shriek and swear like a fish-wife. Temporarily, Bolsheviks and Mensheviks made common cause. They hurled abuse at her in various languages. Some of them shoved their way to the vehicle through a praetorian guard of thespians. Ms Lloyd flailed at her attackers with a cream-coloured parasol. The car began to rock violently from side to side.

That was when the police horses arrived on the scene – a phalanx of them from the direction of Balls Pond Road. The policemen's batons were raised. As I watched, they accelerated from a trot to a gallop, into a full-scale cavalry charge. They must have been held on standby nearby. It is clear from the graphic nature of subsequent reports that several newspaper reporters were present; there would also have been officers from Special Branch and plain-clothed detectives. A group of local protestors had been agitated by a series of stories in the Daily Mail about an "invasion" of undesirable aliens arriving in London. They stood on the pavement opposite the church, jeering.

A single photograph exists of the so-called Music Hall Riots. It was taken by a poor chap who had come to record the historic meeting between Lenin and Ramsey MacDonald, the British Labour leader. The photographer managed to get off one plate before fleeing for safety. The image is somewhat blurred, but I am told that it is a classic of documentary photography. Only one word can describe the subsequent events. Mayhem. I had little stomach for a street fight. I had dropped my leaflets and was looking for an escape route. Seizing an historic opportunity, many Bolsheviks now turned on Mensheviks and began to batter them. The music hall artistes, who had grouped around Marie Lloyd's car, became embroiled in random battles for which they were variously equipped. Little Tich, whose diminutive stature was matched by his ferocity, had made too many enemies. Initially, buoyed by the elasticity of his ankles, he bobbed around like a bar skittle, held up by his boots. When he finally went down and did not come back up a roar rose up from the crowd.

History tells us that Lenin, a tall figure with a gingery beard, was spirited away, that Trotsky sustained a black eye and that Ramsey MacDonald ran down the street, whinnying like a donkey. I did not witness any of this – in any case, I would not have recognised them. I did see a strongman in a spangled costume hoist Marie Lloyd over his shoulder and rescue her moments before her vehicle was turned over. I blush to admit that I caught a glimpse of her white thighs and her blue silk garters before averting my eyes. By the end of the afternoon, when things had calmed down, Southgate Road was littered with pieces of wood, fragments of theatrical costumes and blood-stained banners. Some survivors were clutching their heads, others were lying motionless in pools of blood. It took a fleet of horse-driven ambulances to ferry them away. Marie Lloyd's magnificent Silver Ghost was "arse over tip" to use a vulgar expression – a battered hulk, leaking oil onto the road.

To Sidgwick's great satisfaction, the Fifth Congress of the Russian Social Democratic Labour party did not take place. Most of the delegates were subsequently deported. Lenin and Trotsky slipped quietly out of the country, as they always did. To evade the police, I escaped to the south. I brushed myself down, walked along the Regent's Canal and caught a tram up New North Road. After a pleasant meal in a chop-house and two pints of beer, I swayed tipsily into the park and waited. I was still there long after the housemaids and dog walkers had gone home and the park gates had been locked, hiding fearfully in some bushes.

Sidgwick arrived in his Time Machine, precise to the second. Half-frozen and covered in scratches and mud stains, I was now able to tell him what had happened. He listened carefully to my account. He was delighted by our success. As for the Georgian, Ivanov, also known as Joseph Stalin, an interesting story attached to him. It was not published in any newspaper. Stalin, Sidgwick explained to me, had stayed in lodgings at 77 Jubilee Street, off Whitechapel Road, the night before the congress. He did not make it to the meeting. Why? Because Russian secret police were waiting for him outside. Sidgwick had tipped them off. Stalin's card was marked. He had been agitating in the Caucases the previous summer, denouncing Mensheviks and inciting people to murder them. What happened to him? Sidgwick did not indicate his fate verbally, but simply drew a forefinger across his throat. The Russian secret police were not known for observing the niceties of liberal jurisprudence. The world, Sidgwick believed, would be far better off without the short, foul-mouthed demagogue.

Chapter Twenty

The Brotherhood

The journey back to the Acacia Hotel was uneventful. Neither of us said much. We simply pulled into the drive and got out, as if nothing had happened. I had changed back into my cool, linen clothes.

"Remember, cocktails at six," said Sidgwick. "Please, do not get yourself into trouble!"

I was tired. I knew that if I went to my room I would fall asleep, so I decided to explore the hotel and maybe have a drink in the bar. By the reception desk something caught my attention. It was a black velvet placard, on an easel. Words were stuck onto it, in crooked gold letters. I read the following legend.

Worldvision Corporation: Saving the Planet

Seminars

Politicians – Violet Room.
Engineers – Snowdrop Room.
Doctors – Daffodil Room.
Philosophers – Rose Room.
Utopians – Bluebell Room.

I think I have told you that I am a curious person. What would you have done? Without hesitating, I asked the receptionist where the Bluebell Room was. I then made my way up a broad flight of maroon-carpeted stairs. I proceeded down one of those long, boring corridors that you find in hotels. One door was half-open. I stopped and peered inside. To my surprise, the first person I saw was Sidgwick. His face was flushed with anger.

"How dare you say that I have failed! You whose followers sent the kulaks to their doom! You who consigned whole races to oblivion! Your audacity is breath taking!"

"Gentlemen," said a smooth, unseen voice, with slightly nasal accent. "May I suggest that we adjourn the meeting for fifteen minutes, so that we can all, er, calm down?"

"No, you may not!"

The stentorian command came from a full-bearded face seen through a gap in the door. He turned towards Sidgwick. I recognised him at once, from a thousand photographs. It was Karl Marx.

"Comrade Sidgwick has made certain accusations and I wish to challenge his interpretation of history. Firstly, his allegation that I am merely a materialist ..."

Here, my attention began to wander. If you have ever encountered the more abstruse varieties of Marxist theory, you will understand why. He must have droned on for at least twenty minutes. During this time, I studied what I could see of the Bluebell Room. Eerily, it was all white. It had a white carpet, white walls and a white ceiling. There was little to focus on in the room, apart from the men, a glass-topped table with chrome legs and their voices.

Marx and Sidgwick faced each other at each end of the table. Close to Sidgwick I could see a gentleman in a frock coat, with a voluminous salt and pepper-coloured beard and tired-looking eyes. It looked like William Morris. I could make out some cardboard labels on the table indicating that certain invitees were not present – Plato, Pelagius, John Ruskin and ... I squinted at the unfamiliar name, Mary Wollstonecraft. A gentleman in a stained multi-coloured tee shirt was lounging in an almost horizontal position. I could just make out his name from his place marker – Timothy Leary. He was sojourning in a place where conversation could not reach him.

William Morris's shoulders began to twitch; he was growing

restive. But one could sense that Marx was coming to his peroration.

" ... and this would be credible but for the fact that Sidgwick's interventions have not saved the planet; quite the opposite. We have indulged far too readily his amateur dramatics and his chronospheres – his misguided attempts to meddle in human affairs."

He glowered ahead, looking at no-one in particular. "Sidgwick, I have just learned, has disrupted an extremely important congress of Bolsheviks in London. He has turned it into a circus and made a monkey of me. It is a very serious matter and I shall be making an official complaint."

He glared at the chairman with a face like thunder. Nobody would have dared to interrupt him. "However, I shall not embarrass Sidgwick by taking up the matter in this forum." He looked around. "I told you all during a previous meeting, that only a rigorous understanding of dialectical materialism would serve our ends, not this game of charades, with white robes and false noses."

"You say that I have failed. Upon what do you base this assertion?" Sidgwick stared into the face of the father of revolutions.

Marx glanced away.

"Come now, Sir. What is the problem? I ask you again, what is the problem? Well?"

Marx remained silent.

"The seas have been purified," Sidgwick continued, "the melting of the ice caps has stablilised. People no longer live in dread of war. Flowers and voles have returned to the English hedgerows? Is this not paradise?"

Marx turned to face his interolucter. "Pah," he grunted. "People have become children. They amuse themselves with fripperies and baubles and with the morbid stimulation of virtual reality. Sidgwick and the empirio criticists, Avenarius and his ilk, do not appreciate that it is only in the materialist realm that …"

"Oh for God's sake," Sidgwick interrupted Marx. "This is tosh, Sir. Utter tosh." He looked around the room. "Can you not see what has happened? That I have saved the world from destruction? You are in heaven, but you do not even know it. And why is that? Because your precious ideology has blinded you."

"Rubbish!" exploded Marx.

"Do you not perceive that there is death in your dialectic?" said Sidgwick. "Have you never asked yourself why your followers always divide into murderous factions at the drop of a hat and kill each other? At least I respond to reality as it is, while you occupy a realm of evanescent concepts, like smoke rings. You are the problem, not me!"

"That is preposterous." Marx glared, his brow furrowed.

"Even Leary has a better grasp of the world than you do."

"Hardly!" sneered Marx. "Look at the man. He is asleep!" Leary's posture and breathing confirmed Marx's assertion.

"Aquinas is with me," Sidgwick insisted, "so is Ruskin!"

"Only because he is a fool," sneered Marx.

"I do not think that you should traduce a man who is not here to defend himself." The words were delivered, with quiet gravitas, by William Morris.

"You call him a man do you?" said Marx.

"Gentlemen!" the chairman's voice cut through the proceedings. I perceived from his voice that he was from the English west midlands. "We, the Brotherhood, observe rules, the first of which is that we do not indulge in gratuitous personal insults. I propose this. That we break for five minutes and then take a vote upon the substantive motion that is before us."

"Marx does not respect democracy. He thinks that it is a bourgeois tyranny."

The object of Sidgwick's barb stiffened in his chair.

"Gentlemen!" protested the chairman. "Please …" A hubbub

was breaking out. I realised then that their argument would not lead to a conclusion. The fractious utopians would never be able to agree when, or if, their dreams had been realised. At that moment I lost interest in political science. I wanted to go outside, into a world of light and innocuous conversation. Also, I craved a drink. I turned away from the conference room and made my way to the reception area.

Instinct told me that if I sat there long enough, I was sure to see someone that I knew. And that is what happened. After a few minutes, a tall man in a white suit approached. His long hair draped onto his collar. It was Dean! I tried to capture his attention, but, to my surprise, he ignored me and walked straight past. I followed him. There was a bar next to the reception desk. It was half-empty. Pink spotlights picked out a tiny stage at one end of the room. Dean crossed to it, aware that many eyes were following his progress. It was like a dream. Sid, my old friend, and a female bass player were already in position. They were all wearing silk shirts, with lace ruffles.

The name of the group was written in lurid letters on the drum kit, The Tristars. Dean plugged in his guitar and counted in the band. They began to play a cabaret number. Sid stroked his cymbals languidly, as if his mind was on something else. One thing really surprised me. Sid appeared to have two arms. The bass player, who had a cheerful round face and a perm, looked at Dean admiringly. She was his lover, I could see that. Sid smiled at me. But Dean seemed uncomfortable in his new persona. He did not acknowledge me. He had shaved for once in his life. His face looked tender and vulnerable. He began to sing – quite credibly I thought.

I waited until the set was over.

"Why are you ignoring me?"

Dean looked angry. I had to hold onto his arm to keep him from striding off.

"Why do you think?"

I shrugged.

"I don't know? Really, I have no idea. I thought that we ..."

"The fucking band, The Chosen."

"Yes?"

"I wanted to carry on. Do you think I wanted to do, this!" He looked with distaste at the little stage. "Fucking cabaret!"

"But you died, Dean."

"I didn't."

"You did. I read it in the newspapers."

Dean snorted. "I didn't die. Don't you realise? It was all made up."

"You mean that Sid didn't crash into a wall and lose his arm?"

"Of course fucking not. Look at him!"

I did. He gave the thumbs-up gesture – with two hands. He was grinning like an idiot.

"Look, Dean. As far as I'm concerned, you died, right! Do you think I wanted to lose the band? I loved it."

He looked uncertain.

"Okay," I said. Logic. That is what would win him over. "Let's accept the premise that you didn't die of a drugs overdose and that Sid didn't crash into a wall at Carshalton Beeches. Therefore, someone must have made it appear that these things happened."

"Yes ..."

"But it wasn't me. You have to believe me. I did not want you to die, Okay? You were my best friend."

"Who was it then?"

I think that we both came up with the answer at the same time. Who was the puppet master of Time, the manipulator of human affairs?

"It must have been ..."

"Precisely," I said.

Dean was itching for a cigarette. He was too vain to keep a packet in his stage suit – it would have spoiled the line of the jacket. The bass player, Elaine, was his cigarette carrier. Dean looked at her.

"Sidgwick messed with my head too you know," I said. I thought of something. Had Lara really left me? Had that been a trick too? Elaine came over to us. She had undone her shirt, revealing a triangle of golden flesh. She carried a bottle of beer. Her smile was infectious. Dean introduced us. Elaine was a friendly person and she was easy to talk to. Dean smoked in an exasperated fashion, not saying much.

I reminisced with Sid about The Chosen's last gig in Croydon and ribbed him about his canary yellow shirt. Then I had an inspiration – a band with two bass players! Elaine loved the idea. Sid said that having one was bad enough. I knew that he was joking. We used to be a great combination. My bass lines complemented his rhythms like tendrils of honeysuckle twisting around a hazel branch.

I looked at my watch. It was three minutes to six – almost time for cocktails. I told Sid and Elaine that I really liked their music – I winked – and that I would return for more – soon. Then I made my excuses. Dean returned my smile. We shook hands solemnly. I knew that he had already forgiven me but that he was too proud to admit it. Typical.

Outside, a breeze blew across a perfect lawn, as flat and smooth as a bowling green. The cocktail hour had arrived. Some way off, a white marquee throbbed with violins and cellos. In between, little knots of people were grouped on the neat lawn – the men in straw boaters, the women in long dresses. The smell of cut grass stirred strange memories in me. I felt as if I were at school again, standing nervously at the edge of a sports field. I could almost hear the harsh, mocking voices of the other boys. I wondered where Lara was and began to look for her.

To my left was a lush grassy bank – a tempting place to relax in the dying sun. Curiously, it was covered with khaki-clad men, smoking and drinking tea from their canteens. The soldiers were familiar to me from my brief visit to the Somme in 1916. They bore the distinctive shoulder flashes of the 16th Battalion of the Middlesex Regiment, "the Diehards". A woman came towards me. She was tall and wore a pale silk dress. There was little or nothing beneath it; I tried to avert my eyes. She had large grey eyes and her hair was shaved off in a female version of a crew-cut. She seemed familiar. I did not remember who she was until later. It was Aunt Agnes's maid, Nuala, whom I had last met in Sevenoaks, in 1891.

Nuala did not recognise me. She veered away at the last moment, heading towards one of the soldiers, a handsome, sun-tanned man with a five o'clock shadow on his chin. He wore a Sam Browne belt with a service revolver in the holster. He must be an officer, perhaps Alf's platoon commander, Lieutenant Dixon. I was still thinking about this vignette when I noticed that a man was striding towards me. He was black-haired, with a short, squat build, a swarthy face and eyebrows like hairy caterpillars. I recognised him at once, with a pulse of joy. It was my old friend, Alf. But then, when he spoke, I was filled with confusion.

"Frederick! My dear fellow!" He spread his arms as if to clasp me, then changed his mind. We shook hands, uncomfortably.

"Alf?"

"Not Alf, Alfred, dear boy." His cultivated voice was slightly reproachful; there was still a faint touch of Welsh in it, like the patina on an antique. He was wearing a smart navy blue jacket with a badge of gold braid on the breast pocket, cricket trousers and a creaseless white shirt. What shocked me was the silk cravat. Alf would rather have died than worn a cravat.

"Well, well, well." He looked me up and down. "I really did not expect this. How long has it been, do you think?"

A thousand images jostled in my brain – the Samhain fires; the Ordovice encampment; a cobweb in my uncle's kitchen with a dead butterfly entombed there, forever, by memory. I was lost for words.

"I would not like to hazard a guess, would you?" said the man confidently. "It seems like an awfully long time."

"Your voice has changed," I said.

He looked surprised. "Actually, it hasn't," he said. "This is my real voice. It was the one I was born with. I can't tell you what a delight it is to be able to talk grammatically again. I really hated being inarticulate. It was like trying to build a house with sand, if you see what I mean." He paused. "It don't seem right, do it, Mr Frater?" he said, mimicking his former way of speaking. "Do you remember, I had to hang onto your every word and follow you around with that cow-like devotion! It was humiliating. Still, all of that is behind us now, eh? I must say, Frederick." His brown eyes flicked to mine. "You are looking awfully pale. Are you all right? A stiff drink, that's what you need. Am I right?"

He smiled. I saw that his front teeth were still discoloured and there was still a chip in one of them. It was uncanny; there was a stranger in Alf's body.

"Tell you what. There are a couple of people over here who are simply dying to meet you. Do you remember Nathaniel and Elspeth?" I blinked with surprise. "Of course you do! That party at Spenhurst Hall, when I disgraced myself with the chicken drum sticks. Come."

Alfred grasped my sleeve. He dragged me unwillingly towards a man wearing a striped blazer and a woman in a low-cut blue dress.

As we walked, he continued to engage me in conversation.

"You know that morning when Sidgwick set me down in Spenhurst, after the Welsh business. Guess what? You know the bicycle shop?"

"Yes, I murmured."

"It wasn't there. There was a shop in the high street all right – but it was boarded up."

"Did you see any of the people you knew?"

"Oh yes. But none of them seemed to recognise me. It was as if I had never existed. Even old George up at the forge. He looked straight through me."

"What did you do?"

"What could I do?" He laughed. At least this sounded like the old Alf. "I made my way up to London. Money was no problem. I had a bag of gold Roman coins, thanks to Sidgwick, and two necklaces."

"You mean the torcs?"

"Yes."

My heart skipped a beat. "But the torcs belonged to Lara and me," I said. "Sidgwick gave them to us."

"Did he?" Alfred did not miss a beat. "Oh, I see. Well, there must have been a mix up. Sorry. Anyway …"

I was dumbfounded but I said nothing. He continued his tale. He had moved into one of the swankiest hotels in the West End. I could picture him, a fop, sauntering up and down Regent Street. Tiring of leisure, he had set up in business – importing foreign curios. The enterprise had done well, he said. I guessed from his expression, that his activities had been of dubious legality.

We reached the two people who Alfred wished me to see.

"This is Nathaniel Vane," he said, "and his lady wife, Elspeth. You have met before, of course, at Spenhurst Hall."

Vane languidly held out a striped forearm, allowing me to shake his hand. His hand was as cold as marble. I could not dispel a horrifying image from my mind, that of his body swinging on a rope in Wandsworth prison.

"Good Lord, this is the Druid Elspeth! Do you remember?" he said.

Vane slapped me on the back. Alfred stood at my shoulder. Elspeth emitted a hyena-like sound – a kind of laughter. I felt uncomfortable trapped in their claustrophobic circle. I was forced to stay with them for a while. They talked of Alfred's yacht and about Vane's Hispano-Suiza, which was parked in front of the hotel. I was disgusted by their boastfulness.

During a lull I grabbed my opportunity. "I'm so glad that

you've become friends," I said. "I ..."

My sentence trailed off, for I had glimpsed someone in the distance. It was a tall lady in a green dress, with auburn hair, the colour of horse chestnuts. Could it be her? Lara had been at the forefront of my mind since I had arrived at the hotel. The loss of her had torn something from my soul and I had a million things to tell her. The figure drifted towards a knot of people close to the edge of the lawn. As I watched, it vanished utterly, like a jigsaw piece disappearing into a complicated pattern. I had to speak to her. With a stab of anticipation I made my way towards the group.

Just then I felt a hand on my arm, pulling me back. The hand turned me round. A familiar but almost forgotten face was peering into mine. It was Doctor Wood!

"Freddy!" he exclaimed. "Can it really be you? My boy!"

Before me, indubitably, was Spenhurst's most energetic philanthropist. He was wearing his familiar tweed suit and retained his brisk doctor's manner. However, there was something different about him. The old Doctor Wood had been teetotal. This one smelled of whisky and had moist, red-rimmed eyes. He was also swaying and talking with an exaggerated animation.

"Freddy, there is someone who you must see. You simply must."

"Who?"

He placed one of his hands upon my shoulder as if to steady himself. "Your uncle!"

My uncle? I was disconcerted on two counts. Firstly, Uncle Edward was deceased and, secondly, I could not imagine him in these surroundings. In heaven, his misery and pessimism would be utterly incongruous. He would always be complaining about something – the birds were singing too loudly, the clouds were too fluffy. An image of his baleful face came into my mind.

"Doctor Wood," I said, "I ..."

"Freddy, he is there."

Doctor Wood pointed to a nearby group. At its centre was a jovial man in a crimson shirt. He was holding court to an attentive audience. Every so often, following cues from his voice, the group would burst into appreciative laughter. I studied him more closely. Good grief. It was indeed, my uncle.

"I think you will find that he has changed rather a lot," said Doctor Wood. "Death does that to some people." He guffawed.

My uncle recognised me long before we reached him. This caused him to abandon his anecdote. Soon he was glowing with satisfaction, telling everyone that I was his pride and joy, his long lost nephew.

"Edward, you old devil," said Doctor Wood, "you must let him breathe!" For my uncle was almost asphyxiating me.

"Freddy, my dear Freddy. I am sorry, I am so sorry." My uncle kept repeating the phrase. His face was red from drink.

"Why?"

"Because I was so beastly to you. Let's face it, I was an arse. I was sour and moody. I was arrogant. I had no respect for your opinions. I treated you like a dog. In fact, worse than a dog. Do you remember, I called your girlfriend a harlot? Also, I drank like a fish. Quite honestly, I am surprised that you did not attack me with a carving knife."

"I did."

"Oh yes." My uncle laughed. "Oh well. The thing is, I want you to know that I am sorry. It was not the true me. I was playing a part you see."

"A part?"

"Oh yes." He looked serious. "The one given to me by …" With a finger and thumb he gestured mysteriously towards the hotel. Doctor Wood coughed. My uncle changed the subject.

"You must know that I did not want to be like that," he continued. "It was a real strain, all of that drinking and bullying. I don't even like brandy. I hate the bloody stuff. Do you know what I used to do? I used to fill up a bottle with cold tea. But that was nearly as horrible as drinking brandy."

"At least you could drink!" interrupted Doctor Wood.

"What do you mean?" said my uncle

"Well, my so-called character was a puritan. He was a bloody wine sipper. A water drinker. You know I like a drink, Ted. Well it was murder! And he was so sanctimonious. He was always digging crippled birds out of the bloody snow, that kind of thing. At least your character had some guts to him. You had something to work with."

"You think that getting drunk is fun do you? Arguing with complete strangers. Being terrified of falling asleep because of the nightmares, and then, when you do, burning your house down."

"Oh come on, Ted, you loved it!"

There was a pause. My uncle timed it perfectly. "I suppose you're right."

Everyone laughed. Uncle Edward grasped me in a kind of bear hug.

"Freddy, I love you. I bloody love you. And if I can ever repay you for what I did, you only have to ask. You know that don't you?"

He kissed me on the cheek. Then he displayed me to his entourage, like a fishing trophy. My head was filled with confusion. I began to curl up with embarrassment.

"Agnes here, she feels the same, don't you, Ag?"

I now realised with a start, that the silver-haired lady in a purple kaftan who was standing next to Edward was my aunt. There were signs that her personality had not changed entirely – she was wearing dangling earrings and a string of amethysts around her neck. But she was definitely less rigid and didactic than she had been in her previous incarnation. I commented that it was a shame that her house in Sevenoaks had been partially destroyed during the seance.

She grinned. "It's funny you should mention that, Freddy. Because I still have the repair bill. Think I'm joking?"

She smiled strangely, reaching into a velvet bag. It is fortunate that my aunt was interrupted. But the circumstances were somewhat alarming. Another person had been advancing upon us from the direction of the marquee, and now caught us unawares. She burst into our midst, like a tiger in a jungle clearing. I recall a vivid impression of orange hair and white teeth.

"Where have you been?"

"Sorry?"

"Where, in the name of Jesus, have you been?"

Mary was spitting fire. I started to say something. She sallied at me again.

"Do you think that it is right to abandon a pregnant woman?"

"I beg your …"

"Do you have any idea how difficult it is to bring up a child?" Her expression would have curdled milk.

"A child?" I stammered.

From the cloudy patterns in my mind, an image resolved – of Mary leading me up the stairs to her room, of her metal bedstead and the sloping white ceiling. Good grief, had I really …

"A child!"

That was when I saw you, Isabella. You were still attached to your mother's hand, having been dragged unwillingly across the lawn. Mary had dressed you in a blue and white sailor suit and a sweet little cap. You looked adorable. However, your bottom lip was quivering ominously. You seemed about to cry. I recognised immediately the expression in your face. It was belligerent and fearless – an exact copy of your mother's. I cannot easily describe how I felt upon discovering that I had a two-year-old child. Studying your face closely I started to recognise myself as well as your mother in your features. Your eyes seemed to stare straight into my soul. I had a daughter! An extraordinary feeling took hold of me. It was made up of pride, guilt and euphoria, all mixed together. My poor body could not contain all of them. I am an emotional person. I felt tears welling up.

"Oh for God's sake!"

Mary's hands were upon her hips. Your thoughts must have been as confused as mine. For in the silence that followed you began to whimper.

"Well, well. This is splendid, simply splendid," said Doctor Wood, emphatically. He was beaming. Everyone was. Even Uncle Edward. Soon, I realised, there would be congratulations and the popping of champagne corks.

Mary was shaking her head in disbelief at the fickleness of men. But her expression was softening. I could not take my eyes off you. I looked at Mary. She looked back wordlessly. I picked you up. You snuggled perfectly against my body, as if you had always been there. I kissed your moist cheeks. Mine were damp too. They were streaked with wet lines. But I was no longer sad. They were tears of joy.

Chapter Twenty-one

A Fresh Start

I have reached the end of the story. There is little more to say – it would be fatuous to dilate upon the pleasures of the twenty-first century and I have dwelt for far too long, and perhaps immodestly, upon how I helped to bring them about.

In past few months the emotional attachment that I instantly made with you has grown stronger. Not that you are an easy child. Quite the opposite. Your personality, like that of your mother, appears to be formed around a kernel of stubbornness. For example, when you are placed upon a flat surface you invariably attempt to escape as quickly as possible. Your mother or I drag you back. You begin to howl, emitting ear-splitting shrieks of indignation that could loosen roof tiles. You have some other peculiar eccentricities, like removing your clothes in public. I hope that you will grow out of this habit.

Understandably, Mary feels bitter that I, in her words, abandoned her before you were born. This and the difficulties of caring for a two-year-old have caused us to argue, sometimes violently. But we always make up. We have rediscovered each other. I suspect that whilst our relationship will never be a calm one, it will always persist. The guests at the hotel have made an enormous fuss of you, rhapsodising about your beauty. Dean and I have become friends again. It won't be long before I have a jam session with him and Sid in the ballroom – a Chosen reunion gig. That will blow away the cobwebs! I have also had some pleasant, if surreal, conversations with Uncle Edward, picking up threads from more than a century ago. It is hard for me to accept that he has changed from a churl into a loveable rogue. But everyone assures me that it is so.

Sidgwick's epic disagreement with Marx continues. It has

become a feud, each man trying to outwit the other and to turn the other utopians to his point of view. In one recent argument, Sidgwick broke the glass-topped table in the hotel's conference room while making a point rather too vehemently. He has been suspended from meetings for a month and is concerned that Marx's arguments will prevail. Fortunately, Marx is far more skilled at alienating his natural supporters than making new allies.

I am angry with Sidgwick for various reasons. But I have had neither the opportunity, nor the inclination, to take up my grievances with him. His serenity and plausibility are disarming. This morning, at breakfast, he told me of his next project. He wishes to travel to the island of Atlantis. Atlantis, he insists, really exists, although the ancients disagree on its precise location. There is an urgent, if obscure, reason for this quest. But he would not tell me what it was. Sidgwick beguiled me with a vision of emerald water piling onto black volcanic sands; of white houses festooned with multi-coloured bougainvillea. He claims that the Atlantis trip will be a picnic compared to our foray into first-century Britain. I do not entirely believe him. But still, I am looking forward to a new adventure, perhaps, if Sidgwick will sanction it, you and your mother will be able to come too.

I have written this account largely at night, on the balcony of our hotel room. It has been a blazing summer. On many evenings the sound of Sidgwick's violin wafted from his room as he played Vivaldi or Bach. The music, tender and mournful, formed a backdrop to the clattering of my fingers on the keyboard of my laptop. I would tap away, hour after hour, when you were safely asleep. Occasionally, I would look up from my work to gaze at the jewel box of the sky and at the fields of lights winking along the coast. The night calmed me like a balm, drawing my mind into its corners. It is now apparent that the world, with its scurrying human cargo, has reached a state of equilibrium and that we, the human race, are safe. Want has been largely abolished and we have attained everything that we had ever desired. However, things can change. Each member of the Brotherhood has his or her own agenda and some have access to Time Travel. The dispute between Marx and Sidgwick does not bode well.

Mary has been as patient with me as her nature will allow but I know that she will be relieved now that my book is finished. We are planning to travel up to London tomorrow, to visit some of our old haunts. It will be interesting; I hope that we won't argue. It pleases me to know that, one day, you will be old enough to read these words – that consoles me for having missed the first two years of your life. I must stop now, for it is morning and Mary is calling me somewhat urgently. In these pages I have attempted to describe my world and how I engaged with it. I love you very much, Isabella. This one, my darling, is yours.